Undivided

NEW HEIGHTS PUBLISHING

www.suzannefalter.com

Book cover design by Caroline Manchoulis
www.ladylit.com

Book design by Danielle H. Acee
www.authorsassistant.com

ISBN: 978-0-9969981-7-8

Undivided

An Oaktown Girls Novel

a novel by

SUZANNE **FALTER**

For my friends at Donor Network West

Chapter One

S ally sat up and blinked in the unfamiliar room. Then she gave a stretch of luxuriant happiness.

She looked around, still awestruck at where she was. Frankie had mentioned casually that things in her family home were fairly formal. But Sally had no idea what that actually meant. Until now.

What Frankie neglected to say was that she grew up in a seven-million dollar home with six bedrooms and six baths in Santa Barbara's high-end Riviera neighborhood. The property not only included riding stables, a private pool complete with jacuzzi, and a full staff, it had a spectacular ocean view as well.

In other words, Frankie, one of the least assuming people Sally had ever met, came from big money. It was the last thing she expected from her fiancée.

Sally slipped out of bed, and, still naked, took a few steps toward the French doors, open just enough to let in a breeze. They'd arrived late the night before, so she'd seen little of the estate and now she was curious. Just below her gaze, a gardener in an old straw hat retreated out of sight past a manicured hedge.

The infinity pool before her overlooked a private golf course in one direction and a distant clear-blue sea in the other. Sally turned and studied her love, still asleep in the all-white, king-size bed behind her. Frankie was sleeping deeply, her mouth slightly open, her jaw slack.

Tenderly, Sally looked at her partner in repose. She loved her. She really, truly did. And now, Sally was marrying into all of... *this.* She could scarcely wrap her head around her wild new reality.

Once more, Sally turned back to face the open French doors and the delicious early morning breeze that welcomed her. Stepping out onto the balcony, she yawned and stretched, and looked around. Then she chuckled and shook her head.

Somehow none of this made sense. Frankie was a cop, for Pete's sake. And cops generally were not from serious old money. Sally shrugged as she stepped back into the confines of their bedroom. She'd go with it. Even if it was...well, completely unfamiliar turf.

By contrast, Sally's own single mother had been a folk musician who was seldom home. She sang back up for a rambling band called The Black Hearts that played in bars and clubs all over Rhode Island and the Cape. The rest of the time, her mother waitressed in an all-night diner in Providence called Rosalinda's.

Since it was just her and her mom, Sally was on her own once she turned ten. It was a childhood of learning to stay out of trouble, do the laundry, and make mac and cheese for herself. Eventually, she even figured out how to pay their utility and rent bills. By the age of thirteen, Sally had become completely self-sufficient.

The fact was when she was overwhelmed, she generally called Miss Hart, her beloved fourth grade teacher. Miss Hart was always good for some quick advice, given that Sally's own mother was almost never around, especially after taking up with Danny, the drummer in her band.

It was Miss Hart who gave Sally a lift to the grocery store on the way home from school sometimes and helped her find an afternoon filing job at the school office.

It was also Miss Hart who told her it was okay to be gay.

The year Sally turned sixteen, she dropped out of school a year early and headed straight for San Francisco. Miss Hart secretly blessed Sally's plan to run away, and even drove her to the bus station when she left. Then she handed her a hundred-dollar bill.

Five days later, Sally arrived in the Bay Area with a single suitcase, almost two hundred dollars and a fake ID. After two nights of sleeping in the back room of a bar out by Ocean Beach, Sally found her way to the lesbians and the East Bay. And basically, she never looked back. Her first job was walking dogs.

Frankie stirred now as Sally slipped back in beside her, between the thousand-count sheets.

"Hey," Frankie said softly, reaching for Sally's waist. Frankie pulled her partner to her and they dissolved into a long kiss. "How are you doing?" she asked.

Sally pulled back and looked at her partner. "Stunned basically."

Frankie gave a sheepish grin. "What?" she asked innocently.

"Frankie, come on. Look at this," Sally said, waving a hand around the room. "Why didn't you ever tell me about any of this?"

"What's there to tell?"

"Frankie—seriously? Your mother is loaded."

Frankie rolled away, burrowing in the covers. "It's family money, Sally. Don't get excited. She inherited all of it." Frankie was quiet for a moment, and Sally waited, knowing more was coming. "Look it," Frankie continued, "it's not like it means anything. We don't get a free pass to heaven or something just because there's some money..."

"You probably had horses as a kid."

"Well...yeah," Frankie admitted.

"And you never had to worry about where your next meal was coming from, or how you were going to pay the rent. Right?"

"True," said Frankie, "but I also felt completely oppressed and like I couldn't be myself. I mean, my mother is still working on getting me to wear a skirt! Me!"

Sally burst out laughing, for if there was ever a butch who didn't belong in a skirt, it was Frankie. "Fine, whatever," she said.

"Will I meet your mom at breakfast?"

"Lord only knows," said Frankie with a sigh. "We'll see when Mother can squeeze us in between the dog trainer appointment, the Italian lessons and the benefit committees. And just so you know, Misty calls me Francesca."

"Francesca?"

Frankie turned away for a moment. "Also...there are some things I haven't told her," she added quietly.

An alarm went off in Sally's head. "Wait. What?" She paused, unwilling to embrace the idea now forming. "Frankie—did you tell her about me?"

"Of course. Obviously!" Frankie protested. "And now you're here and everything. And you'll meet. It's just that—"

"She doesn't know your gay?"

"Well, duh. Of course, she knows *that*, Sally." Frankie paused. "There's...other stuff she doesn't know."

"Oh." Sally crossed her arms. "That I'm from the other side of the tracks."

"Sally, please. It's not like that. She knows all about you."

There was now a heavy silence.

"Everything?" Sally finally probed. She got out of the bed and stood there, studying Frankie. By now she knew her partner well enough to sense when something major was being withheld.

Frankie avoided answering the question, and now her gaze was fixed on the ocean beyond their window. "Sally, I haven't told her that we're getting married."

Something gave way in Sally, and she sat down on the bed with a thud. She couldn't believe this. Turning around, she looked at her partner sharply. "I thought that she wanted to be involved in the wedding. You told me she did, Frankie. You lied to me! Why did you do that?"

Frankie sighed and sat up. "I didn't lie, exactly. I mean, Misty will definitely be involved. And she's going to love you once she gets to know you… I just…wanted you to actually meet first. Live. Before we got into all the hoopla."

"Hoopla!" Sally snorted. "I didn't even want a big wedding… I told you that. A quick trip to City Hall is totally fine with me."

"Well, see that's the thing," Frankie said. "I'd be good with that, too. But it's not going to be fine with Mother."

Sally folded her arms and regarded her partner. "Well, right now I couldn't give a rat's ass about your mother and what she wants, Frankie."

Then Sally picked up her panties and stepped into them angrily. "This is wrong and you know it." Her voice skewered up in exasperation. "We've been engaged for six months and this is the first I've heard of this. Or had you forgotten?"

A look of anguish passed over Frankie's face. "Sally, please…"

Snatching a shirt from her suitcase, Sally pulled it over her head. Her angry rant continued. "I'd wondered why nothing was really happening. And now I know. Nothing was happening because you lied to me."

Frankie picked up Sally's bra from a nearby chair. "Here," she said, holding it out to her. "You're going to want this, too." Frankie couldn't meet her lover's offended gaze.

Now Sally glared at the woman who only moments earlier she felt nothing but love for. "What? Now you have to dress me for your mother? Package me up so I'm appropriate?"

"Sally. Please. My mother is—" Frankie stopped herself. "You'll see when you meet her. Just help me out here."

Instead of being sympathetic, Sally laughed at Frankie. "If that's the case, a bra is the last thing I'm wearing to meet your mother," she declared. Sally stepped into her jeans and zipped them up. "She can take me as I am. Warts and all."

Sally strode over to the bathroom as a fiery new confidence coursed through her body. "And so can you, Frankie," she added as she shut the door, her voice wobbling slightly.

Frankie lied to me. Frankie—solid, trustworthy, reliable Frankie—had been lying methodically for nearly six months. All that stuff about finding a location for the wedding…all of it was made up. This explained why she wouldn't let Sally speak to Misty on the phone.

"I want you to meet first," Frankie kept saying, and Sally hadn't given it another thought.

Turning on the shower to mask the sound, Sally stepped in. And as the hot water beat down on her, she began to cry.

Meanwhile, Frankie sank back onto her pillow and stared at the ceiling overhead.

How in God's name did we get here?

And they still had Misty to deal with, which was never an easy task.

Frankie gave the sigh of the doomed. It was going to be a very long day.

*

Gently, Frankie knocked on the library door. "Mother?"

"Francesca?" came the response from within. "Come in, dear."

"Follow my lead," Frankie mouthed to Sally. Sally, in turn, just looked at her.

By now they were barely speaking to each other. There'd been no sign of Frankie's mother at breakfast, a tense affair in which they both ate toast and soft boiled eggs served by someone in a starched uniform in silence.

Frankie pushed open the heavy mahogany doors.

"I have to get off the phone. Someone's here," they heard Misty say as they entered the genteel library. Around them, twelve-foot mahogany stacks of books lined the room, and velvet drapes covered the windows. The tall, thin, impeccably dressed woman put her phone down at the antique Chippendale desk in the corner. Then she rose. On the desk before her, an engagement book spread out. It was filled with entries.

Eyeing Sally carefully, Frankie's mother extended her hand across the desk. "I'm Misty Kennedy," she said with a tight smile. "You must be Sally." She nodded for them to sit in the two wing-back chairs opposite her. Then she studied Sally for a moment.

Sally felt the fake smile on her face tighten as a shiver of discomfort ran through her body. She could already tell Misty didn't like her. Not one bit. Perhaps she even detested her. Taking a breath, Sally lowered herself into the chair.

"Well, then," Misty began with false gaiety. "Have you girls had breakfast?" Suddenly, she assumed the air of a mother talking to two teenage girls having a sleepover. Which, of course, they weren't.

"Ramona served us breakfast," Frankie said.

Misty was studying her daughter. "Oh, of course," she said lightly. "What are you two planning to do today?"

Frankie cleared her throat. "Actually, I thought the three of us might have lunch," she suggested. "Maybe at the club?"

"Oh, the club…hmmm…" Misty said vaguely. Instead of answering, her eye traveled past her daughter's shoulder to the massive flower arrangement on a table on the other side of the library.

"You have a lovely home, Mrs. Kennedy," ventured Sally, wanting to fill the silence, but Misty seemed not to hear her.

"It's Misty," she murmured, her eyes not moving from the point past Frankie's shoulder.

"Sorry. Misty," Sally corrected. Again fake smiles were offered.

The silence was deafening.

"Mother? Lunch at the club?" Frankie began again. "I can call and make a—"

But Misty rose and cut her daughter off. "Just wait a moment," she snapped.

Walking across the room, Misty yanked a wilted, white Asian lily from the elaborate arrangement by the window. "What was

Ramona thinking?" she muttered, dropping the dead flower onto the oriental rug.

Frankie swiveled in her chair and her voice grew more intense. "Mother…please."

Misty still did not look at her daughter. "Yes, Francesca?" Her tone had now changed from false gaiety to undisguised annoyance.

"Can you please come back over here and talk to us? If we can't meet at the club, okay fine. But let's take a walk or something. Please. We really need to talk to you about something."

Misty's voice was strained as she slowly returned to her chair behind the desk. "So, now suddenly you need to talk to me?" she asked. Misty seated herself and regarded them both darkly. "Now I'm intrigued. Is someone pregnant, Francesca?" She gave a scoffing laugh. "Oh, of course not. I forgot. You're lesbians."

Frankie shot her mother a look. "We'll discuss it at lunch. And by the way, lesbians do actually get pregnant."

But Misty wasn't listening. Instead, she was surveying the open appointment book before her on the desk. "I have Arthur, dear. He's coming to the house for a hot stone massage." She glanced up at them. "Would you girls like massages, too? I'm sure he can fit you in."

"No. Mother, no," Frankie began insistently. Reaching over, she took Sally's hand. "Look—Sally and I…" Nervously, she licked her lips and looked over at her partner.

Suddenly, Sally could see that Frankie was indeed trying. Perspiration had now broken out on her brow. She was giving it everything she had to soften this ice-cold woman, which appeared to be a monumental task. Instantly, Sally's anger melted with empathy for her fiancée.

"Mother…" Frankie began again. "I…well, we…"

"Just say it, darling," Misty said, leaning back in her chair. "What on earth are you trying to tell me?"

"We're getting married, Mrs. Kennedy," Sally offered. "I mean Misty."

Frankie's eyes widened beside her, but she said nothing. Now emboldened, Sally carried on.

She leaned forward toward her future mother-in-law. "Frankie was supposed to tell you months ago, but she didn't. I guess maybe you weren't expecting a psychic as a daughter-in-law? Or even—I don't know—maybe not a daughter-in-law at all?"

There was a beat of silence.

Frankie leapt into the fray now. "Look, Mother—" she began. Then suddenly all of them began talking at once.

"I'm sorry if this comes as a shock," Sally rattled on as Misty leaned forward over her desk, her voice low.

"What in God's name are you telling me?" she hissed.

Meanwhile, Frankie was in damage control mode. "Mother—wait! This is not how I wanted this to go… Mother?" Frankie began. Her voice rose with urgency as she tried to stop Misty's verbal assault. "Mother! Mother—don't!"

Still, Sally carried on, her voice relentless. "The fact is, Misty, we're doing this wedding. Right, Frankie?" She turned to her spouse. "At least I think we are. I mean, you gave me a ring and you asked me, remember? Here." Sally turned to Misty, showing off the modest diamond engagement ring to her future mother-in-law across the desk. "Isn't it beautiful?"

But instead of replying, Misty simply rose and, looking at her daughter, she shook her head. "You're marrying a young woman who doesn't even see fit to wear clothes when she steps out in public? On your balcony? Really, Francesca?"

Suddenly, Sally felt a chill run down her spine.

"What?" asked Frankie. She looked at Sally, confused.

Folding her arms, Misty regarded Sally once again. "No," she said flatly. "I'm sure you're a very nice young lady, but there's no way in hell you'll be marrying my daughter."

"Mother! I love—" objected Frankie.

Misty cut her off mid-sentence. "We'll discuss this later." Then with the air of complete self-possession, she walked out of the library and firmly shut the door behind her.

Sally sank back in her seat. "Well, that went well…" Neither of them said anything for a moment. "Maybe I should have worn a bra."

Frankie looked at her sharply. "Did you actually do that? Go out on the balcony nude?"

"Maybe just for a millisecond. No one was there, Frankie—some gardener disappeared over on the other side of the hedge. There was no way he could even see me…"

"Jesus, Sally," Frankie shook her head.

"I swear no one saw me!" Sally protested.

But Frankie only shrugged. "There are cameras all over this place. And someone's always watching. There are three security guards who do nothing but that."

This silenced Sally for a moment. "Wow," she eventually murmured.

The two women fell completely silent now. Finally, Sally looked over at Frankie. "So, Frankie, you could say something, you know. Like I'm so sorry that my mother was so mean to you."

But instead of replying, Frankie leaned forward and buried her face in her hands. "Shit," she said miserably.

At that moment, Sally had had enough. And in a brazen act unlike anything she'd ever done in a single one of her many failed relationships in the past, she rose. Then she, too, made her way out the doors of the library and into the sun, leaving her would-be partner far behind her.

If nothing else, Sally could take a walk on this beautiful day.

Suddenly, there was a lot to think about.

*

The two of them drove home in silence, past the strawberry fields laced with arcing sprays of waters. Past the spinach fields filled with covered up workers, bent over their tasks. And past the technicolor billboards advertising casinos to the north.

Neither had said a word since they left Santa Barbara. Finally, Sally closed her eyes, attempting sleep. But there was no relaxing. The entire trip had lasted less than twenty-four hours. It ended as soon as Misty stalked out of the library.

In this moment, Sally was still furious with Frankie. And Frankie, it appeared, was furious with her.

All because she stepped naked on to their balcony for what seemed like only a second. Sally really couldn't understand it. Was this something to get so up in arms about? She knew, of course, they needed to talk about it. Yet, in this moment at least, that seemed impossible.

Clearly, something far deeper was really at play. For one thing, Frankie never acted like this. Until now, she'd been kind and considerate with Sally, even when the PTSD that came with her police job threatened to drag her under. This hostility of Frankie's was something entirely new.

Sally cleared her throat. "So, Frankie," she began, "what are we doing? Are we just going to be mad all the way back to Oakland?"

Frankie didn't reply. She just stared out at the road in front of her.

"Frankie?"

She was silent for another moment. Then, finally, Frankie shook her head. "That was all very disappointing," she said.

"I'll say," Sally concurred.

"You. My mother. The whole damn thing was just... disappointing."

"Hey, you didn't tell me there were cameras everywhere, and that security people were watching them. How was I supposed to know?"

"Oh, Sally," Frankie replied. "Was I wrong to expect you to keep your clothing on outside of our bedroom?" The security cameras and the guard that came with them were a new improvement, installed after one of the gardeners was found peeing in the bushes by the pool house. Needless to say, the man was immediately fired. "I would hope you'd have better judgement than that," Frankie concluded archly.

Sally was about to say something, but then she clamped her mouth shut. She'd never felt quite so blatantly judged before. By Misty, of course. But also now, strangely, by Frankie.

"Why are you being like this?" Sally finally asked in an anguished voice. Sadly, she looked over at her partner. "Why are you being so weird?"

"I just…" Frankie faltered. Then angrily, she hit the steering wheel with her hand. She glared at Sally. "It's hell going home, alright? You see what my mother is like. I get no slack whatsoever. None. Ever. And I never have! Does that explain why I'm so screwed up right now?"

"Well, alright, Frankie. I accept that. But you threw me under the bus back there." Now tears threatened as Sally took a sharp breath. "You could have at least warned me about her."

"What was I going to say? My mother has ice in her veins and she'll probably hate you and try to block our marriage?" Frankie sighed. "You never would have agreed to marry me."

Sally leaned back against her seat and, once more, closed her eyes.

This was not an argument anyone was going to win anytime soon. And every last inch of it was pure torture.

They drove on in silence.

*

It was late afternoon when their car pulled up to Frankie's house. The conversation had sputtered in and out a few times. By the time they crossed into Oakland, things were hardly patched up.

Frankie had now seen a new, unwelcome side to Sally's personality. It appeared she had no ability to read unfamiliar social situations, including her mother's house. Sally, on the other hand, was still smarting from the fact that Frankie had lied to her. *She lied!* This one untruth now made her doubt everything she knew about her partner.

Sally leapt from the car as soon as it stopped, eager to be out of there. But then something made her stop dead in her tracks as soon as she rounded the corner to the front door. Her mouth dropped open in astonishment.

"Hey, Sally," said the tiny butch in front of her. Her hands were in the pockets of her suit pants. And as usual, all 5'1" of her was dressed to the nines, in a small, custom-fitted three-piece suit in gray gabardine. A lavender silk tie was only slightly paler than her violet button-down shirt.

The look was completed with black and white wing tips she must have scrounged from a consignment shop. The woman looked like a retro 1930's gangster. All that was missing was the Fedora.

"Oh Jesus," Sally said.

It appeared her ex—Veronica, aka Ronnie—was back.

"What?" Frankie said, bringing up the rear. She eyed the woman standing before them.

"I'm Ronnie," she said, extending her hand to Frankie. But Frankie declined to shake.

Instead, Frankie turned to Sally. "Do you know this person?"

Meanwhile, Sally had grown two shades paler. Sally swallowed. "Um...yeah. Hi Ronnie."

"Hi yourself." She eyed Sally appraisingly. "You're lookin' good, sister."

"This is Frankie," Sally explained. "Frankie, this is Ronnie. She's my..." Somehow Sally's voice disappeared.

"It's okay, you can say it," Ronnie chimed in. Once more she extended her hand. "I'm her ex. Two girlfriends ago."

Frankie, once again, declined to shake. Instead, she studied Ronnie with a professional eye. "Aw, come on," Ronnie said to Frankie. "Don't be like that."

Now Ronnie worked hard to put Frankie at ease. "She's a handful, huh? Our Sally's a true original, am I right?" Then smiling, she shook her head regretfully. "And I lost her. But what a woman…"

It was a bravura performance. Sally, meanwhile, stood stockstill, afraid to move. It was unclear to her whether she should run or eject the former lover. Or even, perhaps, invite her in. Sally was simply frozen in place.

"Excuse me," said Frankie, pushing past the two of them with her rolling bag. She unlocked the door. "You coming?" she asked Sally, her voice toughened with annoyance.

"I…uh…just a moment," Sally faltered.

Frankie responded by going inside and shutting the front door with a slam. "Uh-oh, trouble in paradise?" Ronnie wondered aloud. Then turning to Sally, her eyes lit up. "Sally Sally Sally!" she cooed. "Just look at you. You look wonderful!" She held her arms open for a hug, but still, Sally didn't move.

Instead, she brushed a stray strand of hair from her face. "What are you doing here, Ronnie?"

Ronnie shrugged. "I was in the neighborhood."

"No you weren't."

"I was, actually. I'm back in the Bay," her visitor announced. "Maybe for good. Who knows? I'm a rolling stone, if you recall."

Sally did recall, of course, because Ronnie had just rolled right out of her life one afternoon while she was at work without so much as a note. Eighteen months of putting up with Ronnie's maddening manipulations, her intense outbursts of anger, her charm, her brilliance, her originality. Her lies. Even the way she melted Sally with humor.

And then there was the sex that always brought Sally to her knees, and their downright dangerous chemistry. For Ronnie was exceptionally good in bed.

All of it simply ended one Wednesday in July. The entire relationship just disappeared that day with nary a trace. Ronnie had never even returned any of Sally's calls or texts. Forget the fact that they'd practically been living together for the better part of a year. Ronnie had simply ghosted her. Big time.

And now, inexplicably, here she was, three years later, standing on Frankie and Sally's doorstep. Because by now, of course, Sally had moved on.

"How did you know I live here?"

Veronica smiled and regarded the white polished toes of her shoes. Then she looked up at Sally and shrugged. "Just figured it out." She gave Sally a long, melting gaze.

For the tiniest second Sally returned it, unable to resist, but then good sense took hold again. Gripping her overnight bag more tightly in her hand, she made for the front door. "You'll have to excuse me, Ronnie. I have things to do," she said, without looking over her shoulder.

"I bet you do," surmised Ronnie. 'You and Frankie, wow! I hear she's a cop. Nice work."

Sally whirled on her. "Get out of here. Just go, alright? You've done your damage, Ronnie, and you're not welcome. You're just not."

"Oh, but Sally. Honey. That's why I'm here," Ronnie replied calmly. "I know I owe you a great big apology."

This stopped Sally in her tracks. For if there was one thing Sally simply couldn't resist, it was forgiveness. "What?" she asked softly.

"I don't want to disturb you two. Not at all!" Ronnie insisted, hands raised. "That's the last thing I want, sweetheart. I honestly just thought I'd look you up and try to apologize. I know what I did was wrong. The whole thing was ridiculous. Anyway, I didn't have your number for the longest time, so…" She gestured to Frankie's front yard. "Here we are."

Sally looked at her, spellbound once again by Ronnie's piercing blue eyes. It didn't occur to her that if Frankie could find her address now, she'd most certainly could have found her number back then, when it counted.

Fixing Sally in her gaze, Ronnie now leaned toward her and hung her head in shame.

"You were the sweetest woman to me, and I treated you like shit, Sally. Honestly, I am very, very sorry."

That old familiar warmth spread through Sally as she looked back at Ronnie. But then, once again, reason took hold. She couldn't do this. Not now. Not here. Not ever probably. "I…I have to go in," Sally stammered, stepping up to the front door.

Ronnie stuck her hands back in her pockets. "Okay," she said languidly. Then she shrugged. "Just thought I'd stop by. Say what I had to say. But if you have to go, I get it." She paused, tentatively.

Sally looked at her. "Well, I do appreciate it," she admitted. "Closure is always good."

Ronnie nodded. "Yes, it is. Anyway…who knows? Maybe we can actually be friends." She paused and gave her former lover a look. "I sure have missed you, Sally."

Intuitively, Sally glanced over her shoulder to the window behind her. Frankie was silently surveying the scene between them from the edge of the living room drapes. Sharply, Sally turned back to Ronnie. "Really, you have to go now," she muttered, reaching for the door. "But thanks for stopping by."

"Maybe I could come again. When you have more time?" Ronnie pressed.

Suddenly, Sally remembered the fight she'd been in with Frankie only moments earlier, and the cold silence of the drive up from Santa Barbara. And as she did, a sudden breeze of liberation moved through her body.

What am I so afraid of? Sally looked at her former lover with new clarity.

"Maybe you could," Sally said.

"Great! How about tomorrow? Same time."

Sally hesitated. Seeing Ronnie again was going to be nothing but trouble in her life, and she knew it with every fiber of her being.

Still, Sally was incapable of resisting her. Like an opioid, Ronnie raced through her veins, wiping away her pain until she was destroyed. She did it every time.

Dimly, Sally remembered her therapist's words around the time of the break up. *Ronnie is a malignant narcissist, and you need to have no contact with her.* It was advice she'd had a hard time following.

"Okay, come by tomorrow." Sally heard herself say. "I…uh…I may be able to see you. We'll see."

"Great!" Ronnie enthused. "Cheerio!"

Sally closed her eyes. *What have I just done?* Then stepping inside, she quickly shut and locked the door.

She could hear Ronnie's wing-tips tapping down the flagstone path, and the rise of her happy whistle as she walked away.

"Why was she here and what does she want?" Frankie asked as she walked in. And Sally sighed.

"I have no idea," she replied. Though, of course, she knew perfectly well.

"Huh," Frankie said, folding her hands up under her armpits. Shrewdly, she looked at her partner. "Strange you never mentioned Ronnie to me before."

"Oh…" Sally flustered. "Didn't I?"

Frankie shook her head. Then she walked away.

Sally sighed. It was going to be a very long summer.

Chapter Two

Lizzy regarded her barely awake wife, red hair barely visible beyond the edge of the sheet. "Cup of tea, honey?" she asked.

Kate turned a half-open eye on her. "Wha…?" She glanced at the clock beside her. "Oh, murderous hell!" she sighed, sitting up.

In the pearly light of the early morning, Kate looked beautiful. Her pale, naked skin seemed to gleam against the dark sheets. Lizzy felt a swell of pride. "Honey?" she asked her wife again.

"Tea? Yes, love. Tea," Kate said emphatically, rising from the bed. They exchanged a kiss, standing there in the middle of the bedroom. And then another. And another, each one progressively longer. Lizzy ran her hand down Kate's back and began to circle her buttocks with her finger tip. The usual stirring that often led to them making love had already begun.

But there was no time for this now, and both of them knew it. Lizzy still had to make her lunch, and Kate's tea, and eat her eggs. Then she had to get herself over to the garage. Reluctantly, Lizzy pulled back.

"Pick this up tonight?" she asked, looking into her lover's eyes. Tenderly, she brushed a strand of hair from Kate's cheek. Then she kissed it. *God, I love this woman.*

Kate nodded yes and, standing on her tiptoes, kissed her once more. She was like a petite Irish doll, perfectly proportioned and feminine. Her long strawberry-blonde hair softly fell across her shoulders, and a sprinkling of freckles covered her face.

Kate was sexy, smart, kind and strong. And standing there in her pale, curve-hugging t-shirt and her lace panties, she was truly the perfect complement to Lizzy's own glorious androgyny. The two of them fit together like bread and butter, and it made Lizzy's heart swell every time she thought about it.

How did I ever get so lucky? Honestly, Lizzy had no idea. For a long time—years, in fact—it seemed like there had been a curse on her love life. But, really, all this time she was just waiting for Kate to show up. She was simply getting ready for real love. Lizzy really knew that now.

She would never forget the day that Kate drove into her garage. It was Kate's flat tire, all the way back in the beginning, that brought them together. It really had been love at first sight for both of them, and each day still seemed better than the last.

They'd been married for nearly two years now, though the first year they were mostly apart. Kate had been stuck living in a Sanctuary church in Oakland until her green card visa came through, finally making her official enough to avoid ICE deportation. Needless to say, she hadn't been back to her home country of Ireland since. Nor had she left the US at all, just to be on the safe side.

Now, Kate meandered toward the shower as Lizzy turned the kettle on. "You coming in to the garage today?" she asked. Kate handled the marketing and what she called 'the homey touches' at Driven, the garage Lizzy co-owned with her best friend and business partner, Tenika.

"Don't think so!" Kate called. "I have to go see a client in Sonoma midday." Kate's job marketing some vineyards to the north kept her on the road at least a few days a week. It was a niche that had proven surprisingly lucrative.

After several moments, Lizzy could hear the shower shut off just as the kettle began to whistle. She set up Kate's favorite, a dark brown china teapot of P & G Tips—two bags, not one, to steep. Then she sat down to eat her own soft-boiled eggs.

As she ate, Lizzie remembered something that had passed by quickly in the night. Rolling onto her back, she'd woken briefly. Kate was gone from the bed, a light was on in the bathroom, and the door closed. Lizzy almost called out to her, but then she stopped herself and listened.

It sounded like Kate was crying. Her distress was barely audible, as if she was trying not to be heard.

Propping herself up on one elbow, Lizzy listened a little harder. *Yes, Kate is definitely crying.* She sat all the way up in bed, and contemplated going to her wife and asking her what was wrong.

But intruding in this particular way had proven to be tricky so far. Lizzy had been too clingy in the past, too determined to intervene even when her help was not needed or wanted. By now, Lizzy had learned her lesson, and was determined not to repeat it again. She could not, under any circumstances, crowd her wife. Even when she was shut in the bathroom in obvious distress.

If Kate needed help, she'd ask for it. This much she'd made clear to Lizzy, and that was that.

Rolling over and drawing the covers up once more, Lizzy waited silently until Kate came back to bed. Eventually, after what seemed a long time, Kate did return. Curling into a ball beside Lizzy, she tucked herself up beside her. Reaching over, Lizzy caressed her arm, hoping to convey without words that she cared. That she was here.

Kate tucked in a bit closer to her, and the two of them then drifted off to sleep, together yet as separate as ever. Not a word was exchanged about what was causing her tears. Such was the delicate balance they were always navigating. It seemed effortless for Kate. Yet, Lizzy felt like she was working on it all the time.

Kate would tell her what was going on when she was ready. And not one moment sooner.

It felt a little weird. But to Lizzy, it was simply the way things were. And if this was the only hiccup in their relationship, then it was well worth a little discomfort now and then.

*

Lizzy had just scooped the Bustelo into the garage's battered Mr. Coffee machine when Tenika rolled in for work. Usually Tenika was the first one there, and the coffee was fragrant out on the street by the time Lizzy arrived. But not today.

Instead, the garage was silent as a tomb as Lizzy pulled up on her bike. *Perhaps this is to be expected*, she thought, as she unlocked the garage and pulled up the door on the bay.

Tenika's wife, Delilah, was about to give birth to twins, and who knew what those two might be going through. It seemed to Lizzy like having one baby might be hard enough. But two? At the same time? She couldn't even imagine.

"Good morning!" said Lizzy, as Tenika ambled in. She smiled at her business partner.

"Hey, sis," Tenika said, stopping for her customary bro hug. It was the butch in her that made her hugs brief and almost businesslike. Though when push came to shove, Tenika could be a super hugger just like the rest of them. Lizzy knew this because she'd received more than a few.

"How's Delilah doing?" she asked Tenika, as she filled the coffee maker with water.

"Enormous," Tenika sighed, tying her locks up in a well-worn black and white bandana. "I don't know, man. She better have those babies soon; that's all I can say. She looks like she's gonna explode."

Tenkia put her hands on her hips, as she surveyed the manifesto of the day's repairs on the clipboard in front of her. "How are you two doing?" she asked, without looking up.

"Us? We're fine. The usual marital bliss." Lizzy wasn't going to get into the fact that she'd caught Kate secretly crying in the middle of the night. Instead, she'd decided to simply forget she'd ever seen it. Sometimes denial actually was the best strategy.

Tenika smiled at her. Then her smile faded as she glanced up and looked around the garage. "Wait—we got that stinky-ass purple Prius in here again? I just worked on it last week."

Why someone would custom paint any car purple was beyond Tenika. But she tried to remain philosophical. There was no accounting for taste.

"I know…I know," Lizzy muttered, zipping up her jumpsuit. "Came in after you left last night. Someone ripped off the catalytic converter. It's a thing now. Anyway, I'll do it."

Tenika sighed. "Okay. Cool. It's the copper they want, I guess. Jesus. Sometimes I wonder why we're bringing children into this world."

Lizzy looked up. "Seriously?"

"Well, no…but you know…" Tenika's voice faded away, and she left the rest of her sentiment unsaid. Truthfully, she was beyond excited about the arrival of not one but two babies, a boy and a girl.

She and Delilah had picked out their names early on. Their son would be Aiden. Their daughter, Ashanti. Part of her couldn't believe this was actually happening. But it was, any day now.

Tenika liked Aiden's name. It was unusual, but not too unusual in that 'look at me' kind of way that some children's names had these days. Like the people they met in birthing class who were calling their kids Jedediah and River. *What in God's name are these parents thinking?* To her, Aiden sounded dignified, but still cool.

Yet, it was Ashanti's name that Tenika really fell in love with. It was an automatic yes as soon as she found it on Google. Ashanti means thank you in Kiswahili, and that's exactly how she felt about the whole damn thing. *Thank you, great God who moves around us all the time and brought us these babies. Just…thank you.*

It seemed like a million-in-one chance that a single, carefully handled test tube of sperm, for which they'd paid top dollar, could produce not one but two gorgeous kids. She was grateful that she and Delilah had the good fortune, the savings, and the love between them to make this thing real. Without question, Tenika was definitely all in. Even if she had been dragging her feet a little in the beginning.

"Doc says it could be any day now," she mentioned, as she popped the hood on a Nissan Sentra.

"Oh yeah?"

"We went in last night for a check up."

"So how are the kids looking? Did you hear their heartbeats?" Lizzy asked, as the Prius slowly rose up on the lift behind her.

"No," Tenika replied. "We're not doing the ultrasounds, remember?"

"Oh yeah…right," Lizzy mumbled. Delilah apparently heard that too many ultrasounds could be dangerous for infants in utero. Though Tenika had yet to find any real research on this, she went along with it.

"Whatever," Tenika continued. "I figure it can't hurt to err on the side of caution. Anyway, if kicks are any indication, at least one of them is gonna be a pro soccer player."

"Sports scholarship?"

"You got that right," Tenika replied, and both women laughed.

"But the births really are any day now?" Lizzy asked, her eyes now fastened on the Prius' undercarriage.

"That's what the doctor said. Twins come early. And, like I said, Delilah really is the size of a house."

"Wow." She glanced over at her partner. Lizzy stood there, shaking her head. "Just think about it, T. Two more little people are going to be running around here before you know it."

"We could use the help," Tenika cracked, and Lizzy smiled.

If this wasn't a miracle, well, she didn't know what was.

*

Kate tore off the fumbled gift-wrap on the kitchen table before her, and studied the lumpy stuffed animal once more. It was a giraffe, and it was adorable in the toy shop where she bought it. But now it was entirely awkward to wrap into a presentable gift.

Kate sighed. Then she sat down, dejectedly. She put her head in her hands.

Somehow all of this felt wrong. She was glad for Delilah and Tenika, of course. Who wouldn't be? No one deserved a new family more than them, and they would both make wonderful parents. And the baby shower was a perfect, fitting tribute.

That was not the issue. Not in the least.

The problem was in Kate's own head. At this exact moment, she was thinking about her sister Eileen, back in Dublin. The previous month Eileen had adopted a three-month-old—a little girl named Kaeli. Even though Eileen was single and 35. Even though the Catholic Church wasn't so sure about unwed mothers. And even though a major sales job had to be done to get their parents, whom Eileen still lived with, on board. Finally, Mum and Da had grudgingly agreed.

Kate could tell by the sound in Eileen's voice that she'd been completely transformed by this little one. Gone was the sad, tired timbre of her words, worn down from too many years working in the family pub. And gone was the jealous edge Eileen often took when listening to Kate talk about her own California adventures.

But then, babies were like that. They seemed to bring out the best in you, no matter what was going on in your life. The fact that Eileen didn't have a man in her life didn't seem to be a problem either. Somehow, even Kate's conservative parents had managed to get on board. From the sound of it, they were all but raising the child themselves.

So why couldn't Kate be nicer about it?

The whole thing felt strange to her. That's all. It just felt strange.

In fact, it felt so strange, she was entirely distracted. Tenika and Delilah's shower, which she herself was organizing, now seemed like one thing too many in her life. Kate had to admit that she just barely had bandwidth for it.

For here was the real problem. When Kate allowed herself to stop and think about Eileen's baby, the truth surfaced like so much mold in the pantry. Her malaise wasn't actually about her sister and her new baby at all. The truth was simpler, and starker, than that.

For the first time in ten years, Kate was actually homesick.

For the first time since she'd left her home in Dublin, she actively missed her sister. She even missed her Mum and her Da. Her creaky, ancient, highly Catholic parents who still didn't know she was a lesbian. Nor that she was even married. And they definitely didn't know she'd married a woman. Kate had sworn Eileen to secrecy about her relationship with Lizzy, until she could get back to Ireland and come out to them in person.

For that matter, Eileen herself didn't know Kate and Lizzy had married. And all of it made Kate feel extraordinarily sad. Her family was moving on somehow, and she was missing all of it. Despite her blatant rejection of her parents and their values years earlier, when she moved to California, she felt the ache of distance acutely now. She wondered if she'd just been acting young. And rash.

Picking up the giraffe from the table, Kate held it against her chest and cradled her cheek against its stiff, spotted fur. Closing her eyes for a moment, she fought the swell of tears.

She hadn't even sent the new baby—her first niece—a gift. And why? Kate really couldn't say.

How has it come to this? How had she managed to write her own parents off so completely that she couldn't let them know anything real about her life? As far as they were concerned, she was still working as a personal assistant in her old job. And she was single, just like her sister.

Familial guilt streamed over her, like a well-washed riverbed.

Kate knew she needed to go home and tell them the truth, even though there would be some serious blowback. Gently, she put the giraffe back on the table and contemplated her situation once more.

If only she could talk to someone about her troubles. If only she could talk to Lizzy. But if she did, she knew what would happen. Lizzy, God bless her, would try to take the bull by the horns and fix the situation herself. Kate could just hear her now.

Let's just get on a plane and go to Ireland. I'll take a week off! I've been dying to meet your family...

Of course, it wasn't like the two of them hadn't talked about meeting her parents. They'd had the conversation many times. Lizzy had asked and asked to meet them, but each time Kate was evasive. She'd never even told Lizzy that she wasn't out to them.

Instead, Kate usually just changed the subject. Mainly because she doubted her wife would understand.

The truth was that Lizzy's family was entirely different from Kate's. Lizzy's parents were welcoming and kind. They'd accepted their daughter's status as the queer in the family long ago. Kate found she actually looked forward to seeing them whenever they came to visit.

Lizzy's parents weren't devout Catholics who rejected all things gay. They weren't alcoholics, like her Da. At this point, her father was an old, bitter man who'd been consistently disappointed by life, after putting everything he had, including his vitality, into the family pub. Nor were they bitter codependents like her mother, who'd fallen in lockstep behind her father, silently seething all the way.

Kate had no doubt one, or maybe both of them would throw her out of the family for good once she told them the truth.

She brushed away the tears that had gathered on her cheek. Kate had never felt so alone.

Just then, she heard Lizzy's keys turn in the lock. Then there was the usual pause as Lizzy jockeyed her bike into position so she could open the door. Kate took that moment to wipe the distress off of her face, blow her nose and force a smile. Pulling her shoulders back she rose to greet her love.

"Hey!" Lizzy called, as she entered. But then as soon as she saw Kate, she stopped. "What's the matter?"

"Nothing! Nothing... I just...hard day at work, that's all," Kate lied. Going to Lizzy, she took the bike and steered it to the side. Then she put her arms around Lizzy. "Kiss me," she commanded, and Lizzy willingly complied.

This is the game they would play for now.

And that was just fine.

Chapter Three

The last twenty-four hours had been hell in Sally's brain. First came the bleak rain of guilt that settled over Sally as she went about making dinner and unpacking her bag, wishing that everything could just be normal again. Then came a new level of annoyance as she realized Frankie had gone off with a shrug and little else to say.

Frankie was now mostly gone. She spent the evening tinkering with an old motorcycle she was rebuilding with a neighbor up the street, as if not a thing in the world was wrong. That alone was a bleak new reality Sally hated.

For, a lot was wrong.

Even the goddesses seemed to have little to say; this was where Sally, who made her living as a psychic, went for reassurance. In the gloom of their empty living room, she pulled three cards from her well-worn deck of goddess cards and laid them out on the coffee table before her. Immediately, Sally frowned.

First of all, Aphrodite, who spoke to her Inner Goddess, was reversed in the position representing the immediate past, and that was never a good sign. Basically, she was telling Sally to watch out for herself. To focus on self-care. To stay inside and lick her wounds. *Avoid Ronnie*, Aphrodite seemed to be saying.

But then there was Athena in the middle position, reflecting what was happening now. *Listen to your inner wisdom*, she was saying. *You can trust your instincts.* As in…if it feels right to take a walk with Ronnie, maybe she should?

Now Sally was confused. Was Athena telling her to avoid Ronnie or run straight toward her? Sally's tired brain kept arguing that yes, maybe she and Ronnie really could just be friends. After all, they did have amazing chemistry and a shared history as well. Somehow, there was still a connection there. Sally knew that much.

Maybe Ronnie even had something important to share with her. Maybe hanging out with her was actually important for Sally's personal evolution.

The last card Sally drew was Lakshmi, and here the deal was nearly sealed. For Lakshmi was all about Sally's 'bright future', and she tended to represent abundance in all forms. *Head for the light*, Lakshmi was telling her.

Sally tried not to feel hopeful. *Head for...a walk with Ronnie?*

On the other hand, what if 'the light' was staying the hell away from Ronnie? What if 'the light' was self-preservation and self-care?

Uncertainty settled down into Sally's soul, and stayed with her through a sleepless night. In a wordless agreement, Frankie slept on the couch, sullenly trudging out there at bedtime in her pajamas, clutching a blanket. She didn't say goodnight. She didn't even look in Sally's direction.

They never slept apart, so the situation was now officially serious. Sally tossed and turned, unable to sleep. *If only I can get Frankie to talk to me, things could be different*, ranted her tired mind.

If only Frankie would talk to her, she probably wouldn't even feel like taking a walk with Ronnie.

Ronnie. Sally rolled over with a harrumph. Good old quixotic, demanding, but also impossibly alluring Ronnie. She had to be the world's biggest manipulator. And yet...

Sally knew it was a mistake to hang out with her, but finally her big heart prevailed. They really were just friends.

Right?

*

Sally was ready for Ronnie when she returned to their house the next afternoon. She was sitting on one of the chairs in front, freshly made up and primly waiting in her white sundress and her red sandals. Frankie apparently couldn't have cared less. She hadn't even asked Sally what her plans were. Instead, she'd silently made her lunch and headed into work for another day of fighting the bad guys.

Who cared, thought Sally. Frankie obviously didn't.

Now as Sally sat here in the sunshine waiting for Ronnie, her heart beat wildly. It would be typical of Ronnie to stand her up. Ronnie was unpredictable more than anything else.

Yet, somehow this felt weirdly right. And it made absolutely no sense at all.

The moments ticked on. First Ronnie was five minutes late, then ten minutes late. Sally checked her phone again and again, but there was no text. No 'Almost there!' or 'Sorry, I'm running late'.

Why am I doing this to myself? Sally wondered for the fortieth time. And truthfully, she wasn't sure.

Soon Ronnie was fifteen minutes late. At this point, Sally's jangled nerves had been replaced by that old sick sense of anger mixed with regret. She knew what Ronnie was all about, and it was nothing but trouble.

Once again, a benevolent Universe had stepped in to save her from her own worst instincts. Sally stood up, shaking her head, and fished in her purse for the house key to go back inside. And that's when she heard a low wolf whistle from the sidewalk.

It was Ronnie.

"My, my, my…if it isn't my Sally in white. That's a sight I love to see," Ronnie exuded.

Sally whirled around. "I'm not your Sally. And you're fifteen minutes late." She paused. Where was all this righteous anger coming from? She didn't know, exactly, but now, perhaps, the goddess's messages were becoming clear.

Her inner wisdom was dishing up exactly what to say to have a bright future. It would begin with putting Ronnie in her place.

Sally sat down heavily in her chair once more. Folding her arms, she looked at her former lover. "So tell me why I should trust you again when you seriously broke my heart? And I have a fiancée. Why are we even doing this, Ronnie?"

Ronnie held up her hands. "Whoa, whoa, whoa, slow down, sister!" She assumed a casual, 'aw shucks' air. "I'm just here to take my friend Sally for a walk. That's all. I'm not asking for a damn thing more."

Ronnie gazed at Sally, who said nothing, and she shrugged. "Really," Ronnie affirmed.

Sally remained unmoved. She glared back at Ronnie. *Damn,* she thought as she did so. *This feels so right.* "Don't bullshit me, Ronnie."

Where on earth was she getting this confidence, Sally wondered to herself. This abrasive, out-and-out honesty? Saying a silent prayer to the goddesses, she continued. "You know what you're here for, Ronnie. You whistled at me."

Ronnie stuck her hands in the pockets of her well-cut gabardine trousers. "So what if I did? You're the one wearing white, like some virginal princess." Ronnie regarded Sally with a mischievous leer. And for one brief, precarious moment, Sally felt her heartbeat quicken.

"And I have to say, I like it," Ronnie concluded in a low voice.

Sally's heart quickened. *What the hell am I doing?*

Sally stopped for a moment and closed her eyes. She had a loving relationship—most of the time, at least—with the first woman she'd felt solid with in years. It was good love, even with the mother-in-law from hell. She'd finally found the relationship she'd been looking for forever, and it was Frankie. Or so she thought.

That's when a sudden quick replay of Frankie's lie flashed through her mind's eye. The reassurance that her mother was behind their wedding when she didn't even know about it ricocheted through Sally's brain like white lightening.

She paused. Perhaps she didn't know her fiancée as well as she thought she did.

Perhaps they shouldn't even get married.

Perhaps in this moment, the Universe plunked Ronnie down in her front yard for a reason. It was just so Sally could suddenly question everything she'd previously known to be true. Then she really could move toward that bright future Laxshmi kept pointing toward.

Who knew? Maybe her bright future really was with Ronnie, not Frankie. Maybe Ronnie had come back to finally redeem herself after all this time. To even apologize for the heinous way she left all those years ago.

Maybe all of this was right. Remarkably right.

Maybe Sally was exactly where she needed to be.

"So…Sally?" Ronnie was looking at her.

"Huh?" Sally looked up and refocused on her visitor. Ronnie was offering her arm.

"How about that walk?" she asked.

Rising, Sally simply took her former lover's arm and off they went, down the street, heading into the blazing spring sunshine.

Really, in the end, what choice did she have?

The goddesses were almost always right.

*

Tenika slouched against the kitchen counter in a freshly ironed, crisp white button-down shirt and her best jeans. She drained the last of a mason jar filled with cold iced tea. It was bracing, and she needed it at this sluggish moment of the day. Then she glanced at the phone in her pocket.

The baby shower was starting in less than fifteen minutes. And it was definitely bad form to be late for your own baby shower.

"Honey?" she called through the closed bedroom door.

Delilah's voice sounded from inside "I know! I'm coming!" Tenika chuckled and shook her head as she stepped away. Why her wife felt she had to close the door of their bedroom when she was assembling her outfits, she'd never understand. They were just clothes.

Except they really weren't to Delilah. To her, each carefully assembled look, whipped up like a fashion parfait, was an extension of her identity. They actually said something about her.

When she wasn't heavily pregnant, Delilah favored contrasts. Vintage pencil skirts with boxy leather jackets. An ornate velvet bustier with a pair of baggy yoga pants and fantastically huge hoop earrings. Often the ornate tattoos snaking up her arms and across her chest added to the effect.

Somehow the look was always bracing and beautiful. Even in her maternity look, which consisted mostly of soft denim dresses and skirts she'd made herself, Delilah was stunning with her glossy dark hair and her gorgeous cleavage.

Tenika smiled quietly at her good fortune. In her freeform stylings, Delilah was a California original. And she was all hers. So who cared if they were usually late for parties? Really, that didn't matter one tiny bit. She chuckled, thinking to herself that her white wife was the one in this bi-racial partnership who was on so-called 'CPT'—Colored People's Time.

She walked her empty tea glass to the sink and began to wash it. As the water poured over her hands, and the soapy sponge went round and round inside the glass, an image popped into Tenika's head.

It was from a dream the night before. A dream she'd completely forgotten until now.

She was in a dark tunnel, like a birth canal, and she was moving through it slowly. There was a sense she was heading toward the light, but she couldn't actually see it. Instead, she seemed to be moving toward more darkness. Still the light seemed to be in there somewhere—Tenika just couldn't see it. And that was terrifying.

She woke up from the dream in a cold sweat, her heart pounding. It took more than an hour to get back to sleep.

Thoughtfully now, Tenika washed the glass in her hands. Perhaps the dream was significant, even one of foreboding about the birth that would soon happen. Perhaps it was a warning of some kind.

But she couldn't let herself go there. Not with a baby shower to get to.

Everything is going to be fine, she told herself.

Because, well, it simply had to be.

*

Inside the sanctity of their bedroom, Delilah stood before the full-length mirror, turning this way and that.

Today she'd pulled out a stretchy, floor-length navy dress that perfectly outlined her belly and her expanding breasts. It was simple, classic, and its scoop neck and clinging fabric paid tribute to the fabulous, fecund contours of her pregnant body. Around her neck, Delilah wore a large necklace of beads made from slices of red tagua nuts. They formed perfect irregular circles against her pale bosom and the navy of her dress. And they added just the right touch of glamour.

Stepping close to the mirror, Delilah checked her eye makeup. Then she took a deep breath. *This is it,* she thought. Going to the baby shower meant that she was getting near the end of the epic, endless process that was bearing twins. Day after day now, Delilah felt like an elephant as she trundled around their house with this immense load parked on her hips.

The babies had already dropped, even though she hadn't yet made it to thirty-seven weeks. Still, the doctor hadn't seemed concerned. Everything would be fine, she'd said. Still...Delilah had never given birth before. She couldn't help but worry.

Now Delilah touched up her lipstick slightly, and she tried to shake off her ever-present jitters. She was in good hands with

Tenika, she knew that, and the doctor and midwife seemed competent enough. Even her friends were amazing, stepping in to be the ersatz family she didn't really have anymore. Speaking of which, they were now all waiting for her to show at the shower.

So why was she hesitating?

Part of Delilah didn't want to move one inch. She wanted to stand before that mirror all day, studying her body in her stretchy dress, trying to picture Aiden and Ashanti at that very moment, asleep in her womb.

Delilah put her hand on the top of her belly, just below her rib cage, and felt around for the subtle, supple curve of the babies inside. Their babies. She could feel something for sure, as she often had. Perhaps it was a rib cage, or perhaps a tiny pair of buttocks, feet folded up just below. *Which one is it,* she wondered.

Was it her proud warrior daughter who would grow up black and fair? Or was it their son, the color of creamy tea, a splendid blend of them both. Or would their skin color be the reverse? Or would they both be Black, or both White? Either way, Delilah couldn't wait to meet them. To birth them. To hold them. To nurse them.

To love them.

"Honey?" Tenika called through the door.

"I know! I'm coming," Delilah called back. Then taking a deep breath, she picked up a sweater from the chair and walked to the door. Opening it, she made her entrance, stepping into the kitchen.

"Nice," said Tenika appreciatively. "You look beautiful, baby."

Delilah smiled, feeling her wife's love for her come streaming in. This, of course, was why she dressed with the door closed, and insisted on making an entrance. Because every time Tenika said such things, a simple thrill moved up Delilah's spine. It was the shiver of true love.

They kissed briefly, and then she followed Tenika, in her simple white shirt, her bundle of black dreads spilling over the collar, out the door. Pausing, Delilah locked the door behind them. Then she climbed up into their truck.

This was going to be fun.

*

Sally closed her eyes, lulled by the low hum of car wheels on pavement.

The last place she wanted to be right now was a baby shower. She didn't want to be anywhere at all with Frankie, now driving along stoically beside her. Truthfully, they were still barely speaking to each other, a full six days after the disastrous visit to Santa Barbara and their fight. In fact, Frankie was still sleeping on the couch.

Meanwhile, Sally had seen Ronnie twice, each time taking an apparently chaste walk. She hadn't told Frankie about these visits, nor had Frankie asked. It simply hadn't come up, and Sally wasn't inclined to share what she was doing while Frankie was at work. If Frankie was aware she was hanging out with her ex, she hadn't said a word. And that made Sally saddest of all.

Meanwhile, each time Sally met with Ronnie, she had the vague feeling that her ex wanted something. Though what it was, she couldn't figure out. Instead, Sally kept telling herself this was a fantastic opportunity for growth.

Meanwhile, she was beginning to wonder about her future with Frankie.

Frankie pulled up to the restaurant with a sigh and backed into a parking spot. She stared straight ahead. "So now we're supposed to put on our happy face?" she asked grimly.

"Well…sure." She fixed Frankie with a look. "Oh, come on, Frankie! It's not their fault you lied to me."

Frankie's eyes narrowed and she gave Sally an acid look. "Would you just quit it, Sally?" she hissed, her voice lowering. "I wasn't lying. I've told you that fifteen times. I was trying to—"

"Sugar coat the facts so your mother didn't have to deal with me? I know. You've told me repeatedly, Frankie. We discussed this.

You blew it and you know it."

Now Frankie grabbed her arm in frustration. "Look at me," she said, her fingers digging into Sally's sleeveless flesh. "I can't help it that I have Cruella DeVille for a mo—"

But Sally broke free, a new, fierce, nascent liberation running through her veins as she shoved Frankie away. Her arm burned where Frankie's fingers had dug in. "That's right. Just blame it all on someone else." She fixed her partner with a look. "And don't touch me like that," she said, her hand flying to her tender arm where Frankie had grabbed it. "You should just…grow up!"

Getting out of the vehicle, Sally marched up to the door of the restaurant, swung it open and headed inside. She could honestly care less if Frankie followed her or not. Maybe this on-going fight really was all about her liberation.

Meanwhile, up the street, Kate and Lizzy were just rounding the corner in Lizzy's pick up. As Lizzy found a spot to park, Kate was back-peddling like mad.

"Lizzy, please believe me…it isn't that I'm upset. I'm telling you, I'm perfectly fine! I don't even know why you think I was crying," she fibbed.

She had been, of course. She'd been sitting on the toilet just the night before, silently sobbing into a hand towel, as she had so many nights recently. The fact was that Kate had been counting on Lizzy to sleep through her nightly sob, which she conducted as quietly as possible. That Lizzy had found her out was a new, unwanted wrinkle.

Now here they were, about to go off to a carefree, wine-filled afternoon party with all of their closest friends. And Lizzy had chosen this moment to call her on her uncomfortable nightly meltdowns.

Lizzy stopped the car in its parking place, and looking over, she took Kate's hand. "Wait for a minute, honey. Just tell me what it is," she said calmly. "It's okay."

Kate sighed. There really was no getting out of this. She looked over at her wife.

"Okay, okay. Look, I can't really explain it," Kate finally said. She'd be damned if she was going to tell Lizzy every last thought in her head. For the last thing she wanted to get into with Lizzy right now—or ever—was her homesickness.

After all, Lizzy had done so much for her. And sacrificed for her. There was getting Kate out of the job from hell, then paying for her immigration attorneys, and helping her find a Sanctuary church when her former boss turned her in to ICE. She even married Kate, ostensibly so she could stay in the U.S. Though, of course, they did love each other and probably would have married anyway.

Poor Lizzy had to then put up with an entire year of Kate living in the church because she couldn't get a green card. They had to get married in the church, with scarcely any reception at all. And they didn't even get to spend their wedding night together. All and all, it was nearly a year of no sex before Kate finally got her green card, and could move in with her wife.

The list of Lizzy's selfless acts seemed to go on and on. So no, she wouldn't be getting into her crushing homesickness at this point. To Kate, her sadness at this point just seemed shameful.

She looked at Lizzy hopefully. "Haven't you ever just felt like crying for no reason?" she asked.

Lizzy looked back at her quizzically. "No?"

Kate gathered up their gift and her purse, and put her hand on the door handle. "Oh, well, love, let's just not worry about that right now, shall we? Here we are at a lovely party. Let's go and see our friends."

Lizzy stopped her once more, placing a hand on her arm. "But you were crying. Right? I wasn't making that up?"

Almost impatiently, Kate dropped her hands into her lap. "Yes. Lizzy, please. I was crying in the bathroom, alright? But it's truly not important. Really! Now can we please go?"

Lizzy just looked at her. "Alright," she finally shrugged.

Her wife was, basically, unstoppable. Lizzy knew that about Kate.

It was one of the things about her she loved the most.

*

An hour later, Tenika sat back and looked at eight glowing faces around the table. Kate, Lizzy, Frankie and Sally had all made it. And now, two peach Bellinis later, they were all relaxed, happy and animated. An air of satisfied excitement and non-stop chatter filled the room.

Even Rosalind, an Asian-American tech executive and her gender-neutral lover, Monroe, showed up and joined them. Kate had introduced the pair to each other after she met Monroe at the church she lived in during Sanctuary. Tenika and Delilah hadn't really seen them for a good few months, as those two were now soundly parked in their lesbian love bubble. From the looks of it, they had no time, whatsoever, for distractions.

Tenika smiled broadly at the women assembled around the table, then she took Delilah's hand. Her wife smiled back at her. "You okay?" Tenika asked gently.

"Better than fine," Delilah responded. "But God, I'd kill for a Bellini…"

"Here," offered Tenika, holding out her glass, and Delilah took a long sip.

"Thanks, T," she said, giving back the tall, cool, peachy glass. "I needed that." Just a sip couldn't hurt, she figured—not in her last trimester. Sitting back in the chair, Delilah joined her wife in quietly gazing around the table. "This is great," she said.

"Yup," Tenika agreed. Then suddenly, she put down her glass and Delilah's hand, and she stood. Tenika cleared her throat. "Ahem," she said. Suddenly, the animated wall of sound that was six women talking at once ceased, and all eyes were now on her.

"Glad y'all made it here today, and we really appreciate the party, and the presents, and…" Here she smiled at her wife. "Just everything I guess."

Tenika looked around at the group of dear friends, her eyes shining. "I honestly don't know where we'd be without you guys. I mean, now we've got a stroller! A nice one, even. The wheels on it are like a Ferrari! Lizzy, you look at this thing?"

"I picked it out of *Car & Driver*," Lizzy retorted. Some in the group had gone in together on the badly needed stroller, while others, like Kate, had opted for cute baby toys.

The group laughed, and Tenika shushed them. "No. Really," she said, raising her glass, "I'm standing up here because I want to toast my wife. Delilah." She turned to the woman beside her who was slumped back in her chair, her belly a formidable obstacle between her and the restaurant table. "Honey," Tenika said, love beaming from her eyes, "I just want to thank you for carrying these babies, and for all the love you've got for me and for them. You're gonna be an incredible mother, we all know it. So here's to you, baby."

Tenika raised her glass, and the rest of the table followed suit.

"To Delilah!" someone cheered, and the others joined in, with shouts, applause and affirmations. Then they all drank. Even Delilah, though this time she took a much smaller sip.

Now she struggled to her feet and took Tenika's hand. "This is what it looks like when you're having twins," she cracked. "And when you have a partner who really, truly comes through." They kissed then, for it was true. "She had to come a ways, but it's Tenika whose really made all of this possible. So here's to T!" she said, raising her glass.

Delilah's lifelong wish to be a mother really was happening because of Tenika. For not only had Tenika gotten past her fears about being a mother and finally agreed, she'd cashed in her life savings to pay for the IVF.

Eventually, she, too, had realized that having kids was her dream, too. Especially with Delilah by her side.

"Yeah, yeah, okay," Tenika demurred modestly as everyone began to applaud. "Don't get confused here, guys. All I did was pony up the cash. Delilah's the one who's been doing the hard work." She kissed her wife as everyone applauded one more time.

"Whatever you do," Tenika said, turning back to the table, "you've got to take care of your girl. Believe me when I tell you women, it's worth it."

Reaching over, Lizzy took Kate's hand and squeezed it. And leaning in, they, too, exchanged a kiss. It was an immediate referendum on everything that passed between them, a grace note in what had been a touchy day so far. Kate's point had been made. It would only get better from here.

Across the table, Sally stole a look at Frankie who glanced shyly in her direction. She gave Sally a nod, for this was all she was capable of now. Perhaps there was a bridge there. But really, it was just too early to tell.

"Anyway, forget you two," Lizzy joked. "I say let's hear it for those twins!"

"Okay! Okay…" Tenika laughed, as Delilah lowered herself back down into her chair. "We're about to get seriously upstaged, I get it, y'all. Pretty soon you're gonna completely forget about us!" The crowd laughed and hooted.

And so that Saturday afternoon dissolved into a patchwork of sunlight, Bellinis, and the warmest of friends, all together, stitched with laughter, hope, and excitement.

And above all, boundless love.

Chapter Four

Sally rolled on her back and stared into the semi-darkness of their bedroom. She glanced at the digital red numbers on the bedside table: 2:35 am. A low lavender light from the streetlight outside painted strange, ominous shadows on the walls around her.

Great, she thought grimly. It was shaping up to be yet another sleepless night. They were now on day seven since the big fight, and she hadn't had a good night's sleep yet. Honestly, Sally's central nervous system was shot. She'd never been through anything like this before.

Sally glanced at Frankie sleeping soundly beside her. Somewhere around the fifth night Frankie had returned to their bed, but she remained grim and unyielding. She said little and hadn't even touched Sally. Instead, she kept chastely to her side of their bed. Frankie kept her back to Sally, and her breathing was even and undisturbed.

Sally pondered exactly what thoughts kept her awake night after night. Maybe it was the fact that she was now questioning their entire relationship. And the fact was they had yet to have a thorough, honest discussion about what had happened in Santa Barbara. Every time Sally attempted to bring it up, they quickly devolved to anger and shouted accusations. At this point, she had no idea what to do.

Then there was the matter of Misty, Frankie's mother. What was it she had said to Sally?

I'm sure you're a very nice young lady, but you will not be marrying my daughter. The words stung as they recycled through Sally's mind, yet again.

*

Misty had been so definite, so my-way-or-the-highway. There was clearly no chance for reconciliation whatsoever. Misty wasn't even interested in getting to know Sally, not even one tiny bit. It was an open and shut case of refusal. Perhaps even blatant homophobia. Or some sort of weird prejudice Sally couldn't quite put her finger on.

Frankie had said her mother accepted the fact she was gay. Did that mean this was *not* actually homophobia? And if not, then what was it? Was Misty simply against all working class girls with free spirits and a deep connection to the mysterious? Or was all of this really just because Sally had gone out on the balcony nude? And if so, would Misty ever forgive her?

The thought that this could bring down her pending marriage to Frankie boggled Sally's mind.

Rolling on her stomach, she listened to the two opposing voices in her head. One championed her rights—*don't let that priggish old woman boss you around. Be proud you are who you are!* Meanwhile, the other deeply regretted the landmine she'd just stepped on. She couldn't help but feel a twinge of shame.

Briefly, Sally even wondered whether she should write an apology to Misty. She hadn't yet said she was sorry for offending Frankie's very formal mother—this could only help, right? It would be a display of good breeding and decent manners. It was probably the sort of thing Misty expected.

Yet, it was also the sort of thing that made Sally recoil. Why should she play this tortured game when Misty clearly didn't accept her in the first place?

And yet...Sally still didn't understand what was so terribly, terribly bad about stepping out on a balcony nude. Especially when she honestly believed no one could see her. Was it really worth calling off an entire marriage? This argument had circled around her brain again and again, leaving a well-worn path.

Lying there, Sally listened to Frankie breathing steadily beside her. Now Sally couldn't help but wonder where was Frankie in all of this. Why hadn't Frankie stood up to her mother and protected her? And why hadn't Frankie apologized? Where was her champion? Her defender?

These were the real questions on the table now. For on top of everything else, Sally felt acutely abandoned.

She sat up now, more determined to take some kind of action. The first problem to deal with was clearly Misty. Frankie seldom talked about her mother. But now Sally recalled the sweat that trickled down Frankie's brow as she told her mother they were getting married. And how she panicked the minute the woman objected. Clearly Frankie felt powerless, even dominated by her mother.

Sally's newly hatched ire began bubbling once more. *This was so wrong.*

She sat up, feeling like she might explode if she lay in bed for one more moment. Sally just couldn't be held captive by the swirling, undulating thoughts in her head. She simply had to do something about this right now. And if Frankie wouldn't talk to her about any of this, well then…she'd just take matters into her own hands.

No one was going to take their engagement away. Not even Misty.

She thought back to all they had been through the previous year, when Frankie was on administrative leave with the police department because of her PTSD. How many nights had a very depressed Frankie lay inert on the couch while she tried vainly to help?

Then there was her First Responders' PTSD retreat, and how fired up Frankie had been when she returned. That's when hope had begun again in earnest for both of them; that is when Frankie had finally, deeply opened up to her. The thrilling, and deep, almost secret intimacy Sally felt for Frankie left an indelible impression.

She simply had to move forward with her beloved. If Frankie wanted to get married, then marry they would. And yet…

Sitting there, reviewing the events of the past year, Sally felt tears well up in her eyes. An ache began in her chest as she thought of the night they became engaged over dinner in a quiet Oakland restaurant. Her tears began to slide down her cheeks. Frankie had been so vulnerable that night. So beautiful and so strong, and so achingly real. Sally could still recall the thrill that raced down her spine when Frankie handed her the small velvet bag containing the diamond ring.

Sally had been absolutely floored that night—she honestly hadn't been expecting a proposal. And Frankie had been so certain. And oh so mind-blowingly sexy.

Sally felt fury rise up in her. The two of them had worked too damn hard for this to throw it all away. And if Frankie was temporarily disabled by her toxic mother, well then, she needed to take things into her own hands. Sally felt her resolve kicking in.

Silently, she slipped from bed and walked into the alcove where her desk was. She pulled open the bottom drawer. Removing a few pieces of the creamy linen stationery she usually reserved for billing her clients, she sat down at her desk. And she began to write.

Hello Misty,

Thank you for hosting me on our very brief visit to Santa Barbara. Unfortunately, your rudeness to me was so egregious that I left feeling nothing less than traumatized. Frankly, I was shocked. And I still am.

Sally hesitated now, a little surprised at herself. But these words felt remarkably good to write. She kept on going.

People like you think you can spout off about anything you want to say, simply because you have wealth and power. But you don't have power over me, Misty. Instead, you have my pity...

Sitting there in the darkness, Sally did indeed feel powerful as she wrote out everything on her mind. And there was a lot. Not only was she completely furious at Misty, she was furious with everyone who'd ever written her off in her life.

Ten minutes later, Sally was finally done with her rant. She'd laid out exactly what she thought. She'd been one hundred percent honest, and it felt terrific.

Sally sat back as a wave of real relief descended through her body. Suddenly, her mind was clear, and the dark swirl of anxiety that had held her captive for the last six nights were gone. She took a long breath, enjoying her new-found sense of calm.

She'd said everything she'd never been able to say to a disapproving world that had always judged her harshly. Then folding the letter, Sally smiled as she tucked it into a pink envelope. She wrote the name 'Misty Kennedy' on the front.

Then she sat there, contemplating what to do next.

She couldn't mail her letter, of course. For one thing, Frankie would kill her. No, Misty could never see this letter, nor could Frankie, for that matter. Sally knew this without even asking.

Yet, as she wrote the letter, another thing became clear. She did love Frankie—or the Frankie she thought she'd agreed to marry. Now this new sullen, uncommunicative Frankie who'd turned on her was worrisome, yes. But perhaps this, like Frankie's PTSD, was something they could work with. Maybe it was something that might just dissolve and blow away.

It was probably just another 'f***ing growth experience' as one of her friends liked to say.

Wearily, Sally yawned, aware that she needed to go back to

bed. Mostly, the letter was an exercise in getting something off of her chest. She did love Frankie, and she did want to marry her. And Frankie still had some apologizing to do. That much was clear. But somehow the writing of this letter she would never send had broken the logjam in her head. Now she really knew where she stood.

Sally tucked the envelope into the top drawer of her desk. Then she closed it and walked back to bed, thinking nothing more of it. And as Sally climbed back into bed gratefully, a new awareness descended over her.

What am I going to do about Ronnie?

Sally's eyes snapped open in mild alarm. She was glad Frankie couldn't read her mind because, at this moment, some truly dangerous thoughts had just shown up there. Namely, that she wasn't quite ready to send her former lover on her way, even though Sally knew she loved her wife-to-be. And even though she also knew that Ronnie was nothing but trouble. So why on earth was she having such self-destructive urges?

There was just something about Ronnie, though Sally couldn't say exactly what it was. And that 'something' still held her fast.

Perhaps it was simply that Ronnie was a living, breathing person who wanted to talk to her. Unlike her wife at the moment, Ronnie didn't coldly refuse to speak to her. Ronnie was a screamer, yes, and capable of horrific, abusive tirades. But then, almost immediately they were done. And afterwards, she was nothing but sweetness and light. This was simply Ronnie's way.

Furthermore, their walk had been completely benign. Nothing had happened. And if Sally were to be entirely honest about it, it came as a relief. Talking to Ronnie had actually been a balm to her agitated soul. Ronnie had listened thoughtfully, far better than she had in the past. And she'd said remarkably little about herself.

Sally found herself opening up to this person who knew her so well. She told Ronnie all about her relationship with Frankie, how they met and fell in love, and how she helped Frankie cope with the PTSD. She even told Ronnie about Frankie's mother and the disastrous trip to Santa Barbara. And their fight.

To Sally, telling Ronnie all about it was like sliding down a fast, undulating water slide. Once she stepped off the top and let the water carry her, the truth came rushing out in a fantastic whoosh. At the end of which, they just looked at each other for a moment.

"I'm sorry to hear that, Sally," Ronnie finally said, and her expression was gentle and filled with compassion. It was the first time Sally had ever seen her former lover look so genuinely moved. And it shook her slightly.

Now, as Sally thought about Ronnie, she tried to dredge up the appropriate revulsion at Ronnie's past treatment of her. The relationship had ended three years earlier, and its damage left Sally shaken to her core for many, many months afterwards. Yet, now she found she couldn't really hook into that reality. Instead, her mind worked overtime to allow space for Ronnie.

Maybe Ronnie had changed.

Sally badly needed someone to talk to, dammit. Even if it *was* her borderline ex. If that meant she had to go on a few walks with her, and not be entirely honest with her grumpy fiancé about where she'd been, then so be it. Prevail she would.

Sally needed this, for reasons she couldn't entirely explain. And Frankie was going to have to just cope.

No, Sally decided as she rolled over yet again. She wouldn't feel guilty about walking with Ronnie.

Instead, she'd probably do it again.

*

Lizzy poked her head around the shower curtain, startling Kate who was mid-shower. "Hey," she said, "your phone's ringing. It's your sister. Shall I answer it?"

"No!" Kate burst out a little too vehemently. Then she corrected herself. "Sorry, love. Just…just let her leave a message. I'll call her later."

Kate had been lost in reverie as the warm water beat down on her, washing away her worries. The week had progressed slowly since the baby shower. She was grateful to hear her sister was calling because her homesickness had become a steady drone in the background. It wasn't going away until Kate went home, it appeared.

But another thought struck her now as she turned off the shower and stepped out onto the bathmat. They'd spoken just last week—so why was she calling now? The thought worried Kate.

Eileen could only be calling her again so soon with bad news.

Twenty minutes later, from the privacy of their bedroom, Kate pulled out her phone. She tapped on her sister's name and waited for the overseas connection to go through. There was a pause. Then there was Eileen, sounding a little smaller and further away than usual.

"Eileen?"

"Yes. It's me," Relief filled Kate's body, just hearing her sister's voice. But now she paused. Something was off. Eileen sounded somber. She hadn't said much in the message—only to call her. "Thanks for getting back to me so fast."

"What—is it the baby?" Kate began, but Eileen cut her off.

"No, Kate. It's Da. He had a massive stroke."

Suddenly, everything spun out in Kate's consciousness. The words 'massive stroke' swirled around her, surreal, not making sense exactly. "He had a...stroke?" she heard herself say.

"It's not so very terrible as it could be," Eileen continued. "He's going to be alright, and he's talking and all of that. But...he's weak." She sighed. "He's getting old, Kate."

Kate should have expected this. After all, her father was well into his seventies and, honestly, seemed even older than that. Part of her had even been expecting this.

"I'm...oh my," Kate finally said, barely able to speak. "A stroke," she repeated dumbly. "How's mum handling it?"

"Like mum," Eileen said dully. Their mother was as stoic and grim as they came, an angry workhorse. Undoubtedly she hadn't missed a moment behind the bar at the pub in spite of it all.

There was a long silence as two tears slid down Kate's cheek. Lizzy now appeared in the bedroom doorway. "What is it?" she whispered. Kate looked at her and shook her head, unable to say anything. Seeing her tears, Lizzy took a worried step toward her, listening.

"Do you need me to come?" Kate asked Eileen.

"No, stay there. He'll recover, the doctor says. What he needs now is rest." What was implied but not spoken, of course, was that Kate's presence might be too stressful for someone in such fragile shape. Which she understood perfectly.

"Can I speak to him?" Kate asked.

"No…he's uh…he's resting, love." In the background, Kate could hear the baby begin to cry.

"Is that Kaeli?"

"It is." A small warmth crept into her sister's voice, and for a moment Kate was filled with longing to hold her new niece. She closed her eyes against the intrusion of her feelings.

"I'm sorry. I'm sorry I'm not there, Eileen," she said. "Honestly. I am."

"I know," her sister sighed. "But it's alright. Really. He's going to be fine."

"Are you sure…" Kate hesitated. "Eileen, love, are you telling me everything?"

"Relax! Yes, I'm telling you everything, Kate." Eileen gave a brief, unreadable pause. "I just thought you should know."

Kate hung up a few moments later. Then, standing there in the bedroom, she began to weep. By now, Lizzy was sitting on the bed beside her. "Come here," she said, holding out her arm. Kate tucked into it.

"I'm sorry," she finally said, as she curled into Lizzy's shoulder. She laid her cheek against the soft, pilled fabric of Lizzy's shirt as she allowed herself to break down and sob. For once the barrier she'd erected between her and the world had completely melted down.

"Your Dad?" her wife asked, and Kate nodded tearfully.

"You okay?"

"Not really," Kate said. She reached for a tissue and blew her nose. Then she gave a small, ironic laugh. "I'm a mess if you want to know the truth."

"So what happened?" Lizzy asked gently, and Kate headed back into her arms.

"He had a massive stroke," she muffled into Lizzy's shoulder.

Lizzy sat up a little straighter. "Do we need to go over there?"

Here it was, the inevitable question. One Kate knew Lizzy was asking out of concern. She pulled back and looked at her wife "I don't think so. Apparently, he'll be okay."

Lizzy's protective instincts were now, predictably, in high gear. "You sure, honey? Because Tenika would cover for me at work. We could get a flight tomorrow—or tonight, even. We could totally do this, Kate."

"No, no, no!" Kate protested, holding up a hand. "Lizzy, love. Please. Stop. It's alright. Eileen and mum are handling it. We...we don't need to go. She told me that."

Lizzy just gave her a look. "It's your dad," she said. "I mean—I know you don't get along and everything. But if it was mine..."

Kate found she could say nothing more, for right now there was nothing more to say. She didn't have the strength to take on the entire 'taking Lizzy home' issue. Not now. Not when her heart had just fallen down a staircase of circumstance.

Kate dried her eyes and attempted a weak smile. "I'm sure everything's going to be fine," she said firmly. And maybe it actually would.

"But thank you," she added, reaching for Lizzy's hand. Sitting there, she smiled at her partner gamely.

They couldn't even begin to talk about this in earnest.

Not now. Possibly not ever.

Chapter Five

Delilah closed her eyes and focused, as Tenika squeezed her hand.

"And breathe out—two, three, four," intoned the instructor. "Gotta keep it going. That's the key, ladies."

At this exact moment, Delilah was lying on a yoga mat, her belly full of the twins who were totally obscuring her feet. She was having trouble getting her rhythm.

"Breathe, honey…" said her wife. "Come on, Delilah. We know how to do this. Shallow, even breaths, right? Inhale-two-three…then exhale-two-three…" Tenika tried to keep her frustration out of her voice. They'd practiced this twice since the last class. Now she had no idea why Delilah couldn't get this right.

"I know, I know…" Delilah tried once more to even her breaths. But she was distracted.

Who had time to practice intentionally breathing in the whirl of pre-birth? Lately, it felt like every spare moment had been occupied by getting ready for the two babies soon to be born. And that was on top of wrapping up her work at the tattoo parlor for the next three months. Delilah had been totally preoccupied.

But the problem right now was more urgent. There was a new pain, one she hadn't felt before, right in the front of her belly. It felt suspiciously like indigestion. Or maybe gas? The strange pain pinged again, grabbing her gut as if it wouldn't let go. It radiated through her pelvis from the right side of her uterus over to the left. It felt like a menstrual cramp on steroids. And it worried her.

Maybe this is the beginning of my contractions? Delilah set her jaw, determined not to go into labor yet. Because if this was the beginning of real contractions, those babies could just hold on. It was still a good four weeks before her official due date.

"I don't—" Delilah began to say. "*Ow!*"

Tenika's eyes widened. "What?"

Delilah just shook her head. "Nothing. Nothing. Let's try it again." She gripped Tenika's hand hard and began breathing in earnest, while her wife counted. "Inhale-two-three…" But still she winced again.

Tenika peered at her. "Hey, you okay?"

Delilah only shook her head. She exhaled, then she winced again. "Shit," she muttered.

"Delilah?" asked Tenika, looking her over more closely. "Honey?" Then suddenly she was up and moving, leaving Delilah in her spot on the floor.

Within a moment, the birthing class instructor was standing over her, a worried Tenika by her side. "How are you doing, hon?" she asked gently.

"I'm fine, it's just…OW!" Delilah clamped her eyes shut. "It's this pain that keeps on coming."

"Great—let's get that breathing going again," said the instructor. "Perfect chance to practice. And one, two, three, fou—"

"But what about the freaking contractions?" Tenika interrupted.

The instructor gave a shrug as she finished counting. "Five, six, seven…" Then she turned to Tenika. "Let's see what happens. Maybe these are just Braxton-Hicks." It was not uncommon for women at Delilah's stage to have false labor pains, and so now here they were.

Maybe.

Delilah closed her eyes and took a few steadying breaths. She returned her focus to her wife, resigned.

"T… please," Delilah panted, eyes still closed. She patted the carpet beside her yoga mat. "Sit down…next…to me." Delilah's breaths were coming short and sharp now.

The last thing Delilah wanted was to kick up a whole lot of unnecessary baby drama at this moment. Things were already anxious enough with the mere prospect of twins.

Twins. How in the hell was she going to actually give birth to not one but two babies? And how were they ever going to take care of them both? Two was a lot of babies.

Delilah tried not to think about it as she focused on the breathing. Once more, Tenika took her hand. "One, two—" Tenika began, but this time Delilah cut her off with another groan of pain.

"Shit," she murmured as she rolled over heavily to her side. Delilah drew her knees up slightly. "This feels bad," she said in a small voice.

Tenika pushed her glasses up her nose and gave her wife an assessing look. "Like…*bad* bad?"

"Yeah." Delilah's eyes met hers and now she looked scared. "Bad," she repeated grimly. Suddenly the instructor was by their side again, responding to Tenika's urgent signaling.

"Everything alright here?" she asked, ever perky. Tenika shook her head grimly.

"I'd say we'd better get over to the ER," Tenika said as she stood up.

The instructor looked slightly stricken. "You sure?"

"Oh, we're sure alright," Tenika replied. Bending over, she helped Delilah slowly rise to her feet. Now the other breathing mothers in the class were all looking at them. A few were beginning to sit up in concern.

Delilah leaned on her wife heavily as she moved toward the door. She waved to her classmates as they headed off, and a few waved back.

"Okay...don't forget to breathe!" the instructor called after them. "And good luck!"

But they were already out the door by then, heading for the hospital.

*

An hour later, Delilah's contractions were classified as Braxton-Hicks, and so they were told to go home. Not only had her water not broken, but her cervix wasn't even dilated. Their midwife did a very cursory check on Delilah before sending them both right back out the door.

Now the two of them drove home in silence. They pulled up to a stoplight, and Tenika drummed her fingers on the steering wheel. Anxiety had been pulling at her all day. It was the anxiety of anticipating every last thing that could go wrong, beginning with Delilah having emergency surgery to deliver the babies.

Could they actually have the natural birth Delilah kept talking about?

Given how enormous she was getting, and how slight her frame was, the prospect seemed downright impossible to Tenika. That's where the c-section came in, and with it frightening features like anesthesia and heavy bleeding. The list of things that could go wrong with a surgical birth went on and on, parading in an endless conga line through Tenika's mind. She wished she'd never looked it up on Google.

Now Tenika remembered her dream from the night before. The darkness of that tunnel was so oppressive as it closed in around her, a heavy velvet blackness she could practically feel. It was almost as if she was suffocating.

She couldn't think about this now. She really couldn't. She had to stay strong and positive for her wife. Reaching out as if to steady herself, Tenika put her hand on her partner's knee. "How you doin'?" she asked.

Delilah was looking out the window. "I'm okay." she said, eyes not moving. She seemed quiet. And resigned.

Tenika nodded and put the truck into gear, they began to drive again. Above all, she had to keep on moving forward.

*

Two evenings later, Tenika slid onto the stool beside her business partner and ordered an Obsidian from the woman behind the bar.

The two women sat silently for a moment, relaxing in their shared, end-of-day fatigue. It had been their ritual for several years now to have a beer together after work at least once a week. This was usually on Tuesday nights for some reason neither of them could still remember. They talked, and drank, and hashed out life together for a while. It seemed as essential to the running of their business as keeping up their inventory of auto parts.

"So…" Lizzy began, taking a swig of her Corona. "How are you doing, T?"

"What do you mean, how'm I doing? You just spent the damn day working right next to me," Tenika groused. "You know perfectly well, Lizzy. I'm hella shitty." The last few days she'd kept her head down and kept working in an attempt to keep her anxieties at bay. But her workaround wasn't working.

"Well…more like keyed up, I'd call it," Lizzy noted. "But hell. You're supposed to be scared, T. This is big shit you two are dealing with. Extremely big."

"How reassuring," Tenika said darkly. She shook her head and took a long pull at the cold, dark beer that arrived on the bar before her. The Obsidian slid down her throat like frosted gold. She closed her eyes for a moment, savoring it.

Who knows when I'll get to have a nice, cold beer with my best friend again? I should do my best to enjoy it.

Tenika's eyes flew open. Where'd that thought come from? Once again, the dark doomsday feeling from the dream slithered through her body, unsettling her. "Yeah, well I'm fine, okay?" she insisted, trying to push away the sensation with her words. "And everything's gonna be fine. For real." Tenika turned toward Lizzy. "I know that, alright?"

"That bad, huh?" chuckled Lizzy. "I never really pegged you as an optimist, T."

"Lizzy, shit. Come on. I'm just doing what you have to do when you and your partner are about to have two damn babies at once, and all hell's about to break loose. You gotta stop and just assume the best. Am I right?" Tenika paused and looked at her best friend expectantly.

"Of course you're right. I'm just giving you shit, T. That's all." Lizzy chuckled at her own humor. "But yeah…of course. It's all going to be fine."

There was that word again. At this point, it meant nothing. And no one felt particularly 'fine' at all.

Taking another long pull that basically finished off the bottle in front of her, Lizzy didn't stop to think about her own situation at home. Better, she thought, to keep the focus on Tenika and the approaching births. Because the last thing she wanted to do right now was dwell on her own wife, or even talk about the strange trouble simmering between them.

If there was trouble. Anyway, Lizzy wasn't even sure what it was about. As usual Kate was an enigma, albeit one whom Lizzy deeply loved.

"Hey—did Sally give you guys that reading yet?" Lizzy asked.

Sally's goddess card readings had become something of a cause celebre among the lesbians of the East Bay. With a little flourish, she'd presented Tenika and Delilah with a free reading at the baby shower. Some flocked to her for the psychic readings whenever something big was about to happen. Meanwhile, others hung back, eyeing the process skeptically.

"Uh oh…" Quickly, Tenika dug her phone out from her shirt pocket. "Was that…damn!"

Putting the phone away, she gave Lizzy a crestfallen look. "I screwed up. The reading just happened. It was an hour ago and I missed the whole thing." Tenika shook her head and sighed.

"Why was it scheduled on a Tuesday?" Tenika complained. "I completely forgot about it—you know I'm like a damn rat looking for the cheese when it comes to my Tuesday drinks with Lizzy."

"Hey, I didn't schedule it," Lizzy protested.

"Delilah is not going to be pleased," Tenika grumbled.

Picking up the last of her beer, Tenika drained it. Then putting the bottle back on the bar, she stood with a harrumph. "Better get home and face the music," she said. Once more she shook her head. "I can't believe I missed the damn reading."

"Oh, you're going to be okay," Lizzy said, giving her old friend's shoulder a reassuring pat. Then, throwing down a twenty, she stood and settled up their tab. "This one's on me, T. Get home. I'll see you tomorrow."

Tenika shot her a grateful look as she grabbed her backpack. "Thanks, Lizzy. Night."

"Night."

Still shaking her head, Tenika slung her messenger bag over a shoulder. "Only brain I got," she said to no one in particular as she pushed through the door to the sidewalk.

*

Sally laid the cards down on her coffee table with a definitive air. Then she paused, unwilling to admit exactly what she was seeing. Sally looked again at the cards. Then she glanced at Delilah and hesitated.

What she was seeing was completely disturbing.

"What?" Delilah leaned forward a little too eagerly. She could always smell trouble on the horizon. And given that she'd known Sally since college, she could see something was not right. "Sally...what is it?"

A professional veil dropped over Sally's face, and she composed herself. She glanced up at her friend. "Interesting..." she said vaguely. Silently, she surveyed the array of goddess cards spread before her.

"Why don't you pick two more?" Sally proffered the deck to Delilah, who chose a few more cards and laid them down.

It was now well past the time that Tenika should have arrived, so finally they'd started without her. She hadn't responded to Delilah's two texts, nor had she even picked up the phone when she called. Delilah had no idea where her wife even was. Still, she carried on, unconcerned.

Tenika would show. Or not. That was her way.

"Um," Sally began hesitantly. "So it looks like the twins birth may bring the...uh...unexpected."

"Unexpected?" Delilah's voice rose slightly with worry. "What do you mean by that?"

Again, Sally hesitated before she spoke, trying to choose her words carefully. "Things don't always turn out as we wish, Delilah. But that's not necessarily a bad thing." She pointed to the first card. "You have Isis, the signifier of past life. So there's a big completion going on, as there often is with babies. They come to us from other times, and other challenges, and we finish our business with them karmically during their lifetimes. That is, we do this if we want to evolve. Some might even say it's part of our life purpose."

"Okay, okay, Sally. I get that part. But why do you look so worried?"

Sally paused and took a breath. "Most of the cards are reversed," she finally said. "So there's some very intentional stuff going on here. A sorting out, I'd say. You have to pay attention, Delilah. Look for the lessons. Tune in to what's happening on a very deep level."

Delilah sat back and surveyed her friend. "So it's not all sunshine and unicorns, you're saying. These are not going to be easy births."

Sally glanced at her and hesitated. Now was not the time to seed doubt with her friend, who already had enough to deal with. "I'm saying what I just said, Delilah, and nothing more. Pay attention and take it one step at a time. Be intentional. That's all I know."

"Intentional..." murmured Delilah, wishing like hell that Tenika was there as well at this moment. "What does that mean exactly?"

"It means, well...look; here's Sekhmet in the final position, saying 'Be Strong'. That's clear, right? Even if it doesn't all go smoothly, you will gain in strength and understanding." Tenderly, she looked at her old friend. Delilah and Sally had known each other since the first day of college, when they became roommates all those years ago. "I know you will, hon. I'm sure of it."

Sally continued on, looking for cards that would bring her friend some encouragement. "And here, in terms of what's happening now, is Bast. She's all about independence. Doing the right thing for you."

Delilah thought immediately about how they'd bucked the trend toward multiple sonograms, despite their midwife's suggestion to have one last one. They'd had one in the beginning and then they'd both decided that was enough.

"Well, yes," Delilah agreed. "I guess we are doing these births our way, you could say." But now she peered more closely at the cards. "Why do you think the Home card—Vesta—is reversed? Our home life is perfectly happy."

Sally bowed her head, eyes closed, waiting for the usual hit of intuitive guidance that carried on its separate narrative in her head. "It's about caution," she said, looking at her friend. "And it's reversed because you have to be careful right now. I'm not sure if this is about tripping and falling, or starting a kitchen fire, or what. But just...take care, alright? This is when people get stressed and make dumb mistakes."

Delilah swallowed. This was not reassuring. Pulling out her phone, she texted Tenika again. *Where are you?*

Sally continued. "Overall, it may be a hard time initially. You're going to have a challenge. But you're going to prevail—I can feel it. And you two are going to become closer, and become better parents because of it. All in all, these births are going to be incredible life changers. That's often what happens with so many reversed cards." She paused. "It just may not turn out the way you expected."

"Oh God," Delilah murmured. She closed her eyes, trying to stop the tears that threatened. But then, she was often on the verge of tears these days, fighting the swell of big-hormone emotions that were always threatening to envelop her. "Okay," she whispered. Letting out a little sob, Delilah hiccuped.

Then she blushed, embarrassed to be crying in front of her friend.

Reaching over, Sally took her hand. "Hey," she said. "This is not all bad, Delilah. And why wouldn't a pair of twins be life changing? I'm just saying, keep your eyes open and keep doing the right thing. Because they will challenge you…that's all."

Sniffing back her tears, Delilah shook her head. "Okay," she agreed, taking a tissue from the box Sally offered her. Delilah laughed at herself as she blew her nose. "I just wish it was going to be easy. Why couldn't I pull those cards? Now look at me, I'm already a mess and they aren't even here yet."

Sally gave her hand a squeeze. "You're both going to be amazing mothers. I know it. You just need to trust yourselves, and be intentional. That's the big takeaway here. Make every move count. Nothing hurried, rushed or wasted. Okay? Be as present as you can."

"Okay," Delilah said. Then she pulled out her phone one last time, scanning for a message from Tenika. There was nothing. "I can't believe she missed this," she said. "But it's probably good she wasn't here."

"Oh?"

"T's worried. I mean, she hasn't said anything, but I can tell." Delilah gazed at her friend. "Don't say anything to her about this, okay? I'll fill her in."

Sally smiled. "I won't say a word. I never do."

"Good." Because Delilah wouldn't tell Tenika anything she'd just heard. Nor would she share the deep sense of foreboding that was now building in her own body. Instead, she would tell Tenika the reading was exactly what they were hoping for.

The births would be sunshine and unicorns all the way.

This was the humane thing to do.

*

An hour later, Tenika's truck pulled up to their house, and Delilah heard her come in the front door. She trundled over to the kitchen doorway, as Tenika strode forward.

"I'm an idiot!" Tenika began. She took her wife in her arms and kissed her. "I'm so sorry, honey…honestly. I don't know what happened."

Delilah noticed her kiss tasted like the beer she'd clearly been drinking. "You were having a beer with Lizzy? Seriously?"

Tenika grimaced. "It's Tuesday and I'm a damn rat in a maze. Like I said, I'm an idiot. I completely forgot." Pausing she looked at her wife. "So… what did she say? We gonna have two little champion birthers? They gonna come sliding down the birth canal no sweat?"

"Mm-hmm," Delilah answered tightly. "It's all going to be just fine," she lied. "The reading was great. We've got this."

Tenika gave a big sigh. "Thank God!" she said. Then she gave a laugh. "'Cause I've had my head in all the wrong places lately. It's been lookin' bleak."

She took Delilah's hand. "We're gonna get through this, right? We're going to have the world's cutest twins and sail right through the whole damn thing, right?"

Delilah smiled back at her. "You know we are."

It really was a good thing Tenika missed the reading, Delilah noted then, as they kissed once more.

The last thing she could deal with was a freaked out wife on top of everything else.

Chapter Six

Sally peered out the curtained window in front of their house. Ronnie was standing out in front, hands in pockets, waiting patiently. Today she was wearing her vintage Harris tweed suit. A cranberry-red polka dotted, silk hankie was visible in the breast pocket. She'd had the suit for years, and Sally recognized it. Ronnie only wore it when she dressed to impress.

Standing there, she had the air of someone who had all the time in the world to wait for Sally. For one split second, Sally pondered whether seeing Ronnie again was such a good idea. But then reason got tangled up with old fleeting emotions, and she wavered.

Of course it is a good idea, she chided herself. Being compassionate and forgiving was always the right thing to do. *Right?*

Being a good person was fundamental to Sally. Some might even argue that spending time with her former girlfriend certainly qualified on the scale of one's goodness in life. Especially after the way Ronnie had ghosted her. It was certainly the right thing to do. As long as the encounter was all about forgiveness and nothing else.

"Ronnie," Sally said as she opened the door and stepped outside.

Ronnie struck a pose. "My my my!" she murmured as she looked at Sally from head to toe. "I've got to say…you look cuter than ever."

Sally blushed as she locked the front door. Then she joined her former lover in the sunlight.

Today Sally was wearing a pink oxford cloth button-down shirt, a pair of close-fitting jeans and simple black flats. Her makeup was modest, and her cascade of ash-blonde curls were as wild as ever, even when pulled back in a modest clip behind her head.

She intentionally wanted to be understated. There would be no flouncy skirts or obviously femme come-on heels today—and no big earrings, either. Sally chose today's look to signal she was showing up strictly as a friend, and nothing more.

The last thing she wanted was to lead Ronnie on about her intentions. Though, if Sally were to admit the full truth, she wasn't entirely clear on what her intentions were.

"Where shall we go?" she asked. Quickly, they settled on a nearby dog park and began to walk.

The Piedmont Dog Park was a quiet refuge that featured a meandering walk along a lush creek. Several small waterfalls dotted the path beneath towering eucalyptus and oak trees. And the path had the occasional wooden bench, inviting a rest. It had been a walker's destination for more than a century, and the trees had the canopy to prove it.

Sally resisted the urge to take Ronnie's arm as they moved along the sidewalk. This was how they'd often walked, back in the day. So, no, she wouldn't be going there.

When Ronnie actually did offer her arm, Sally put her hands in the pockets of her jeans instead. She knew she had to be careful here, for her ex really was capable of anything.

Yet, it was her sheer unpredictability that had first drawn Sally to her. They walked on in silence.

"How's your girl doing?" Ronnie asked after a while.

"Frankie?" Sally had forgotten they'd met, ever so briefly.

"Yeah…Frankie."

"Frankie's fine," Sally replied, wondering where this was going.

In fact, Frankie was anything but fine. They were now on the ninth day of their cold war, and it appeared they were drifting apart irreparably. Though Frankie had agreed, grudgingly, to see a counselor with Sally early the following week, this, alone, was a tiny ray of hope.

They avoided each other in the kitchen, the bedroom, the living room. When they were together, Frankie bristled at nearly everything that was said. It had taken everything Sally had to patiently sit and talk to her partner about the mere prospect of seeing a therapist. And when Sally suggested they both had things to talk about in the session, Frankie nearly blew up.

"Oh…that's rich. Rich!" she retorted. "You're telling me I have things to own up to?" After muttering something about the pot calling the kettle black, Frankie disappeared out the door for the rest of the night. But the next day, she reluctantly agreed to couples counseling in a tired voice. "Okay. Fine," was all she said.

Clearly this was a side of Frankie that Sally hadn't seen before. But perhaps Frankie could say the same about Sally. Around and around they went, trying to convince the other of their point of view. At this point, both of them were truly exhausted.

Yet here was Sally, strolling once more with Ronnie. Frankie still didn't know about her walks with her former partner, and at this point, it appeared she didn't even care. The pair of them turned in to the dog park and headed for the cool, tree-shaded path just ahead.

"Remember all those walks we took back in Golden Gate Park, back when we lived in the city?" Ronnie mused as they passed by some especially tall eucalyptus trees. "Remember the tea garden?"

"Mm-hmm," Sally replied. *Keep it light*, she chided herself. *Noncommittal.*

"I loved those walks," Ronnie continued, unabashed. "You were so light and beautiful. So positive. Like a ray of sunshine in my life." Turning back, she smiled hopefully at Sally. "Guess you still are."

"Ronnie—" Sally warned, but Ronnie cut her off by holding up her hand.

"I know, I know. You're 'occupied'." Ronnie made little air quotes with her fingers. "I get it, Sally. I'm not trying to start anything. Honest," she insisted.

Immediately, Sally had her doubts. They passed a knot of dog walkers, owners and their pets milled around. The dogs sniffed each other out, and the humans chatted pleasantly. Yet, both Sally and Ronnie fell silent as they moved through the small crowd.

Strangely, there didn't seem to be that much to say today, even to each other. Sally wondered now if she'd made a mistake, coming out with Ronnie.

Eventually they climbed a set of concrete steps leading to a small cascade. The waterfall had been flowing for years, centuries even, as it spilled endlessly into the afternoon. The air was cool and refreshing, and the shade from tall trees was deep. It was a welcome respite from the relentless, dry Northern California sunshine.

Ronnie stopped. Then she studied the waterfall. Ronnie cleared her throat, then her voice grew quiet as she spoke. "If I didn't have problems of my own, I guess I wouldn't have even reached out. But I never want to be a pest," she said gravely, turning to look directly at Sally.

She gave a small ironic chuckle. "Guess you're about all I've got left, Sally."

Something about Ronnie's manner pulled at Sally, disturbing her. This wasn't just Ronnie being dramatic. Clearly something actually was wrong. "What do you mean?" Sally asked with concern.

But Ronnie put up a hand to stop her. "It's nothing. Forgive me. I shouldn't have even brought it up. Here…" Ronnie gestured expansively around them. "Let's just enjoy this beautiful spot." Her eyes moved up to the towering canopy of eucalyptus trees above them, as her hands slid back into her pockets.

Moving on, Ronnie began to quickly walk up the path ahead. Sally hurried to keep up behind her. "Ronnie?" she called after her. "Tell me what's going on."

"It's nothing, nothing— I shouldn't have mentioned it," Ronnie replied over her shoulder. She kept walking.

"Well, something's going on, obviously, or you wouldn't have said a thing," Sally insisted. But Ronnie just shook her head. Raising her hands in a dismissive gesture, she kept walking up the path, now at an even faster pace.

Sally paused. Something really bad must be up with Ronnie. Why else would she be acting so weird?

She'd sensed something was amiss since the first day Ronnie appeared on their doorstep. Ronnie's visits to Sally were about something—some bit of information that was just out of Sally's reach. Maybe she needed help and she was afraid to ask for it. Sally's curiosity, and her empathy, were piqued. She needed to know what it was.

Meanwhile Ronnie continued along briskly, walking as if she hadn't heard Sally's entreaties behind her. "Come on, Ronnie," Sally cajoled, now breathless. "Please…stop." Reaching out she grabbed a fistful of tweed from Ronnie's sleeve. "Wait. Please."

Pausing, Ronnie gently removed her hand from her sleeve. Then she continued on, pausing only when she reached a waiting park bench ahead.

Ronnie lowered herself on to the bench, wincing slightly as she did. She patted the empty part beside her. "Come sit," she said.

Sally immediately sat and studied her former lover earnestly. "Would you please just tell me what's going on?"

Ronnie looked straight ahead, refusing to meet Sally's eyes now. "I'm sick," she said in a quiet voice. "Really sick."

Alarm surged through Sally's body, and she grasped Ronnie's hand without even thinking. "What? What's the matter?" Sally leaned forward, peering at Ronnie, trying to understand what she was saying.

Ronnie closed her eyes and seemed for just a moment to be on the brink of tears. "Like…mortally," she half-whispered.

"Mortally!" Sally's jaw dropped open in shock. Then quickly she recovered, squeezing her former lover's hand even more intently. "Ronnie, what is it? Please tell me. It isn't…cancer?"

Opening her eyes, Ronnie leveled a look at Sally. "It's a blood thing," she said vaguely. "I can barely remember the name of it. Very rare apparently. But they say I have less than a year. Maybe eight months?"

"Oh, Ronnie." Sally just stared at her ex lover. She didn't know what to say for a few moments. Then she recovered slightly. "It's not cancer?"

Ronnie just shook her head, eyes downcast.

"They don't know," she continued. "Turns out you can look perfectly fine one day and be on death's door the next." Now she turned a seasoned eye toward Sally. "You're the only person I've got left, Sally," she said. "I mean it. I always knew you were one of the good ones."

Ronnie shook her head slowly. "I never should have let you go." Leaning back, she tipped her gaze up to the sky. "What the hell was I thinking?" she asked the sky in despair.

Sally was still staring at her, mildly confused. "But—but why are you here? Right now, I mean. Shouldn't you be at the hospital, or at home resting. In bed even?" She glanced around them and lowered her voice. "Should you even be taking a walk?"

"Oh, it's not like that," Ronnie quickly explained. "I actually feel fine. The whole thing's been a huge shock to me as well. I just …" Ronnie closed her eyes and lowered her head. "Honestly, if I had a decent home right now, I'm sure I'd be there. Resting, like you say. But you know how it is."

"No. How is it?" Sally didn't actually even know where Ronnie was living, beyond just being in San Francisco.

Ronnie cleared her throat. "Well, 'home' isn't actually that homey these days," she said slowly. Then she looked at Sally. "Basically, my stuff's in storage. I've been living in an SRO hotel in Mid-Market."

"Mid-Market?" This was a San Francisco neighborhood Sally hadn't heard of before.

"The Tenderloin." Ronnie's voice was barely audible. "They rebranded it."

"The Tenderloin? Oh, Ronnie! What on earth…" She'd heard Ronnie had fallen on hard times after her work as a music promotor dried up, but the Tenderloin? That was where San Francisco's most desperate and down and out congregated. People shot up on the street there and collapsed on the sidewalk as by-passers stepped over them. The Tenderloin was clearly a last resort. "Really?"

Ronnie just nodded, refusing to meet Sally's eyes. She folded her arms across her chest and stared at her lap somberly.

Sally placed her hand on Ronnie's arm. "Ronnie. Just tell me… are you using drugs?"

"No! Oh hell no! Sally—please. It's me! Do I look like a druggie to you?" Ronnie yanked her arm away and gave her an exasperated look. "It was the only rent I could afford in the city. I'm living on vapors to begin with. I don't even have health insurance. I don't have a job right now. I don't have anything!"

"Oh, Jesus. Okay, so what can I do to help?" Sally asked, squaring her shoulders. "Just tell me, Ronnie. God, this is terrible—I have to help you. Just tell me what you want me to do."

A new light of possibility shone in Ronnie's eyes as she slowly turned to look at Sally. It appeared her face was lit with gratitude. "You're so kind to me," she said humbly. Ronnie seemed on the verge of tears.

"We have to get you out of there, obviously. What can I do?" Sally repeated, as pure horror ricocheted through her brain. "I'll do anything."

It never occurred to Sally that Ronnie could have chosen a less expensive city to live in. Or reached out to San Francisco's long list of public resources for those in need. Instead, when she hit the skids, she called Ronnie.

Sweet, pliable Sally was a soft target whose heart was reliably huge. And all Sally knew was that, in this moment, she had to help.

Ronnie looked at her and said nothing.

"Wait!" Sally said suddenly, reaching for her phone. Impulsively, she dialed Frankie at work, half knowing she wouldn't pick up. The call went to voicemail and Sally hung up. Then once more she took Ronnie's hand and gazed into her eyes.

"You're coming home with me," Sally announced, inspiration spiraling up in her body as she squeezed her hand. "We're going to help you get better. It's part of our karmic contract, Ronnie. I know it is!" She stood up, ablaze with purpose. "You can sleep on the couch—it's actually incredibly comfortable. And I'll give you part of my closet. I'll take care of you. You look so thin, Ronnie. I'll cook for you."

Ronnie looked up at her hopefully. "Well, it all sounds amazing. I mean…thank you, honey. Really. But what about Frankie? How's she going to feel about this?"

"Frankie will be fine with it," Sally said tightly. She'd deal with Frankie that night, but at this point part of her didn't even care what Frankie thought. Sally was eager to get going on the new plan. "Go back to the hotel, get your things together and check out," she directed Ronnie. "Then BART back here, and I'll pick you up tonight at the 19th Street station."

Sally looked at Ronnie with a satisfied smile as she stood. "Your new life begins now," Sally announced.

One slow tear of gratitude slid down Ronnie's cheek, and she gazed up at Sally fondly. "How can I ever thank you?" she murmured.

And Sally gazed back at her, convinced this was the next right thing.

*

Frankie climbed out of her car, sleepy from her after-work work-out and the three beers she'd had with her burger at a local bar.

She'd been in no hurry to return home to another round of arguing with Sally. Frankie turned her key in the door, noticing the lights were now dark in the living room.

"What the fuck?" she muttered. Most likely Sally had turned off the lights on her, so she'd have to stumble her way back to the kitchen and the bedroom. *This was completely passive aggressive,* she thought grimly, stepping inside.

As the door gently shut behind her, Frankie suddenly stopped, sensing something was different. Suddenly, all of her cop training cranked into gear.

Someone was in here.

Frankie was now on high alert as she stood stock still, assessing the situation. Something was definitely wrong. She listened in the darkness, the short hairs on the back of her neck vibrating at attention. Then she heard it. Another person was definitely breathing just around the corner from where she stood.

It didn't sound like Sally.

Slowly, silently, Frankie slid her backpack off her back. Then reaching into the open compartment on the side, she withdrew the loaded pistol she always carried, just for moments like this.

Gripping the gun in both hands, Frankie took a breath. Then she swung around the corner, bracing her feet on the floor, and raised her weapon, pointing into the darkness. "Freeze!" she yelled, attempting to alarm whoever was hidden in her living room.

The naked woman before her screamed in alarm. "Don't shoot!" she yelled, as Frankie snapped on the table lamp. The intruder stared back at Frankie, clutching a blanket to her chest. Apparently, she'd been asleep on their couch.

"Oh Jesus," she said, for she recognized Sally's ex. It was the same ex who'd been lurking around their house when they got back from Santa Barbara. Frankie lowered her gun and stood there, dumbfounded.

"I'm Ronnie," the woman in front of her said. "Sally's...

uh…." She didn't complete that sentence. Then in a helpless act, she thrust a hand forward as if to shake Frankie's, the other hand still clutching the blanket to her.

When it became clear Frankie wasn't interested in shaking, Ronnie withdrew her hand quickly.

"Sally!" Frankie bellowed just as Sally came running out of the bedroom in her pajamas.

"What's going on out here?" she asked. Then she stopped when she saw the weapon, now limp at Frankie's side.

"Frankie—what are you doing? It's only Ronnie!" Sally exclaimed. Then she paused awkwardly as she surveyed the scene. "Oh. Okay, so you met again. Good. Ronnie—Frankie. Frankie—Ronnie." Sally looked searchingly at Frankie. "Remember?" she asked weakly.

"I called you about this, honey," Sally explained. "But you didn't pick up."

Putting the gun back in her backpack, Frankie just shook her head. "Sorry," she said tersely, as she headed off toward the kitchen. She passed Sally coolly without even looking at her.

Sally looked at Ronnie helplessly. "Is this alright?" Ronnie asked. "I mean, if it's not, I can go right now."

"No, no!" Sally burst, and in that instant, she realized something. She needed Ronnie here, in this silent war she was now in the middle of with Frankie. She badly needed an ally, even if it was Ronnie. "Don't go. We'll work it out. She's just…jumpy."

"Apparently," Ronnie said dryly, as she lay down once more. She looked at Sally from the couch. "You sure this is okay?"

"It's okay," Sally assured her. Though, of course, she was far from sure.

*

Once back in the bedroom, Sally closed the door and looked at her partner who was now sitting on her side of the bed in her underwear. She had her arms folded across her chest, and she was staring out the window, as petulant as a child.

"What is that person doing here?" she asked without looking at Sally.

"Look—I tried to call you this afternoon, Frankie. Twice. You never picked up. It's an emergency or I wouldn't have invited her to stay."

Frankie looked unimpressed. "An emergency, huh?"

Sally took a step toward her. "You don't have to be so skeptical. I know this woman. Ronnie's like my sister."

"Then why didn't you ever tell me about her before?"

"I just—" Sally stopped without answering her question. She didn't have to get into this with Frankie. Not now. Not when everything was so raw between them. She hadn't told Frankie about her because the break up with Ronnie had been so devastating. It was hard to talk to anyone about it.

And now...well, here they were, with Ronnie soundly camped out in their living room. Yet, Sally still had hope that all would be well. Perhaps in some weird way, Ronnie's presence would actually help her and Frankie repair their disintegrating relationship.

In Sally's mind, the right path was obvious. It was as if all the goddesses had aligned to give her and Ronnie a chance to complete their relationship and bring some kind of closure. Or, at the very least, for Sally to somehow let go of the past and forgive her.

This was what active karma looked like, Sally told herself. It was often messy and imperfect. If Frankie couldn't wrap her head around it, then so be it. Which would be too bad, because this certainly could be Frankie's growth experience as well. If she chose to engage.

But this wasn't a thought she shared with Frankie. Instead, she gave an inward smile. Tonight was just another one of the Universe's infinite variations on grace. Sooner or later, Frankie would get used to it.

But Frankie, on the other hand, wasn't so sure. Standing, she gave a small harrumph.

Then, once again, she began to put on her clothes.

She was going out.

*

Half an hour later, Frankie was on her motorcycle, heading straight for Ocean Beach.

She always found solace in her ride. The trip across the Bay Bridge into San Francisco was bracing as she sped along, weaving around what little traffic remained at this hour. She needed the salt air. She needed the speed. And she needed the embrace of the cold night air, damp as a marine layer of fog settled in.

In no time, Frankie was on Fell Street, tearing along with the perfect rhythm of green lights in sync. It was well past midnight by now, and no one was out. There was no one to monitor Frankie as she sped along faster and faster in a straight line toward the beach.

Why the hell Sally hadn't even thought to ask her if she could bring this…this person into their home? It was Sally's ex-lover, for God's sake. She never would have done that to Sally, that was for damn sure.

Frankie hadn't liked Ronnie from the minute she laid eyes on her. Everything about her screamed 'con job', from her stupid little suit to the fake smile she kept flashing at Frankie.

Frankie had met enough out and out grifters in her career that her senses were finely tuned. She could sniff them out at fifty yards, and Ronnie was a class A example. And why was she even there—on her own damn couch, no less?

Clearly Sally had been either talking or texting, or God forbid, hanging out with Ronnie. And when had all of this been going on? While she was at work? When she asked Sally about this, she'd said nothing. And that, alone, was a huge red flag.

Frankie had asked again, and once more Sally just shrugged. That's when she left. Or 'stormed out' as Sally put it, the bedroom door slamming as she called, "There you go again. Storming out."

As she'd passed by the couch, Frankie caught sight of Ronnie peering at her from behind her blanket. And a deep stab of fury kicked it. *Don't look at me!* she'd wanted to scream.

It's my goddamn house and my goddamn couch and you shouldn't even be here, Frankie thought indignantly as she locked the front door behind her.

Now, as she headed for the ocean, Frankie had a sobering thought. Why on earth was she leaving, yet again? What was the point? Even within the well-worn grooves of anger, she knew that if she and Sally were to have any chance at all, they had to sit down and truly talk things through. And they had to do so calmly and rationally.

Frankie believed the relationship was still worth preserving. For one thing, she needed Sally. And when she'd proposed and Sally accepted, it had filled Frankie with the deep, warm delight of knowing, once again, she was loved. Sally was going to be her reboot. Her reinvention.

That feeling, alone, made up for the lost year and a half just after her beloved Dree died. That's when she was so disabled by grief, Frankie couldn't even work, let alone go through the motions of life.

Frankie knew what she had to do. She had to stop getting so angry and so defensive. There was no other way to get back to the stability of the committed, married life she'd once had with her late wife. That was Frankie's personal gold standard, and she'd still be there if Dree hadn't died of brain cancer.

No, Frankie knew she had to do this, which was why she'd agreed to go to the therapist in the first place.

Otherwise, there would be no happy home to come back to at the end of the day, complete with a waiting, willing wife. A woman who wanted only to be with her. This had been Frankie's vision, her dream. But now…well, who knew what was going to happen.

Especially now that this mongrel of a person was sleeping on her couch. *What the hell was Sally thinking?* A new wave of righteous anger rattled through Frankie's brain as she pulled up to the end of Judah and gazed at the dark ocean, straight ahead.

Not a soul was around as she parked her bike. Walking down the steps from the sea wall on to Ocean Beach, she took off her shoes and socks and plunged her feet into the sand. It was cold, and soft, and slightly damp, and it felt completely refreshing. Something real she could sink into.

Before her, the Pacific pounded grandly, waves pushing in, thundering in the dark. A half-moon rose majestically overhead. *Nature really does seem so much mightier in the dark,* she thought.

Frankie found a spot and sat down in the sand. Then she hugged her knees to her as she studied the waves. Lowering her head to her knees, she felt herself give way and soften. She really did have to talk to Sally. The ex-lover showing up was the last straw. This relationship was going to be over before she knew it if she didn't do something.

In fact, it felt like it was already disappearing before her eyes, and it scared her. Frankie closed her eyes, trying to ignore the sting of tears. *How did I get here?*

Until now, Sally had been her guide. Her teacher. The wise voice in her ear. Yet, seeing the stark contrast of Sally in her flip flops, her sun-kissed skin and her Namaste necklace against the formal backdrop of her family home had been unsettling. Even more so when Frankie introduced her to Misty.

Things had gone about as badly as they could go, and now Frankie felt truly stuck. If she was going to marry Sally, she would probably never get Misty's blessing. That would be the end of hope for any kind of a relationship with the last living relative Frankie had left.

Furthermore, Frankie could just forget about receiving any kind of inheritance when her mother died. Even though there were no other heirs, she'd be written out of the will for sure if she married Sally. Misty was like that; she made massive decisions in a heartbeat. And she'd have no problem deeding the house and her millions to whatever charity struck her fancy at the moment. Frankie was certain of it.

In the end, perhaps it didn't even matter that much. Frankie was happily self-sufficient without her family's money. But it had been convenient at times. It had been a big help when she got her degree in criminal justice, a career choice her mother disparaged but paid for all the same. And it had definitely been useful when Dree died and Frankie couldn't work.

Once her disability benefits ended, her mother had supported her—mainly because Dree was a lawyer from a good Boston family who Misty had approved of. Her mother had been downright empathetic then.

But Sally was another breed altogether. Frankie could scarcely believe she'd fallen in love with her. Yet she had. When they'd touched each other, the connection was electric and had been getting more so as they began their second year together.

Until now, Sally was always reliable, and beautiful, and wise. So erotic, and yet so real as well. But now, Sally had become someone else entirely. Suddenly, she was feisty, angry even. And so fed up with Frankie that she'd invited a former lover into their home. She knew why Sally did it—because Frankie, herself, had been such a raving bitch for the last ten days.

A few more tears ran down her face as she sat there listening to the surf.

What am I doing? This was Sally, not some chaotic monster she was taking out her rage on. And Sally had her weaknesses just like everyone else.

Couldn't she just give the poor woman a break?

She thought of her beautiful golden curls and her heavy-lidded eyes as she looked at Frankie, and a pang of empathy rose up in her chest. She thought of Sally's devastated face, sitting in Misty's library, watching her mother walk out. And how utterly bewildered she'd been that Frankie hadn't stood by her that terrible afternoon.

Frankie sighed and lowered her face to her knees. She needed to apologize to Sally. She really did. But first, the monster on the couch was going to have to go. That was just totally over the line.

Frankie stopped herself. No…she'd blown it and she was in no position to dictate Sally's moves at the moment. She could tolerate the ex being around for a few days if she had to.

Couldn't she?

Frankie would apologize tomorrow night. She'd take Sally out for a beautiful dinner, and they could start all over again. Maybe she'd even surprise Sally with flowers after work.

When push came to shove, even Frankie could be a romantic.

Chapter Seven

Kate had just loaded three bags of groceries into the back of her car at Berkeley Bowl when her phone rang. Pushing the empty cart to the corral with one hand, she dug out her phone with the other.

Her sister was calling her from Dublin. Again. That was three times now in less than two weeks.

Alarmed, Kate answered quickly. "Eileen? Did something happen?"

"Hello to you, too," her sister retorted. Yet her voice wasn't jocular or even slightly wry. Instead, it sounded flat. And worried.

"Something's wrong," Kate said. It was more a statement of fact than a question. One that she could feel straight down to her gut.

There was a pause. She could tell her sister was composing herself on the other end.

"Come on, come on. Tell me! What is it, Eileen?" Kate asked more urgently. She was stopped now in the middle of the parking lot, the cart and the traffic around her forgotten. "Is it Da?"

"Yeah," her sister said in a small voice. "He's worse. He had another stroke, Kate."

Kate swallowed and stifled a cry. "Is he going to die?"

There was another pause. "Yes," Eileen said simply.

Kate didn't really know how she got back to her car at that point, or what happened to the errant shopping cart. Cars had begun to beep at her. That's all she remembered. Then suddenly she was sitting in her car, gamely trying to figure out what to do next.

For a long time she was silent, her thoughts a jumble as she listened to Eileen explain the situation. She could hear her sister crying softly on the other end of the line.

Finally Kate spoke. "How is mum coping?"

"The usual. Stoic," her sister said. "She can't even cry. Won't until it's all over, I expect."

Kate cleared her throat. "Alright," she said, feeling all caution slip away. "I'd better come then. Maybe I can book a flight tonight." She half expected her sister to fight her on this. But instead, Eileen agreed immediately, her voice awash in relief.

"Alright. Good," she said. "They need the both of us, Kate, Ma and Da."

"I'll make a reservation and email it to you."

"Hurry," urged her sister. "We don't know how long it will be."

Kate hung up a moment later with a promise to get there as soon as she could. Then she started her car, resolute and moving forward.

In the back of her mind, Kate did the calculations. Could she reasonably leave with only her new green card to let her back into the U.S.? Yes, she was married to a U.S. citizen now, and she had her papers. That had to be good for something. At least, her lawyer had told her it would be.

But then there was Lizzy. She was certain to insist on coming. And that would be disastrous. Kate pulled out into the traffic and chewed her lip as she came to the first stoplight. What in God's name could she say that would help her wife understand that this time she really had to go home alone?

And how would she feel once she was up at 30,000 feet, going to see her family without the comfort and the strength of her wife by her side?

It wasn't fair to Da or Ma to spring Lizzy on them. Not now, in the midst of their worst family crisis ever. Which meant, of course, she'd have to finally tell Lizzy the truth.

Her parents had yet to learn they were married. Or even that Kate was queer.

Who knew what kind of upset that would unleash? Lizzy would definitely be pissed. But even worse, she'd be disappointed. This made Kate's gut churn even more, for up until now Lizzy had been nothing but supportive.

Without Lizzy, Kate wouldn't even be here. And now she was going to have to disappoint her beloved. There was no way around it.

Kate gave a loud sigh as she drove up the ramp onto 580 East. She merged into the fast-moving traffic, feeling a knot of tension in her stomach. One way or another, they'd get through this. They had to. The key was just taking all of this one uncertain, rocky step at a time.

She'd breathe and pray her way through it. A wallow of grief opened up inside of Kate now.

If only it wasn't her father. Her Da. She sped along, thinking about climbing onto his lap as a little girl. Snuggling in his scratchy wool sweater in front of the fireplace and pulling at the many pills in the wool with her small fingers. It became a game between them, her sneaking snatches at his sweater and him laughing and brushing her hand away.

Those times were rare and precious, when he was actually home from the endless hours required by the pub. Sometimes, when he'd had a few whiskeys, he'd even sing to her in his sweet tenor voice.

I'll buy my child a saucepan
I'll buy my child a spoon
I'll buy my child a writing desk
And she shall go to school
Dance to your Daddy-o
Dance to your Mammy-o...

She laughed at his off-key, croaky singing then, but it was so dear that thinking about it now nearly broke her heart. Tears began to slide down Kate's cheeks as she drove on. What had happened to her father, what had changed him all those years ago? Surely it wasn't just the drink.

There was always the smell of alcohol and mothballs around her Da, and the uncertain feeling that he might be loving and kind. Or he might not be so kind. Honestly Kate never knew what to expect. And now…well. This time the outcome sounded certain.

She thought about the fact that she'd been gone from home for so long.

Unlike her sister, Kate had grown up to become a terrible disappointment to her parents. And that was without knowing about her sexuality. Kate had left home and gone far away, no explanations offered. She'd turned her back on the pub, and Ireland, the church and them, and this was the biggest sin of all. She'd scarcely heard from her parents in years.

Now she couldn't even imagine what she would say to her father on his deathbed. Or what frame of mind, if any, he'd even be in.

Goodbye, Da. Thanks for everything…

The prospect was chilling, and, for a moment, Kate wondered if she even could go home.

Couldn't her sister possibly do this without her?

Kate knew the answer and steeled herself to what lay ahead, as she pulled up to park outside their house.

She let herself in the front door. Lizzy's bike was not yet hanging in the front hall; she wasn't home from work yet. Immediately Kate felt a wave of relief. Swiftly, she put away the groceries. Then, purposefully, she sat down at her laptop. She had to look for airline reservations.

Kate paused as she clicked open the website, and it demanded to know her travel dates and destination. 'One person, one way. SFO to Dublin', she typed in. Then she stopped. *Really?*

But buying a one way ticket was correct, because the return could only be booked upon her father's death. *Right?*

Now a new tangle of thoughts descended on Kate. What if he had a miraculous recovery? What if her sister was wrong, and he actually survived? What if he came away sufficiently chastened to stop drinking, improve his diet and lose weight? What if Da became a changed man from all of this?

And what if he forgave her for leaving, and even was open to hearing about her new life...and her new wife? Kate was sure such things happened in life. Which would be an incredible relief.

And yet...what if she ended up needing to stay there for a month or more, and her father grew progressively worse? How and when, exactly, could she leave? She'd have to wait for him to die...and that could take time. In the meantime, how would Kate keep Lizzy from getting on a plane and showing up as the weeks began to tick by?

Would she simply tell them about Lizzy before she left Ireland, because there was no other choice?

The various prospects felt terrifying to her, and all too real. For the truth was that Kate didn't want to leave Lizzy like this. And she most definitely didn't want to confront the sad spectacle of her father, dying in a hospital bed. And she absolutely didn't want to share the details of her life in the States with any of them.

Yet, she also didn't want to miss this. She simply had to be at her father's deathbed. That was all there was to it.

Kate began to scroll through the airlines' options. Aer Lingus had a number of flights each day to Dublin, as did a few of the other major carriers. As she read through them, questions bombarded her tired brain.

Should I just book the ticket for tonight? Or tomorrow? And if I did, what would be the best way to tell Lizzy about it? This was her first hurdle.

Back and forth, Kate's head swam, combing over the different possibilities. It all felt like entirely too much to process, and for the briefest moment, she shut her eyes. And that was when she began to cry, shoulders shaking as tears poured down her face.

On the other side of the room, Lizzy's key suddenly turned in the door. Abruptly Kate stood up, dabbing at her wet face with her sleeve. "Hi!" she called with forced cheer as she rushed for the bathroom. Then closing the bathroom door behind her, she sank to the floor and hugged her knees. Silently, Kate began to cry once more.

"Hey there!" she heard Lizzy call. Then there was the rustle of something being placed on the counter. Kate heard water running, and a cabinet being opened.

Breathing deeply, Kate tried to calm herself, but it was no use. She simply had to cry. There was no avoiding it. Yet, she was also aware she couldn't stay in the bathroom for long. Kate wondered if she could get away with not explaining herself when she finally emerged.

She returned to the kitchen a full five minutes later, after rinsing her face and flushing the empty toilet in an attempt to erase her breakdown in the bathroom. Pulling herself together, she'd given herself a little shake and squared her jaw as she regarded herself in the mirror. *I can do this. I have to.*

"Hi, love," Kate said as nonchalantly as she could, giving her wife a kiss. Lizzy turned around to face her, and immediately she sized her up. Her expression moved fast, from happiness to concern.

"Honey? Are you okay?"

"Me? Oh, fine. Lovely!" Kate lied, looking away. Still Lizzy was not fooled. She leaned toward her and cocked her head. Then she stopped Kate and turned her toward her.

"You've been crying again," she said. Kate tried to pull away, but Lizzy wouldn't let her.

Instead, her strong arms came around Kate and pulled her in. Kate lay her cheek on the rough flannel of Lizzy's shirt. And methodically, rhythmically, Lizzy began to gently rock her. It was all Kate could do not to dissolve once again into heaving, racking sobs. She looked up at Lizzy's sweet, concerned face and it made her heart melt a little more. Then past Lizzy's shoulder, Kate saw something that was cherry pink.

A voluptuous bouquet of pink peonies now sat on the kitchen counter. Lizzy stepped aside. "I thought you needed cheering up," she explained, sticking her hands in her pockets and smiling shyly. Then she gave a half laugh. "Guess I was right."

"Yeah," said Kate, blowing her nose. "They're lovely."

Lizzy folded her arms and cocked her head at Kate curiously. "You gonna tell me what's going on?"

Shaking her head, Kate sat down at the kitchen table, trying to compose herself. Trying to string together some set of words that would make the impossible possible. "I—" she began. But that is where she stopped.

Now Lizzy sat down across from her and took her hand. Wordlessly the two of them sat there, until finally, restless, Lizzy got up and began to wander around the kitchen. A moment later, Lizzy stopped at the laptop on the counter, still open to the *Aer Lingus* page.

Sharply, she looked at Kate. "You're going to Dublin?"

Stricken, Kate looked back at her. Still she could say nothing as dull shock settled in. This was not going well at all. She buried her face in her arms on the table and began to sob loudly.

"Hey, hey, hey…" Lizzy soothed. "Honey?" She stood beside her now, stroking her back.

Finally Lizzy sat down across from Kate, her face painted with a mixture of fear and concern, and she took her hand as Kate finally looked up at her. "Babe, you've got to tell me what's going on. Are you leaving me?"

"Leaving you? No! No… God no!" Kate exclaimed, sitting up. "I'm so sorry Lizzy. It's only…my father. He's…he's…" But then suddenly, Kate broke down again as sobs overtook her. Once again, she was mute with grief. She shook her head helplessly.

"What, honey?" Lizzy took her hand, as her concern took over. "Is he worse?"

Kate nodded. "He's dying," she whispered.

Immediately, Lizzy stood up. "Okay," she said, taking charge. "Let's go to SFO right now. I'll call Tenika—it'll be fine. We can get a plane tonight."

But just as fervently, Kate was shaking her head. "No, no. Lizzy. Stop. That's the thing!" she cried in anguish. "You can't go with me."

Kate looked at her wife and the gentle, confused expression on her face. Now Kate's words became barely audible. "I have to do this alone," she explained.

Lizzy stood stock still. "But I'm your wife," she said evenly. "Obviously I have to go." It was more a statement of fact than anything else.

A sudden, feverish new feeling poured into Kate's body, one of being uncomfortably hemmed in. Shoving back her chair, she stood abruptly. It was as if all of the deliberations of the past few days had coalesced inside of her suddenly, filling her with Vulcan strength. "No, Lizzy. You're not coming and that's all there is to it. You'll simply have to trust me on this."

Lizzy looked up at her, still plainly confused. "What—is this about immigration or ICE? What the hell is it?"

Kate shrugged off her question, and, walking back to the laptop, she began to angrily tap out commands. She was doing it—booking a ticket for tonight. For herself. Silently, Lizzy regarded her from the kitchen table.

"You're not going to even talk to me?" Lizzy wondered aloud.

Kate continued on defiantly, choosing her seat assignment,

typing in her credit card number and her identifying details. Finally, she became aware of the leaden silence in the room, and Lizzy's eyes still fastened upon her. Kate turned back to her.

"I'm sorry, sweetheart," Kate said. "The fact is that my parents don't know about you. They don't even know I'm married. Or even that I'm gay." Kate gave a heavy sigh. "They just wouldn't know what to do," she finally said.

Lizzy's jaw dropped open slightly. "I thought you told them. You told me you did. The day we got married. You said—"

"I know what I said!" Kate snapped. Then her voice dropped. "And it was all a lie, alright?"

Looking at her wife with her eyes brimming, Lizzy just stood there. She shook her head back and forth. "Wow," was all she could say.

A little stab of fear rang up through Kate's body, as Lizzy turned away and began to move slowly for the door.

"Sweetheart, I'm sorry," Kate called. "I really am. Lizzy— Lizzy?"

But now Lizzy was unhearing, advancing more and more rapidly on the front door. She hadn't even stopped to say good bye. Grabbing her keys and yanking open the doorknob, she left. The door slammed shut behind her.

A moment later, Kate walked to the window and looked out. She could see the last of Lizzy, disappearing down the road on her bike.

Now she truly was on her own. Whether she liked it or not.

*

"This better be good," Tenika began, swinging onto her stool at the White Horse.

"Delilah could drop those babies at any minute, you know."

Tenika glanced over at the young gay man behind the bar and, catching his eye, ordered a dark beer. Then she looked at her troubled friend. "So...what's up?"

Lizzy set her jaw firmly. "I think this is worth it," she said in a small voice. It wasn't Lizzy's practice to hang at the White Horse on a Wednesday night, nor was it to demand command appearances from her best friend on a moment's notice. But in her mind, this qualified as an emergency. "It's Kate," she said. "She's going back to Dublin."

Tenika's eyes grew wide.

"She's not leaving me," Lizzy added quickly. "I guess her dad is dying."

"Oh, well—Lizzy, what do you freaking expect?"

"No, no. It's not that. There's something much more…" Her voice drifted away, helplessly. Then finally Lizzy turned to her business partner with tears in her eyes. "She's never told them about me," she said in exasperation.

A look of alarm washed over Tenika's face in the red bar light. "She never told her mom and dad?" Lizzy nodded miserably. "Whoa."

"Yeah, right? I mean…" Lizzy shook her head helplessly. "I don't know what to think."

Tenika was silent, listening appraisingly. After a moment, Lizzy continued. "This is so fucked up. I'm supposed to give Kate all this unconditional love and support. And I've been doing it, T! I've done every last, damn thing you told me to do. I've been empathy on steroids. And it turns out she was lying the entire time."

"Lying? What do you mean?"

Now Lizzy looked at her darkly. Her eyes were blazing. "She said she told them all about me—sent them pictures of us and everything." Lizzy sniffed derisively. "I wondered why I'd never actually spoken to her parents. But she's never even come out to them, T, let alone told them she has a wife."

Tenika looked mystified. "Kate did that? Our Kate?"

"Yep. And who knows where the fuck she is now. Probably half way to Dublin."

"Well, now look, Lizzy. Don't get ahead of yourself. She has to go say goodbye to her father. You'd do the same, right?"

"Well, yeah," Lizzy conceded.

Tenika took a pull of her beer. "And who knows what the hell is going on back home. Maybe she's afraid. Her parents are probably hard core Irish Catholics, right? They'll disown her or something. You know how it goes."

Lizzy sighed. "Maybe," she said dubiously.

"Girl, please. Put yourself in Kate's shoes for five minutes—"

"No, T. That's all I've done!" Lizzy's cried. Her hand slammed down on the bar, and a few concerned patrons glanced over. Embarrassed, she removed it and put it back in her pocket. "Over and over and over again I've given her slack," she added in a lower voice. "And what did it get me? Fucking lies."

"Okay, I agree," Tenika conceded. "That is not cool, but you've got to keep it together here, sister. You seriously do. There's big shit happening." Tenika took a long sip of her beer.

The two of them sat there silently.

"I mean I know you're mad. I'd be mad too," Tenika continued. "But you just gotta go with the flow, Lizzy. You know what I mean?"

Lizzy did. For that was the toughest part of the whole thing. There was nothing more she could do but wait.

*

An hour later, Lizzy rode home through the quiet back streets, a low beer buzz clouding her senses. She dreaded reaching the house and finding that Kate had left, suitcase in hand. She'd texted Kate as soon as she left the bar, but there was no reply.

Pulling her bike up to the house, Lizzy noticed the living room light was still on. At least that was a hopeful sign.

But as soon as she steered her bike through the front door, Lizzy could feel the stark, emptiness of the house. She was alone. Standing there in the front hall, her bike in her hands, Lizzy was uncertain what to do for a moment.

Perhaps she was wrong. "Honey? Are you here?" she called out.

But there was no answer. Only the silence of a now empty house.

Lizzy now felt empty as well.

Chapter Eight

Recently released from the plane, Kate rolled her bag down the long, windowless airport corridor. She'd arrived in Dublin half an hour earlier, and her heart was beating wildly. Somewhere out there, past all the barriers and bulletproof glass was her sister, Eileen. Or at least Kate hoped she was.

If their father was stable enough, Eileen said she'd come to pick Kate up.

Da. Kate still couldn't believe she was here, or that he might die, or that any of this was actually happening. Trudging along the corridor, her brain fried from no sleep for the last twenty-three hours, she glanced up at the sign directing her to Customs.

Immediately Kate smiled. Green letters in Irish Gaelic directed them to *Imréiteach Custaim* above the usual official-looking sign in English. After nine long years, she was most definitely home.

Kate was genuinely glad she'd come back, regardless of the circumstances or how long she'd been away. Or even what the reception might be to her arrival, for it wasn't like she was close with her parents these days. She quickened her step to get through the border requirements as quickly as possible. Then she stepped into line and waited, her fingers tapping nervously on the maroon Irish passport in her pocket.

Moments later, Kate passed through Customs and arrived at Baggage Claim. Eagerly, she scanned the waiting crowd of restless children and searching adults, looking for her sister. But there was no sweet, smiling round face with the green eyes, nor was there anyone whose red hair matched her own. Kate surveyed the crowd again, making sure.

Briefly, she wondered if she'd even recognize Eileen. She'd barely been twenty when Kate left, and in a phase of dying her hair the strangest of colors. Kate would know her own sister…right? She brushed the thought away with annoyance. The fact was that she had to.

On the other hand, Eileen might not have been able to leave the hospital. Without a working cell phone, Kate couldn't be sure exactly what was happening. Standing there, hands on hips, Kate silently scanned the crowd once more to be sure. Her sister was not there.

Now Kate looked around for a place to buy a Sim card. At least that way she could get her phone working again. Then she would find a cab and go directly to the hospital. For who knew how long Da actually had.

Getting the Sim card was easy. Walking out of the shop, she parked her luggage and texted Eileen. *I made it*, she typed.

A thumbs up was all she got. *Okay*, she thought. Now for the hard part. Going to the hospital.

Moments later, as she pulled her huge bag off the conveyer belt with two hands. Kate felt a sudden, deep pang of longing for Lizzy. Fleeting thoughts of her wife had been a constant companion on the plane ride here. She thought of her coming home, seeing their apartment was empty. And then, most likely, sitting down on the couch in dismay, or maybe even tears, trying to figure out what to do next.

She could practically feel Lizzy's disappointment and frustration at not being able to come here with her. But then…what was she supposed to do? By now, perhaps Lizzy got the point.

There were no welcoming arms for her here in her parents' home. Not yet, at least.

Kate thought about their fight, just before she left. And the fact that she'd never been entirely forthright with her family—or Lizzy—about their marriage. There were mistakes made right and left, and they kept on rampaging through Kate's mind. She felt terrible about all of them. Not to mention inept.

Why was she so terrible at relationships, even with Lizzy? This was the one that was supposed to be different.

Kate did her best not to give in to the abject guilt that was building once again, but it was hard. She would text Lizzy as soon as she could get a wifi connection. And then, after she put her phone away, she would do her best to be there for everyone else, beginning with her parents.

When the time was right, she would tell them about her gay marriage in California, and the fact that she was trying to become a U.S. citizen. And she would tell them all about Lizzy and how wonderful she was. She really would.

At least that much she could bring home to her wife.

This visit, with its predictable highs and lows, was bound to be much more difficult than she'd bargained for. Still, Kate held out hope. Ultimately, Lizzy could get along fine without her—that much she knew.

The rest, presumably, would take care of itself.

*

Frankie pulled out her keys, tucking the big bouquet of summer flowers under her arm. She was whistling at this moment, anticipating the light returning to her life as she gently and lovingly apologized to Sally. Her inspiration on the beach to do the right thing was now stronger than ever, almost twenty-four hours later.

She'd slipped out that morning while Sally slept, and waited all day to make her apology. Picking up the flowers after work, Frankie knew it was critical to get the moment just right. She had the whole scene mapped neatly out in her mind.

Sally would be in kitchen puttering around, or maybe making dinner, and in she would come, spectacular bouquet in hand.

She'd present them to Sally. Then taking her hands, she'd look into her eyes, and say something like, "Honey, I've been a complete and total idiot and I am very, very sorry. Can we please not fight any more?" Sally would dissolve in her arms, and they'd kiss.

And well, cut to the curtains gently blowing in the window. Frankie had this. No problem.

She smiled in anticipation as she unlocked the door. Then stepping inside, she gave a jaunty hello. "Hon?" Frankie called. But there was only silence.

In fact, the house appeared to be empty. Frankie walked into the kitchen, and then the bedroom, calling Sally's name. No one was home. Not even Ronnie, whose clothing and shoes were now neatly piled on a living room chair along with her pillow.

It was just her and the dust mites, suspended in the ray of sunlight coming through the kitchen window. Frankie even walked outside into their tiny backyard, "Sally?" she called, looking around, uncertainly.

There really was no one there. Where the heck was her fiancée?

Feeling a little deflated, Frankie walked back upstairs, the flowers still clutched in her hand. Maybe Sally would be home soon.

For now, Frankie would just have to wait.

*

"Have whatever you want," Sally said, her eyes taking in the vast menu before them. "My treat."

Taking Ronnie out for dinner at the Guru Curry House had been a sudden, spontaneous idea. There was Ronnie, standing in the kitchen a little awkwardly, hands in pockets, as the dinner hour approached. Frankie wasn't home yet from work, and Sally had no idea if she'd even be home any time soon.

It occurred to Sally then that Ronnie probably didn't have money for food, or even groceries. Maybe she was even too shy to ask for help. Which wouldn't do at all. Not if she was really stepping up to to comfort Ronnie in her time of need.

Briefly, Sally scanned the contents of the refrigerator, which was emptier than usual. She'd been meaning to get to the grocery store, and yet, she hadn't. That was a direct result of her ongoing annoyance with Frankie. Her line of thinking went like this: *Why should I bend over backwards to support my very grumpy partner? Let Frankie do the domestic chores for a change.*

"Do you want to go out for dinner?" Sally suddenly found herself asking Ronnie. "There's an Indian place nearby..." she began.

Then suddenly, they were walking to her car and they were getting in. Then off they went. Gripping the wheel as she turned onto Grand Avenue, Sally reminded herself of her new litany:

We are just friends, doing what friends do. This is nothing more than karma.

It's all perfectly fine...

She had no idea that only moments later, Frankie would come walking in the door with an enormous bunch of flowers and an equally large apology. Instead, Sally was carried along in the momentum of the moment with Ronnie. All of which was deliciously uncertain. And even a little forbidden.

The two women began to chatter easily, bantering along as they arrived and parked. Ronnie and Sally were seated at a table beneath an enormous wall print of the Dali Lama's former palace in Nepal. There they sat, sipping chai from the small chai bar nearby.

Suddenly, Sally found she was overcome with shyness.

Something about sitting here, across from Ronnie, unsettled her completely. It wasn't just that Frankie almost certainly wouldn't approve. That was the least of Sally's concerns right now. Instead, she felt Ronnie was observing everything about her—every hair on her head, the cut of her blouse, the frown wrinkles on her brow. And the way she'd aged ever so slightly. Diverting her eyes, Sally licked her lips and shifted primly in her seat. "What?" Sally finally asked.

Finally, Ronnie looked away and shook her head, a little embarrassed. "I'm sorry, Sally. I just… I just can't believe we're sitting here like this." She shot Sally a look that was tender and nearly vulnerable. Somehow, it contained their entire shared history. "I mean, of all people, you're the last one I'd expect to be so kind to me at this point in my life."

Sally blushed under the honesty of Ronnie's words. "Well, anyone would—"

"No, that's my point, Sally. Anyone would most certainly not take me in, or even want to help me. I've burned a lot of bridges, you know. It's—it's hard being a person like me…" Ronnie floundered a little. "'Bigger than life', as they say."

Reaching across the table, Ronnie took her hand and gazed at her. "I just want to apologize to you one more time, Sally. You're so good. So kind—"

Gently, Sally released her hand from Ronnie's hot, slightly sweaty grip. She cleared her throat, hoping to change the subject. "I'm sure you have more friends than you think, Ronnie," she asserted. Then Sally picked up the oversized menu and fastened her eyes on it, in an effort to put a barrier between them.

"No, I really don't." Ronnie insisted. "And given how I've rolled, what do I expect?" Ronnie laughed bitterly and shrugged. "Guess I'll always be a work in progress."

"Aren't we all?" Sally asked from behind her menu.

"Right!" Ronnie exclaimed. Then she leveled a look at Sally. "You are no work in progress, my dear. You're all cooked, I'd say. And you've turned out beautifully."

Sally closed her eyes, trying not to listen and fighting off her descent into the loving attention of her ex. *None of this is real,* she reminded herself. *That was then. This is now.*

"What are you going to order?" Sally continued evenly, eyes once more on the menu.

Ronnie picked up her menu distractedly, as if she'd forgotten they were here to eat dinner. "Oh...uh..."

"Chicken tikka!" Sally announced, putting her menu down on the table. "It's amazing here. You'd love it."

Ronnie put her menu down. "Fine," she said, still gazing softly at Sally. Sally could swear she saw tears in Ronnie's eyes.

The two women fell silent. Sally crossed her arms in front of her. "I'm sure you have friends you can call," she said more gently. "I can't be the only one."

"No. You actually are. I'm not kidding, Sally."

For a moment, Sally imagined Ronnie making the rounds to, perhaps, all of her exes. Could it be they all refused to help? All of them but her? For this had always been the problem with Ronnie. She was brilliant, gifted, edgy, strong, and funny—a complete original. Yet, Ronnie also had the capacity for tremendous mendacity. She could make up entire worlds in a heartbeat when it suited her, and so convincingly. And she was no stranger to gaslighting.

Her lies had made Sally's head swim in the past. As had her narcissism. The words 'borderline personality' had been applied to Ronnie again and again. But none of that really mattered now to Sally. She considered Ronnie her narcissist. Her borderline. And no matter how much damage she'd done in the past, Ronnie could be forgiven, once again.

Perhaps, Ronnie had turned over a new leaf, Sally thought hopefully. Maybe this time she'd truly been humbled and would behave with more maturity. More consciousness.

More kindness.

For here was where hope sprang eternal: in the intersection between love and experience. And Sally was always big on hope. Despite all the break ups and traumas of her past, and the never-ending parade of committed relationships she'd been in, Sally still had yet to become wise.

Apparently, there was still more work to be done.

*

Laughing, Sally and Ronnie let themselves back into the house. It had been a relaxing, fulfilling dinner. After they'd ordered and Ronnie's intensity had waned, the rest of dinner was full of easy chatter, remembered stories, and shared laughter. And the best *pakora* Ronnie had ever had, or so she said. She kept thanking Sally on their leisurely drive home.

Sally's guard was not only down at this point. It was dismantled into pieces on the floor. In its place was her old willingness to trust Ronnie and invest in her ongoing travails. Sally could practically taste the satisfaction of saving Ronnie.

As long as no one crossed a line, what could the harm be? Sally was sure it would all be different this time.

She flipped on the light in the foyer. "Hello?" she called out a little cautiously, as Ronnie locked the door behind them. "Frankie?" Frankie's car had been outside, so they both knew she was here.

Still, Sally was cautious. She wasn't sure what mode Frankie would be in. And now, suddenly, she became aware of just how bad their entrance together looked. She and Ronnie had gone out to dinner and not even invited Frankie to join them. Immediately, Sally's good mood dissolved. She swallowed nervously.

Frankie appeared in the kitchen doorway, a strange look on her face. *Okay*, Sally thought grimly, *here we go*. She tensed, wondering what caustic remark Frankie would hurl her way.

But instead of saying anything, Frankie took a long breath and leaned against the door jam. "Hi," she said simply. Her voice was quiet. She sounded utterly defeated.

Sally burst into explanation. "We just went out for a quick dinner at Guru Curry. I was going to call you, but I figured you were probably still working, and we'd be home before you got back—"

Urgently, Sally walked toward Frankie, placating as she went. Meanwhile, Ronnie tried to disappear into the shadows of the living room. But now, surprisingly, Frankie dismissed Sally's concerns with a wave of her hand.

"Just come in the bedroom," she said simply, leaving Sally to follow her. And for an instant, Sally felt the flash of desire that always came swimming up when Frankie took that tone with her. It was so strong. So commanding. So...irresistible. Her heart quickened in her chest, and Sally followed, obediently.

As soon as she walked into their bedroom, she saw the arrangement. A huge profusion of cream, lavender, white and blue hydrangea, roses, lavender and stephanotis sat on her bureau. They'd taken over the space completely with their commanding presence. It was breathtaking.

"Whoa..." Sally said, awestruck. Then she looked up at Frankie. "Is this...for me?"

Frankie walked over and stood before her. "Of course it's for you. I was going to surprise you. Take you out to dinner. I guess I should have called."

They gazed at each other, their eyes rapidly smoothing the hurt that had persisted between them. "Oh, honey," Sally said softly.

"Sally. Honey," Frankie said, taking her face in her hands. "I'm tired of fighting. We need to stop. And I'm sorry. Sorry for every last, stupid thing I've done and said. You were completely right. I should have protected you in Santa Barbara. My mother is so difficult—I was just cowed by her. Like I always have been." Frankie faltered. Then her voice dropped away in shame.

"I don't know what I was thinking," she whispered, her eyes filled with regret. She looked at the floor for a moment, while Sally stood there, listening. Finally, Frankie's gaze returned to Sally's face. "I have a long way to go with Misty. I know that. But I'll marry you tomorrow if you'll still have me."

Sally's heartbeat was still beating fast in her chest, and she could feel her longing for her partner painting every fiber of her being. This was exactly what she'd been waiting for. And this was exactly where she belonged. It was all going to be okay.

Her momentary distraction with Ronnie was forgotten now as she dissolved back into her connection with her love.

"Will you have me?" Frankie asked.

"Yes! Yes, of course I will," Sally agreed, reaching for Frankie. They kissed then, mouths finding each other, bodies coming together as they stood in the dim light of the bedroom.

Frankie's hands moved over Sally's body, caressing her, celebrating every last voluptuous curve of her body. Reaching up inside her shirt, she unfastened Sally's bra, and stepping back Sally pulled off her top in a single sweep, her bra following it. They fell on the bed together, their bodies showing them the way back.

They'd found each other again. And that was all that mattered.

There was a knock on the door, and the two women stopped abruptly. They looked at each other. "Just a minute!" Sally called, scrambling to put her shirt back on.

Rolling on her back, Frankie sighed. Meanwhile, Sally got up and hurried toward the door.

"Hi," she said a little breathlessly as she opened it.

Ronnie stood before her, looking slightly pale. "Do you have any antacids?" she asked.

In a flash, Sally was off to the bathroom cabinet. Frankie, meanwhile, was staring at the ceiling, trying to will herself to be patient. To be kind. The task seemed impossible.

"There," said Sally, handing the bottle of tablets over to Ronnie.

"Sorry to interrupt," Ronnie murmured. Then she gave Sally a wink.

"It's okay." Looking at her houseguest, Sally felt a strange sensation now. It was guilt, entwined with empathy. *What the hell am I going to do with Ronnie?* Suddenly letting her into their home seemed like a massive mistake. Turning away, she shut the bedroom door and headed back to Frankie.

Yanking off her shirt once more, Sally joined her partner on their bed. Frankie slipped an arm around her as Sally snuggled up to her. "Honey, she's got to go," Frankie said quietly.

"I know," Sally said, in between kisses. "I'm working on it."

"You're working on it?" Frankie pulled back and glanced at her. "What's that mean?"

"I mean...I'm working on it," Sally explained. Then she paused. "I can't just kick her out, Frankie. Ronnie's sick—she's in seriously bad shape. She has nowhere else to go."

"Or so she says," Frankie remarked tartly.

"Frankie..." Sally said, dismay washing over her face. "Honey, please."

Frankie exhaled, trying to calm her rising ire. "Okay, okay," she said tightly. Then she lowered her voice in case Ronnie was listening to their conversation through the door. "You know how I feel," she whispered. "This woman is a total phony, a con artist. I can feel it, Sally. I know it in every cell in my body."

Sally sat up abruptly. "Actually, you don't know her at all, Frankie. And if you could just stop being so jealous for five minutes, you might actually like her."

Frankie gazed up at her partner for a minute. "Babe—" she began plaintively, but then she stopped herself. *I need to hold steady if we are going to stop fighting.* "Fine," Frankie finally said, remembering once again how much she needed Sally. "Okay."

Whatever Sally said, for now at least, would have to be fine. Frankie really got it now.

She had some serious making up to do. And reaching out, she caressed Sally's naked back.

"Come back, please," she said.

*

Tenika turned off the TV with a snap of the remote and gazed at her wife nestled beside her. "Okay. Bedtime?" she yawned.

Beside her on the couch, Delilah also yawned and gave the tentative stretch of a person whose body was under siege. She folded her hands on her massive belly and closed her eyes. "Tell me a story, honey."

Tenika smiled in her wife's direction. "About what?"

"Tell me again how easy all of this is going to be. How I'm going to have five labor pains and the babies are just going to come sliding on out."

She opened her eyes and looked over at Tenika, hopefully. "And how you're going to bring me lots of ice chips and massage my feet and tell me how great I'm doing."

"Well of course you are going to do great. Right? Even Sally said so."

Delilah looked down, and a small tear suddenly slid down her cheek. "Mmm-hmm," she tried to say lightly.

Tenika studied her face with concern. "Hey…" she said. Taking Delilah's hand, she kissed it. "What's the matter?"

Delilah gave an embarrassed laugh, pushing the tears away that gathered on her cheek. "Oh, it's silly. It's nothing. I mean you know I'm a hormonal wreck…" Her voice drifted away.

Tenika continued to study her wife tenderly. "Delilah. Tell me what's wrong."

Delilah looked at her, and she could feel her fortitude dissolving. The truth was always impossible to conceal from her wife. Sooner or later, it always came tumbling out.

Delilah said nothing. Instead, her eyes were fastened on the vast round bulge of babies that protruded in front of her. She couldn't even see her swollen legs on the ottoman in front of her.

"It's about the damn reading, isn't it?"

"What?" Delilah looked up with eyes that said it all. There was the fear, the anxiety, and the steely glare of someone trying to obscure the truth.

Tenika shook her head. "What'd Sally say? When she read

your cards? Just give it to me straight."

Now Delilah began crying in earnest. The truth now came spilling out, unstoppable. "Oh T... I think something is really gonna go wrong. She kept saying all this stuff about how hard it was going to be. We have to be intentional she kept saying. All the cards were reversed—even the stuff about our home life. I mean, it couldn't have been worse. I don't know if I'm going to fall or what, but we've really got to watch it."

Tenika sank back against the couch and stared at the ceiling. For a long moment she was silent, too, melding all of her thoughts together. "Yeah," she finally said. "We are definitely in for something, babe." She took Delilah's hand in her own. "Those two are planning to give us a hard time. I can feel it, too."

But then she looked over at her wife, with a look that spoke of their shared mission. It was both tender and strong, just like Tenika was. "But listen to me, Delilah, we're the adults in the room. We've got this, right? And we know how to call the doctor if we have to, and we've got medicine on our side. So let's just get you the last damn sonogram, okay? We'll go in on Monday. Just make sure everything's fine."

"You sure?"

"I'm definitely, positively sure. It's going to make us feel better."

Delilah gave a sigh of relief. "Okay... yes. Yes. You're right."

Tenika continued, "I mean, you stressing and everything— that's probably worse than the damn sonogram, right?"

This was, of course, what had to happen next. At least, it did if Delilah was going to get any sleep at all before the births.

Holding hands they sat there, staring straight ahead, imagining their future.

And it was unimaginable.

Chapter Nine

The Sunday afternoon walk out to Tennessee Valley Beach had been rambling and beautiful. The mile-long dirt path wound through the Marin hills, still green with scrub oak and wild grass. The air was moist and misty, as the perpetual Bay Area fog settled in for another day.

At the end of the trail was the Pacific, framed by a cliff on one side and a massive, fifty-foot rock outcropping on the other. A spread of pale sand and smooth dark gravel formed the small, intimate beach. The scene was stunning.

Sally had planned the walk as a way to help Frankie get to know Ronnie, and Ronnie had readily agreed, in spite of her illness. That much Sally found nothing less than heroic. They'd walk slowly, she'd assured Ronnie, in case she felt weak.

Frankie, on the other hand, was being grudgingly tolerant of Ronnie's presence, and that was about it. As they rounded the last bend of the winding dirt road, things weren't going well at all. For one thing, their drive across the Richmond Bridge to Marin County was uncomfortably quiet. No one seemed to know what to say.

Then, as they began hiking out, Frankie's achey hip immediately flared up. It was the remnant of a fall she'd taken years earlier while scrambling over a chain link fence in pursuit of a car thief. Not that Frankie complained about it. Instead, as usual, she was silently stoic. And suffering.

Eventually, Frankie got that drawn, tense look on her face—the one that said she was in abject pain and don't ask her about it. So the trio slid toward uncomfortable silence. Neither Frankie nor Ronnie seemed to have anything to say to each other. As a result, Sally was now non-stop talking, trying like hell to salvage the afternoon. She just hoped an argument didn't start.

"So," Sally asked Ronnie as they walked, "when's the last time you hiked?" Then she stopped. "You're okay to hike, right?"

"Huh?" Ronnie looked over at her, slightly confused.

"You're sure this isn't too much? Given that you're sick and everything. We could walk more slowly."

Ronnie waved away her concerns. "Oh. No, no. Really, it's okay. The doctors said fresh air is actually healing."

Frankie cleared her throat and looked over at Ronnie. Today, Ronnie's carefully chosen outfit was a pair of classic Levi's, cuffs rolled, with a fifties bowling shirt and her black and white wing tips. The shoes seemed ill-suited for hiking, and their whites were now pale brown with a layer of trail dust.

Ronnie had completed the look with a bit of hair gel for the slicked back Fonzie look. The entire costume made Frankie want to roll her eyes.

"So, Ronnie," Frankie began slowly. "What's wrong with you again?"

Ronnie shrugged. "It's a blood thing," she said vaguely. "The doctors don't really know."

"Like…leukemia?" Frankie probed.

"Oh, well, I wouldn't exactly call it Leukemia. It's a rare condition apparently, but they're not even sure." Ronnie now smiled at Frankie. "You know how these things are."

Frankie kept looking at her. "No, actually, I don't. Why don't you tell me?"

"Frankie—" Sally interjected.

"No, I'd love to hear more about your illness," Frankie

continued. Ronnie smirked and looked away at her tone. Then a moment later, she turned back to her inquisitor.

"I have nothing more to say about it, actually. It's private," Ronnie remarked.

Frankie stopped. The ocean was now visible just ahead of them. "Oh, really?" she asked. "You're sleeping on our couch but you can't even tell us what this mysterious disease is that you've come down with? Seriously, Ronnie? Surely you can do better than that."

Sally fastened her hand onto Frankie's forearm. "Frankie, don't go there," she warned. But Frankie shook her off.

Tipping her chin up defiantly, Frankie faced Ronnie in the middle of the path, blocking her way. She put her hands on her hips and studied Ronnie for a moment. "I don't think there's a damn thing wrong with you," she said in a low voice.

In an instant Sally was on her. "Excuse us," she said over her shoulder as she fast-walked Frankie at least twenty yards away. Then Sally turned to her would-be fiancée. "Would you just stop it, Frankie…" she hissed. "If you genuinely care about me, cut it out."

Calmly, Ronnie stuck her hands in her pockets and watched the couple quietly bicker. Meanwhile a pair of hikers passed them on the trail. She gave them a shrug and kicked at a small stone in the path.

Frankie and Sally returned a moment later, and Frankie took a deep breath. "Forgive me," was all she said. She could barely look at Ronnie.

Sally leaned toward Ronnie sympathetically. "She didn't mean it, Ronnie. Of course, you're sick. We're both incredibly sorry." She looked at Frankie. "Aren't we."

Frankie looked at the ground. "Yeah," she barely said.

Ronnie gave a little cough, as if to testify to the fact that she was, indeed, ill. "It's alright," she said easily. "No harm done. Let's get to the beach, shall we?"

Protectively, Frankie slid an arm around Sally's waist and glanced back over her shoulder, skewering Ronnie with a very dirty look.

Ronnie simply gave Frankie the smile she'd been saving all afternoon.

It was the one that said, *You really can't get rid of me. No matter how hard you try.*

*

The Radiology tech pushed open Delilah's powder-pink robe, exposing her swollen belly. With a squirt, she applied the cold, slippery ultrasound gel, and Delilah gave a little gasp. "Sorry," the tech said with a sympathetic smile. "That's usually the hardest part."

Clasping Tenika's hand, Delilah just nodded, eyes closed as she sent up a silent prayer. Meanwhile, on the monitor beside them, a gray, flickering screen yielded a shot of their two babies. They were squeezed together, occupying every last bit of space in Delilah's uterus. What looked like a leg, a hip, and then a hand with a thumb zoomed into view.

Tenika peered closely at the screen right alongside the tech. Then she took a breath and shook her head. "Oh…wow," she said slowly, as the reality of her nearly born children began to sink in.

The tech smiled at her. "Exciting, huh? They're almost here."

"The last time I saw them they were just little blobs. But now these are…these are definitely babies." Tenika couldn't take her eyes off the screen.

Rolling the transducer around, different parts of the babies were revealed as they curled together. The last sonogram had proven they were fraternal twins, so each had their own placenta, which appeared as a thick shadow clinging to the uterine wall. One of them, their son, was positioned closer to the front of Delilah's belly, partially obscuring his sister in the sac behind him.

"There's our boy," Tenika said, giving Delilah's hand a squeeze. "There's Aiden." Delilah finally opened one eye cautiously, then the other, as the tech continued to roll the transducer around on her belly.

"Oh my God," Delilah whispered, and she gripped Tenika's hand hard. "There he is. Oh, honey…" Delilah looked up at Tenika, as tears began to pour down her cheeks.

"See? Everything's cool," Delilah said. "I told you. He looks great!"

"When was your last sonogram?" the tech now asked.

"Oh, months ago. This is only the second one," Delilah replied.

Silently, the tech gently rolled Delilah on her side, then she whirled the transducer around on the other side of her belly. Again, she peered at the monitor. Then she glanced at their file. "I'm not getting a complete picture of the baby in the rear position. Your daughter?"

"Yes, Ashanti," Tenika confirmed. "But everything looks fine, right?"

Wordless, still absorbed by the image on the screen, the tech just gave a little nod. She appeared to be taking measurements. "One of the floor doctors will be in in a moment, after she's seen the sonograms," she said lightly.

"Oh, well we're working with a midwife."

"Yes, I see," said the technician, "but it's protocol to show one of the doctors. Since I can't completely see your daughter," she said.

"Okay, fine. That's good." Tenika was beginning to feel more reassured. All that so-called predicting of Sally's was just psycho-babble sometimes…wasn't it?

Meanwhile, the technician left the room. Delilah blew her nose on a tissue and took a long, shuddering breath. The slow twisting burn of a charley horse had begun in one of her calf muscles. Bending her legs, she put her feet on the table, trying to press it out.

"Hon?" she said after a minute. "I've got a wicked cramp in my calf." Delilah winced. "Ow…owww! This hurts!" Without warning, she suddenly leapt from the examining table, landing hard on her feet. Furiously, Delilah braced against the wall and began to stretch her calf. "Owww," she groaned again.

Then suddenly, there was an unmistakable sensation. "Hey…" Delilah said. "What the—?" A gusher of pea green liquid now poured down her thighs, collecting in a large puddle on the linoleum floor beneath her. "Shit!" she cried. "What did I do? My water broke—and something's wrong with it. It's green! T, help me…get someone."

"Stay right there," Tenika commanded, rushing for the door of the examining room. "Hello? Help!" she called into the void of the empty hallway. "Emergency!"

But no one seemed to have heard her. Instead, the hallway was utterly silent. "Some freaking hospital," Tenika muttered under her breath, as she slipped back into the exam room. Delilah was just standing there, the puddle of something resembling pea soup growing beneath her on the floor. She looked completely stricken.

Quickly, Tenika helped her back up onto the table.

"Stay here and don't move," she commanded. Then she set off for help down the hall. Seeing a flash of blue scrubs go by, Tenika hustled up and flagged a stout Chinese woman who appeared to be a nurse.

"Hey! My wife's water just broke, and it looks weird. She's supposed to have twins in a month but this is way too early. We need a doctor—it's an emergency!" she said. Stabs of panic began to race through her body. This was bad and she knew it.

The nurse hurried down the hall after Tenika, and as soon as she stepped into the room she visibly blanched. "Oh dear," she said slowly, surveying the now dripping wet Delilah and the strange liquid on the floor.

"Are you having contractions?" the nurse asked. Delilah shook her head, and the nurse's mouth tightened. She asked who their doctor was, and they told her they had a midwife outside the hospital.

"Let me get a wheelchair. We'll get you up to Labor & Delivery to get you evaluated," the nurse said. Then she took off quickly.

Delilah was now white as a sheet. She gripped Tenika's forearm. "This is it," she said grimly. "This is exactly what Sally was talking about. It's happening, T. It's happening."

"Okay, okay, honey. Shhh…just stop. They know what to do. We're in the right place. We're gonna be okay."

"I want the midwife we've been working with!" Delilah cried.

"Well, baby, that ain't gonna happen, alright? So just stop and breathe. We're going with the flow here. That's all we can do."

Tenika seated herself beside the examining table. Then she took Delilah's hand and they both sat, silently waiting for the next thing to happen.

Moments later, the nurse arrived with a wheelchair, and she and Tenika helped lower Delilah into it. Then the three of them took off, the nurse rolling her briskly through the hallway.

"Don't worry, miss. It's all going to be fine," she remarked. Then she patted Delilah's shoulder as they came to rest before the elevator.

Neither Tenika nor Delilah responded. They both knew that simply wasn't true.

*

The obstetrician had salt and pepper hair and a stethoscope around her neck. It had been nearly an hour since Delilah's water broke, and a trio of monitoring straps spanned her belly in three different locations. So far there were no contractions, and the babies' vitals were reportedly stable.

The doctor removed the straps and, once again, prepped Delilah for an ultrasound.

She rolled the head of the ultrasound over Delilah's belly, and peered at the screen before her, saying nothing.

"I feel so stupid," Delilah muttered. "I should have just stayed put on the table."

"Hey, it's thirty-six weeks. It's not the end of the world. You know how many twins I've delivered at thirty-six weeks? Lots." The doctor took a reassuring tone. "And you're not the first mother who had a premature rupture. You did nothing wrong, okay? The thing I'm concerned about is the meconium in the fluid."

"Doctor, we'd actually like to deliver with our midwife—" Tenika began.

"Well, actually, the babies are both breech," the OB said as she removed the transducer, "so I think we're going to have to do a Caesarean. I can confirm first baby, your son, is butt down. But I can't quite see your daughter, but my guess is that she is also butt down."

Wiping the transducer gel off of Delilah's belly, she snapped the monitors back in place. "The fact that your son has lost all of his fluid, and it does have meconium in it, and the breech presentation… I'd say it's pretty clear that—"

An alarm sounded from one of the machines over Delilah's head, and the doctor looked up immediately. The pattern on the screen clearly showed a decelerating heart rate. "Wait a minute," she said. "Okay, scratch that. Nurse, call a Code C."

Instantly, a sudden flood of activity began around them. "Your son's heart rate is falling," the doctor explained while two orderlies hurried into the room and snapped up the sides of Delilah's gurney. They paused only briefly and looked at the doctor.

"Can you sign this please? We have to put you to sleep," she said to Delilah, thrusting a clipboard at her. Delilah scribbled a fast signature.

They were already wheeling her out the door as the doctor turned to Tenika. "I'll be doing an emergency C-section on you. Right now." The doctor then disappeared, scurrying off in the direction of the fast-moving gurney.

Tenika watched a swarm of nurses rush her wife down the hallway. They disappeared behind a pair of swinging doors. "Hey! Wait!" she called after them, but a nurse restrained her.

"You can't go in there," the nurse said. "I'll show you to the waiting room. But don't worry. Everything's going to be fine."

As if, thought Tenika. And an ache began in the pit of her stomach.

Their shared destiny had just arrived.

*

Lizzy pulled off her grease-covered latex gloves, tossed them in the trash, and wiped her brow. She hated radiator work. Something nasty inevitably dripped all over her. Today's repair involved pulling out a radiator that had been destroyed when the Honda Fit hit a feral cat going seventy. Yanking this particular radiator had been particularly unpleasant.

And now here was Tenika, calling again. It was her second call in less than five minutes, and she wasn't one to call incessantly. Something was definitely up. Lizzy picked up.

"Hey, T. Everything okay?"

"Definitely not. Delilah's in emergency surgery. She's about to give birth."

"What?" Lizzy's mouth suddenly grew dry. It was too early for these babies to be born. "I'm...am I...what can I—" she stammered. Lizzy found she was having trouble talking. Tenika had told her with twins anything was possible, but this seemed extreme. It was just eight months.

Still, her business partner sounded weirdly calm. "I want you to get everyone to the hospital," she instructed Lizzy. "Just get them here. Everyone, even Rosalind and Monroe. Get 'em all here and get them praying. We're on the third floor at the Kaiser, Fabiola Building on Howe. Labor and Delivery."

The two were quiet for a moment. "Thanks," Tenika said simply. Then she hung up.

Numbly, Lizzy found a piece of paper and started scrawling out the hospital information. She couldn't believe this was happening. Not now. No one was ready for this, least of all her.

Lizzy paused, studying the paper she'd scribbled on. She needed Kate right now. She really, really needed her. *Why did everything have to happen at once?*

It had been only four days since Kate left, but already it felt like months. Especially because so far Lizzy had only gotten one text from Kate, saying she had arrived safely. Lizzy didn't even know if her father-in-law was still alive.

Father-in-law. The phrase stuck out at Lizzy. Because, yes, Kate's Da was definitely her father-in-law. Even if he didn't know that she existed. Yet.

Still...maybe everything would be alright. Maybe somehow all of this drama would resolve itself. Kate's father would pass away, the babies would be born healthy, and Delilah would be fine. Then Kate would come home grateful for their marriage, fully out to her family, and life would return to normal once more after a whole lot of upheaval.

Cause that's what usually happened, didn't it? Everything was almost always okay in the end.

Wasn't it?

Rousing herself from inaction, Lizzy now began a text to everyone she could think of. Her hand was shaking as she typed.

Delilah just went in for emergency surgery. The twins are on their way. Not sure what's up, but T asked us all to come and pray or whatever you do.... 3rd floor. Fabiola Building on Howe. Meet me over at Kaiser ASAP.

Lizzy pulled off her coveralls, pulled on her jeans and shoved the phone in her back pocket. Then grabbing her backpack, her helmet and the keys to the garage, she locked up and headed out.

She'd get there as fast as her bike could carry her.

*

Kate picked up the handful of faded old photographs from the white hospital bedspread and dimly smiled as she thumbed through them again. Her mother had dropped them off earlier for a look-through with her father. Then, once delivered, her mother promptly left.

It seemed Sheila Morahan couldn't quite tolerate sitting by her husband's deathbed. Better for the girls to do it, especially now that Kate was home. Or that was how it seemed to Kate. But then, she wasn't surprised.

"Someone has to keep things going down at the pub," her mother explained briskly, as if the imminent death of the man who owned the place might not be reason enough to close it for a few days.

But that is pub life, Kate thought with a sigh. Always there, and always open. Like the police. Or the church. Or McDonald's. Someone always needed their dram of Jamesons or their Guinness on tap. And that's how her mother was, decidedly ignoring reality most of the time in deference to work.

Her father stirred slightly under the covers in the dimly lit room. He opened his eyes and gazed at her. His eyes had sunken into his head, giving him a stark, disturbing appearance. She realized it was the look of death, and she wasn't prepared for it. Nor was she ready for the fact that her ordinarily robust, red-faced father would be so pale and drawn. But he was, and weak as well.

Da had little to say to her, naturally, but more out of illness than anything else. All of the fight had gone straight out of him by now, and for this Kate was grateful. In his infirmity, he'd been reduced to a placeholder, though Da did manage to pat her hand weakly a few times. It was an acknowledgement of sorts. His other daughter was finally home.

Her Da knew her, and he loved her, even after all this time. That, in and of itself, was something. It was enough to make Kate cling to his side, refusing to leave his room.

"I have some photos, Da, look," she said, holding up one of the yellowed, square photos so he could see it. The ailing man squinted, trying to make out the picture before him. In one of the shots, Kate is playing with a dog, a border collie, while her father smiles at them both, hands in pockets.

"Do you remember Jack, our collie, Da?" she asked. "Must have been twenty years ago. Mum brought me these for us to look at."

But rather than recognizing the image she held before him, her father simply closed his eyes again. As if he hadn't even the strength to muster up a memory. Lowering the photograph into her lap, she sat there, once again uncertain what to do. There was an abundance of time and of quiet in the hospital room of a dying man.

This is what the last three days had been for Kate. Long, tedious and filled with almost moments, where she tried to engage with Da, but he was just a little too far gone to really hear her. Perhaps he was already on his way to the afterlife, she reasoned. Settling back in her chair, Kate searched for acceptance. It was best she do nothing more than hold space.

He would get to that place of release soon, she knew it. Earlier, the nurse had said it could be that very day. And for this reason, her sister, with a baby in tow, was busy tracking down their mother and forcing her to come to the hospital. Eileen had sworn she would get her mother to close the pub and come to the hospital, even if she had to drag her there herself.

There was a ping, and Kate glanced over at her phone on the table next to her. A What'sApp text flitted across the screen.

Delilah is delivering. Bad situation, emergency C-section. I wish you were here. Pray.

Kate closed her eyes and felt a pang in her gut. With every fiber of her being she wanted to be in Oakland right now. She wanted to be at that hospital, with Lizzy by her side, supporting her dear friends. She wanted to do whatever she could, whether it be consoling the inconsolable or perhaps to help mind two brand new infants.

But she was here now, on the other side of the world with a dying man who happened to be her father. Never mind that she couldn't be fully who she was with him. Never mind that she'd been forced to move five thousand miles away to build the life she wanted. All of that was irrelevant now, for Da was her own flesh and blood. And in this moment, that meant the world.

Without him she wouldn't even walk this earth. Kate was acutely aware of this now.

Searching his face, she looked for any kind of sign of life. Then suddenly, slowly, her Da opened his eyes and he, once again, looked right at her. And then he smiled, nodding silently. It was the first time she'd seen him smile since she'd arrived.

She was so glad she had come. "Da?" she asked hopefully, thinking maybe he'd just needed a rest.

But once again, her father closed his eyes. Kate settled back once more, resigned, and reread Lizzy's text. In her mind's eye, she could see her wife, slightly baffled as she held the swaddled, crying bundle of baby in her arms, and Kate almost laughed out loud.

But this sweet scene was not what Lizzy was texting about now. Not at all. First they had to get through the births, and at this point that was some kind of a problem. The situation actually sounded serious. She could even feel the panic in Lizzy's terse text. *I will pray.* she texted back. *What's happened?*

There was no immediate reply. Once again, Kate was left to sit by Da's bedside, wade through the passage of time and wait for the inevitable.

This was, of course, exactly what she'd come for.

Chapter Ten

Tenika was standing by the window, the phone pressed to hear ear, waiting to leave a voicemail. Down below, she could see some boys playing one-on-one basketball in a lot adjacent to the hospital parking lot. There were some baskets made, some hoots. A fist bump or two.

They were probably supposed to be in school at the moment, but the four of them were filled with life. She couldn't keep her eyes off of them. Somehow watching them was soothing her.

"Keisha? It's me. Call me. Delilah just went in for emergency surgery." She paused, not sure what else she should tell her cousin in a message. "Just call me, okay?"

It was her second message to her cousin in the last ten minutes, but at this point Tenika wasn't sure what else to do. She'd texted everyone she could possibly think of, but Keisha was probably the most important one. Not because she and Keisha were so close or anything. Keisha had been a royal pain her butt for most of her adult life, hovering over her like the mother she always thought she was, but clearly wasn't.

But right now she needed Keisha more than ever, mainly because she was the one person Tenika knew who actually went to church. If anyone could pray their way out of this, it had to be Keisha. Other than that, Tenika had no idea what else to do. And in that moment, she felt utterly and completely alone.

It was the doctor's manner that did it. The OB was being way too reassuring, kind of like an airplane pilot when they're about to fly you through severe turbulence. Then, she practically took off at a run when she coded Delilah. And where the hell was their midwife? At this moment, she was totally MIA. Tenika had left at least three messages for her as well.

And why hadn't she ever told them that both babies were breech?

A creeping sense of disaster—the disaster she'd already had a premonition of—was settling in for a long stay.

Tenika turned her attention back to the boys playing in the lot below, thinking she might surf on their positive energy. Or at least get distracted for a while, but a voice behind her called her away.

"T!" It was Lizzy.

The two woman fell into a long hug. "Thank you, sister," Tenika said, giving her friend an appreciative look. Seeing the tears welling in her eyes, Lizzy hugged her once more.

Now Lizzy ran a nervous hand through her cropped, dark hair. "So Delilah's in surgery, right? Heard anything yet?"

"No word." Tenika checked her watch. "They've been in there almost an hour. I thought these things were pretty fast, but what do I know? Nothing, as it turns out. And where the hell is our midwife? The woman's not even returning my calls or my texts. She said she'd be here the minute anything happened."

"I get it, this really sucks. But seriously, T, everything's probably going to be fine. These people do this all the time."

"So I hear," Tenika said dryly. She turned back to the window. "It's a fucking crisis is what it is. Just like Sally said. The babies were breech. Breech! Why didn't the—"

"Sally predicted this?"

Tenika nodded. "Yep." She turned back to her friend. "That's why we need everyone now. Who knows how the hell this is going to turn out. It's going to be 'challenging'," Tenika said, using air quotes.

She turned back to the window, not wanting her business partner to see the tears that were now streaming down her face. Tenika was not generally one for overwhelm. But if she had to be, this was definitely one of those moments.

"I can't do this alone," she finally said to the glass, as Lizzy's hand landed firmly on her shoulder.

"We got you, T."

Turning around, Tenika shook her head woefully. "The whole thing's a damn shit show," she muttered.

But at least her old pal was here, and more friends were on their way. That had to count for something.

*

The OB held her scalpel poised over the patient's prepped and shaved belly, waiting for the signal from the anesthesiologist to begin. The patient had gone down loudly, complaining that she wanted her wife, but then, that was sedation for you. These folks always had something interesting to say just before lights out.

The anesthesiologist looked up from his work. "Go."

Cutting into the belly, the surgeon deftly made her way across the bikini line and through the intervening layers of tissue. Here was Baby A, dry as a bone without his amniotic fluid. She guided and scooped and the baby's butt emerged followed by its legs, its arms and finally its head.

Handing Baby A off quickly to the purple-gloved hands of the waiting pediatrician, the OB didn't even glance at the baby. A few seconds later, she heard the baby's wail and felt the usual small thrill of satisfaction as she worked. There really was nothing better than hearing a newborn give its first cry.

Clamping the cord and cutting it, the surgeon quickly moved on to Baby B in the rear position. Cutting into its still full sac, the doctor released a gusher of fluids and felt around for body parts.

Once again, a small, perfect pair of buttocks presented themselves in the uterine opening and she pulled. Then she eased its arms into place as she pulled them out, scooping Baby B's legs along as well. She gave a final tug and the baby's entire body now appeared. Once more, she handed the infant over to the waiting pediatrician, her eyes fastened on the open, bleeding pelvis of the patient in front of her. There was still quite a lot to do.

"Oh, wow," she heard the pediatrician say seconds later, but the surgeon did not look up. Now she was reaching in to extract the placentas, handing them off to a waiting nurse to check. Then she was clamping and cutting, and yet again, keeping her eye on the patient's bleeding.

Around her, she began to notice something. There was a low murmur in the OR—a sound the doctor had only heard a handful of times in her twenty-seven years. It was the subtle buzz of alarm.

Something was clearly wrong.

She realized then she still hadn't heard Baby B cry. And briefly, she raised her head. "Baby B still alive?"

The pediatrician was working hard to keep his voice even behind her. "Yes. But…uh…Baby B is anencephalic."

The obstetrician blanched. It was only the second time she'd heard this birth defect mentioned in the OR.

Baby B was missing most of her brain.

*

Sally sped toward the hospital impatiently, snapping off the spew of irritating non-stop ads on the radio. Again and again, the array of reversed goddess cards she'd seen in her reading with Delilah kept flashing through her mind. She remembered her words to Delilah at the time.

All in all, these births are going to be incredible life changers.

So here they were. The Universe, as usual, was delivering on its promise. There would be chaos. There would be challenge. The veritable bottom would, indeed, drop out. Still there was some semblance of hope.

No matter what happened, they would get through this. Each of them would heal, just as they always had. Delilah would be just fine, as would Tenika. And Sally and all of their friends would stand by, doing what they could. Perhaps they would even be healed as well.

But the babies…those poor little babies. For them, their fate was far more uncertain.

A tear now ran down Sally's face, and then another, for she could feel what was just ahead and she dreaded it. At least one of the babies would not be fine at all. Sally sighed heavily as she drove.

How could life carry on, unabated, doling out such tragedies as if they were nothing? The sweeping pace of the world, barreling along at such times, never failed to shock her. Accelerating along San Pablo, Sally picked up speed and passed the two slower cars ahead of her. She had to get a grip.

These infants have their own karma, Sally reminded herself. They would ebb and flow in their lives, just as we all did. Furthermore, their path was already preordained by the Goddesses, or God, or the Universe, or whomever they answered to. Just like the rest of us, they had no choice but to comply.

No, there was nothing for Sally to do here, but try to stay calm and be supportive. She reminded herself of this once more. All she had to do now was be a good friend and help however she could. That would truly be enough.

Sally pulled up to a stoplight and shifted uncomfortably in her seat. She could feel the ache of helplessness deep in her body. Reaching for a tissue, she wiped her eyes and blew her nose. Then she drove on, doing her best to pull herself together.

Sally had run out the door quickly, just moments earlier, leaving Ronnie alone and baffled in their living room with little explanation. By now Lizzy was probably already at the hospital.

So far, she'd only been able to text Frankie at work. Ideally, Frankie would come, too, as soon as her shift was done.

She knew Frankie would want to be there with all of them. And being a cop, the first responder in her would certainly rise to the occasion. As for Tenika—well, perhaps she was still in the waiting room, waiting to hear the status of her new family.

Together they would all get through this. They had to.

Sally drove on in silence.

*

Sally hurried down the hospital corridor toward the Labor and Delivery waiting room.

Monroe and Rosalind were the first to greet her. They'd been sitting on one of the modest couches in the fluorescent-lit waiting area. Both of them leapt to their feet when they saw her. "Sally!" Monroe cried.

The three hugged. "Nothing yet?" Sally asked, and the couple gave each other a worried look.

"Tenika just got called in by the doctor," Rosalind explained. "She wouldn't tell her what happened in front of us."

"So basically something really terrible has happened," Monroe observed. Sally could feel her stomach drop to her knees.

"And Lizzy? Is she here?" she managed to ask.

"She's just left to try to get Kate on the phone," Monroe said.

"Yeah, it's past midnight in Ireland. Anyway, who knows when we'll really find out anything."

"How's Tenika so far?" Sally asked.

"How do you think?" Monroe shrugged.

"Terrified. Fearing the worst," Rosalind said. She took a breath and sat down once more. "Can't say I blame her."

Sally sank down into an orange plastic seat beside Monroe. "So I guess…we just sit here and wait?"

Rosalind nodded. "This whole thing…wow. I mean…I just feel so helpless."

"Me, too," Sally murmured, thinking to herself that they didn't know the half of it. Not yet at least.

And she dearly wished she didn't know as much as she did.

*

A fierce shaking woke Delilah.

"Ma'am, we need you to wake up," someone was saying. She could smell them, an antiseptic smell. And though her eyes were still closed, she could sense the warmth of their body close to her face. She could hear a beeping in the background. *Who is this?*

And where am I, anyway?

Delilah wished fervently that this person would simply go away because right now all she wanted to do was to sleep.

"Delilah, please wake up," the urgent voice insisted.

It was a voice she really couldn't place. Whoever this was, it wasn't her wife. It was someone strange. Someone she didn't know. And where was Tenika?

Delilah shook her head slowly, wearily, unwilling to open her eyes. Her mouth didn't seem to quite be working correctly, but somehow words made of thick cotton managed to ooze out.

"I need a nap," she groaned. "Leave me alone."

The shaking simply continued. "Time to wake up, Delilah. The doctor's coming in."

Groggily, finally, she opened her eyes, squinting at the bright light. She was barely conscious. Looking up she saw the source of the urgent voice. It was a nurse. "What's happening?" she asked.

"Ah…here's your wife," said the nurse.

"Honey? Gotta wake up, baby." Tenika leaned in and her voice came sliding over her like warm, melted chocolate.

Delilah squinted up at her. "T?" she said. Tenika's beaming face stopped right in front of her.

"Yep…look over here, honey." She was trying to get Delilah to turn her head and look beside the gurney she was propped up on.

"It's your baby boy," the nurse added. "Isn't he beautiful?"

Slowly, Delilah turned her head.

A bassinet was parked beside her, and inside it, a small bundle was swaddled tightly. Only the tiny, perfect face of a six-and-a-half-pound baby boy was visible. He opened his eyes and looked right at her, and she gasped with wonder. His expression was simple, open and wide-eyed with trust.

This was her son.

"Aiden," she whispered. *Aiden*. Here he was and he was looking at her. A huge smile spread across her face, as Delilah leaned toward him. "Oh my God…" Delilah said softly, instinctively reaching for him.

"Wait," the nurse cautioned. "You need to stay right there, ma'am. You're full of stitches."

Looking up, Delilah squeezed Tenika's hand. "Oh, T," she said. "He's here."

"Yep." Tenika was smiling more than she'd ever seen her smile. It was like her face was lit with sunlight. "He's here."

"And he's so…oh my God. He's so beautiful." Both of them were now crying and talking at the same time. "Can I?" Delilah said, reaching for the baby.

But the nurse stopped her. "I'm afraid he needs a few more hours to stabilize in the bassinet. Because he came early. Then you can hold him and nurse him all you want."

"Okay," Delilah said dreamily. She couldn't take her eyes off of this perfect child, nestled beside her.

Her son her son her son… It was like a song that just wouldn't stop playing through her heart. Her son was here. *Her son, Aiden.*

Delilah lay there quietly, as she gazed at the scene with a fuzzy sense of wonder. Then she heard Tenika ask the nurse a question that made her pause.

"Where is our daughter?"

The nurse looked up sharply. "The doctor will be here soon," she said, a forced smile now in place. Her reply seemed strange. Off somehow. Yet, Delilah noticed this as if she were on a cloud, floating somewhere up by the ceiling.

Tenika took her eyes off the baby and leaned toward the nurse. "What is it—is something wrong?" Delilah heard her ask.

There was a pause now, and the recovery room grew deathly still. Delilah suddenly felt herself plummeting back to earth as the collective sense of alarm grew around her.

"The doctor will be here soon," the nurse repeated, looking urgently toward the door as if she were trying to will the obstetrician to magically appear. The air in the recovery room was now thick with the unsaid.

Something is clearly wrong.

Delilah closed her eyes, willing the entire scene to become soft and gentle again. She wanted to go back to the fuzzy reality she'd been enjoying only a moment earlier. Once more, she focused on the baby beside her.

Yet her wife continued, undaunted. "So where's the doctor? How long are we going to be waiting here?" Her voice had an unmistakable edge that Delilah knew well. It was fear, if not panic.

"What's happened to our other baby?" Tenika asked.

The nurse did her best to placate Tenika "The doctor's on her—" she was saying as the double doors to the recovery room swung open, and the obstetrician now appeared. Notably, their second baby was not with her.

Tenika's eyes grew big as she watched the doctor approaching empty handed, a grave look on her face. Suddenly she sat down on the edge of Delilah's gurney. "Shit."

"Where's our other baby, doc?" Tenkia burst as soon as the doctor neared them. "Just tell us! Is she dead?"

The doctor and the nurse drew close to Tenika and Delilah, as the other nurses and orderlies in the room seemed to slip away. The nurse put her hand on Tenika's arm, as the doctor leaned in toward them.

"Your baby is still alive," she said quietly. "But barely." The doctor paused and took a breath. "I'm so sorry," she began, "but your baby girl has a serious birth defect, anencephaly. She is missing a significant part of her brain and her skull, and she will not survive more than a few more hours. Or maybe overnight."

The air was still and the room was dead quiet. Even the customary background beeps and whirs of the recovery room had fallen silent.

"I'm so sorry," the doctor repeated; there didn't seem to be anything else left to say.

Suddenly reality dropped in, and Tenika let out a howl that filled the entire room. Beside her Delilah gasped. Everything became disconnected, as the doctor continued on about rare birth defects, genetic mutations in twins, and the chances being one in ten thousand that something like this might happen.

But Delilah wasn't listening now. Instead, the doctor's voice got smaller and smaller. And she found herself drifting far away, on a golden plane of light that wasn't quite here or there. Delilah had no idea where she was because, for one brief, brilliant moment, a vision consumed her completely.

In this golden zone, her daughter was a tiny, far away speck glowing in the distance. And she was still her mother, no matter what happened. It was as if instant understanding poured down through Delilah's consciousness at that moment, and she drank it in eagerly.

She knew this truth now. Ashanti would die, perhaps that very day. But she would always be Ashanti's mother, whether her baby got to live her life or not. Though her daughter soul was floating away, Delilah could feel the entirety of who she was, this baby who came directly from her own body.

For just one small moment, she knew her daughter's passions. Her loves, her preferences, and even the things that disturbed her. She knew everything about this half-formed child, this child without much of a brain. Delilah instantly knew all of it; this was the silver cord of maternal love. And it was strong between them.

With every fiber of her being, Delilah knew every bit of this to be true.

Reaching out now, she took her wife's hand as she dropped back into the moment. Beside her Tenika continued to sob loudly, a broken sound that Delilah had never heard before. She gazed at her almost impassively.

"Can we see her?" Delilah asked the doctor calmly. It wasn't post-op drugs, or cosmic bliss, or even serenity she was surfing on now. Instead, it was inevitability. There was no avoiding this tragedy, and they had no choice but to embrace it. There was nothing else to do.

"Of course you can," the doctor said. "They will bring her to you in your room." The doctor added gently. "I've arranged a private room for you both. You can keep her with you as long as you want tonight."

They both noticed then what had been left unsaid.

You will need the time and space to say goodbye.

In a strange way, Delilah felt she already had.

Chapter Eleven

Lizzy listened to the strange, tinny ring of the international call as it attempted to connect. Then she looked at her watch, knowing full well the time had scarcely changed from a minute ago. It wasn't even 4AM in Dublin.

Kate would almost certainly be asleep. Unless, like Lizzy, she was having a rough time and big things were happening there as well. Then…well, who could sleep? Lizzy hoped against hope, as the phone rang on and on, that Kate might miraculously pick up. But there was no answer.

In defeat, Lizzy pushed the disconnect button and slid the phone back into the pocket of her jeans. Whatever might be happening to Tenika's babies, Kate wasn't going to help her get through this, and that's just how it was. Lizzy would have to go this one alone.

As she slowly ambled back up the hallway toward her waiting group of friends, she pondered Kate's particular situation. To be losing her own father had to be gutting her. Perhaps that was why Lizzy had heard little to nothing from her since she'd left. Kate probably didn't have the bandwidth for even a supportive call to her wife.

She could only assume Kate was grief-stricken and over-whelmed. Maybe there was nothing to say on the phone. Lizzy suspected it would be hard for Kate to communicate the intensity of everything she and her family were going through. That had to explain a lot of her silence. Still it was strange, and it ate at Lizzy in her off moments.

The other bleak scenario, which Lizzy tried not to think about, was that Kate had fallen back into the comforting warmth of home. Perhaps her life in Oakland now just seemed too different. Or worse, like a problem that Kate would now want to avoid.

Maybe coming to America had only been a temporary dream for Kate, an adventure that was now suddenly over. The mere thought made Lizzy's mind race.

Maybe Kate would never come back. Maybe marrying Lizzy seemed like a necessary convenience at the time, which would need to be completely undone. Maybe all they'd really had was a Green Card marriage—one that Lizzy had mistakenly convinced herself was real.

Perhaps this was the end of their whole damn story.

But that just couldn't be so.

Lizzy believed all of Kate's ecstatic sighs when they made love, and how deeply and soulfully Kate looked into her eyes. She believed in their shared laughter, their household jokes and the fun they had together. And she believed in the joy of watching Kate make her Irish stew on Sunday afternoons, after they picked out the ingredients together in the farmer's market. Lizzy believed in their love one hundred percent.

She thought about their work together at the garage. It was Kate who'd saved their business back in the first days of their relationship, and Kate who'd suggested and then outfitted the all-important conversation corner at the garage. That, alone, had pretty much saved their business when it was hurting—that and her famous Valentine's Day Lube Job Sale.

It was Kate who kept the cream in the mini fridge and the customers coming through the door. Just in the few short days Kate had been gone, at least three customers asked when she'd be back. Simply put, Kate was her soulmate. Lizzy knew it with every fiber of her being.

Both of them had leapt into their life together with such abandon, Lizzy had been entirely gobsmacked, announcing to whoever would listen that this was the relationship she'd been waiting for all her life. So much so she'd even been willing to spend their first year of marriage apart, while Kate bided her time in a Sanctuary church until she could get a Green Card.

Lovingly, thoughtfully, Lizzy had tended to Kate's every last need while she was in the church, never once even getting to sleep with her. (Well, okay, there was that one fast and furious, very illegal lovemaking session just before her time at the church ended.) Still, Lizzy had spent countless hours and thousands of dollars on immigration attorneys. She'd helped Kate fill out forms and stood in line herself to file them time and time again.

Lizzy had stuck it out to the bitter end, being the most supportive wife she could possibly be, until the glorious day finally came when Kate got her Green Card. And then, once more, she was free to live her life in the U.S. in perfect ease as Lizzy's wife.

But now Lizzy wondered at Kate's ongoing silence. Had all of that so-called love and romance just been an illusion?

With all her heart, Lizzy believed they'd been in love…how could they not be? And how could she doubt all of it so quickly now? Lizzy had no answer. Instead, she shoved her hands in her pockets and made her way back to her waiting friends.

She needed to focus on what was happening here and now, in this moment, in this hospital. Lizzy was actually grateful for something else to think about entirely.

*

As Lizzy walked up to the small group in the waiting room, they clustered together in a tight group. Sally was sitting there with her head in her hands, crying with great, racking sobs. Rosalind looked over at Lizzy, shaking her head with dismay.

"What is it?" asked Lizzy, making her way to the corner they'd taken over. "What's happened?"

Monroe turned back to her with a plaintive look. "Nothing so far. At least no one's telling us anything."

"Tenika hasn't come out yet. We're still waiting to hear," added Rosalind.

Sally shook her head and looked up at Lizzy with reddened eyes. "It's going...it's going to be bad," she said, trying to stem the flow of her tears. "It's everything I saw in the cards. Oh, Lizzy. I know it is."

Bewildered, for they were not a believer in such things, Monroe looked over at Lizzy and shrugged. But Rosalind took a different approach; sitting down beside her, she put her arm around Sally. She began to whisper soothing, shushing sounds into her friend's ear.

"It's going to be okay," they could hear Rosalind say. But this just elicited furious head-shaking on Sally's part.

"Oh, no no no, it's not, Rosalind," she insisted. "That's what I keep trying to tell you people. This is going to be very, very bad. We've got to prepare ourselves."

"Shit." Lizzy put her hands on her hips and began to pace in small circles, shaking her head. Her entire being was now about to explode from so many assorted pressures at once.

Monroe reached out and touched her arm. "Hey. Did you manage to get Kate? How's she doing?" Monroe had worked in the Sanctuary church that housed Kate. In fact, it was Monroe who'd arranged for Kate to move in. And it was Monroe who'd had the misfortune to fall in love with Kate, as well.

The fact that Lizzy was an ever-present fixture in the background of Kate's life was something Monroe had finally come to accept, albeit begrudgingly. And now Monroe and Lizzy were friends of a sort.

"No, no. It's like 4AM there. I think her phone is off." Lizzy gave a defeated sigh. "That or maybe she's ignoring me."

"I doubt that," said Monroe. "You heard much from her?"

"Not since she got there. And it's been…what…three days?"

Monroe gave Lizzy a sympathetic pat on the shoulder, to which Lizzy folded her arms and tried to focus on Sally. Anything to change the topic.

"So, you gonna be okay, Sally? Or what?" she asked.

Sally nodded and blew her nose. Then she gave a small, crooked smile. "Sometimes I…uh…just need to meltdown. But I'm here. I'm okay." She cleared her throat and wiped the tears from her face with a wavering hand.

Sally gave a small embarrassed laugh. "And we are all going to get through this," she announced. "But I'm telling you, I've seen what's happening here. And just…just prepare yourself."

Lizzy folded her arms and looked down at the floor. She never knew quite what to make of Sally's mystical pronouncements. She wanted to be respectful, but sometimes it all seemed like a whole lot of hype and delirium.

To Lizzy, Sally was…well, excitable. Maybe that was the most polite way to put it.

"Is Frankie coming?" Lizzy asked now.

Sally shrugged as she blew her nose. "Maybe," she said. "She hasn't answered my texts. I'd hope she'd make it here. I've called and texted, but there was nothing. And, to be fair, she is at work." Sally pulled out her phone and took another glance. "Yeah. Nothing so far. But she's getting off soon, so maybe we'll see her."

Sally's voice didn't sound optimistic. Lizzy wondered for a moment if they were having love troubles.

In fact, Sally didn't mention what was foremost on her mind about her partner, which was that they still hadn't fully recovered from the disastrous walk with Ronnie the previous day. Nor had they recovered from any of the ongoing tension in the house. They were barely speaking as Frankie left for work that morning.

Frankie had been sullen, almost businesslike as she moved around the kitchen, making her coffee and toast. It was as if she'd given up trying, even after that enthusiastic offering of summer flowers and the big apology. This was the same bouquet that now sat dying in a vase on Sally's bureau. It felt like the clock had rewound to a few weeks earlier, when all the trouble between them was new.

Yet, one thing Sally knew for sure—Frankie was her own worst enemy at such times. She had demons in her head that neither Sally nor anyone else could appease. And now it was Frankie's jealousy that was the problem. Frankie would have to do that work herself. Sally, herself, was powerless.

She glanced around at her friends, all seated nearby. The other women rested in a resigned silence, some looking at their phones while others simply sat there, biding their time. And she was grateful for the comfort of good companions.

They were all waiting for God knew what. And it was hard.

*

Tenika and Delilah waited in the hospital room. It would still be a few more hours before Aiden would be released from his bassinet and brought to their room. Then he would finally be free to nurse on Delilah's breast.

They still had yet to see Ashanti.

All Delilah knew as the post-anesthesia grogginess began to wear off was that she was extraordinarily tired. And bewildered. Where were her babies? At least she wanted to see and hold her damaged daughter. Delilah closed her eyes against the nightmare the two of them had now been presented with.

Tenika, meanwhile, was staying to herself for the moment. Arms folded, she just kept looking out the window, trying to come to terms with things. Her brain kept going in circles.

Why the hell hadn't they brought Ashanti in by now? Restlessly, she looked at her watch once more. It had been nearly two hours since the birth. Two hours of their precious daughter's life that had now been wasted by God knows what.

The dark thought that Ashanti had already died briefly flitted through her brain. *They couldn't do that*, her mind sputtered and whirred. *They couldn't fucking do that.*

But, of course, they could. And they certainly would if they wanted to. She was used to all the prejudices the overly White world of institutions regularly dished out to Black people like her, not to mention those who were queer. Wearily, Tenika expected nothing less.

Tenika looked up then at a sound in the doorway. A nurse was wheeling in one of the babies in a plastic bassinet, as the pediatrician, a clean cut younger doctor, followed close behind.

"Sorry that took so long," he began. "We were keeping your daughter with us to try to stabilize her breathing." The pediatrician stood there almost awkwardly for a moment, as if he wasn't sure what else to say.

Tenika regarded him skeptically. "You seriously had to keep her for two hours? Or was it just like…hey, this one's going to die soon, so no big deal?"

"T—" Delilah sounded a warning tone from the bed.

"Ma'am—" the pediatrician began.

"No, really," Tenika continued. She fixed him with her furious gaze. "It's not like she's going to have some long and healthy life, right? Just be straight with me, doctor."

The doctor paused delicately, and then let out a defeated sigh. "Well… no. She may be able to make it through the night. But no longer than that, I'm afraid."

All three of them were silent for a moment. "I am sorry we had to keep her in the nursery for so long. And we did stabilize her, for now. But…" His voice drifted off, the sentence unfinished.

"Can I hold her?" Delilah asked.

"Yes. Yes! Of course." He paused. "Do you have any questions?"

Tenika just looked back at him with an expression that was heartbroken. She shook her head grimly, and the doctor practically backed out of the room, eager not to disturb them for one moment longer.

Reaching into the crib, the nurse handed over the small bundle of swaddling, placing the baby carefully in Delilah's arms. Ashanti was beautiful, with creamy-coffee colored skin and features that were tiny and perfect. A small rosebud mouth lay just below her tiny baby nose. Her eyes were closed, as if she was sleeping. And a white cotton cap covered her head which was nestled in thick swaddling.

To the casual observer, she looked like every other newborn. Small, whole, perfect.

Yet, as Delilah held her in her arms, this baby's passivity was unmistakable. Ashanti didn't make a sound. She didn't stir, or cry, search for the breast or even flutter her eyelids. She was like a human doll, asleep and utterly devoid of expression. Delilah tried not to notice the extra swaddling around the back of her head, where her brain might have been had she been a normal baby.

She looked up at her wife as tears filled her eyes. "Oh, T…" she said brokenly.

Tenika came over and stood beside her now, and for the first time she really looked at this baby who was her daughter. "Oh, man…" she said, and she, too, began to cry. "She's fucking beautiful. Beautiful, D… look at her."

"Yeah. I know," whispered Delilah.

"What a waste," Tenika said bitterly, and Delilah nodded. "What a waste of a perfectly good life."

The two of them were silent; there was nothing else to say.

Finally, Tenika broke the silence. "We're going to just sit here with her," Tenika finally said. "Let's just both hold her. Cause this is all we get with her, honey. I don't want to miss one minute."

"Yeah, me too."

"And when Aiden comes back, we'll get everyone in here, and we'll all hold the babies. We'll do this together, right?" Tenika continued. "They've got to meet her, too. We've all got to." Her words broke off as silent sobs overtook her. She realized she didn't even know what she could say.

It is fucking tragic. That's what it is.

Delilah began to unwrap her swaddling across her body now. Ashanti's skinny, listless legs didn't kick or squirm. Her small arms lay inert across her body. Her ten perfect fingers and ten perfect toes were motionless, but, again, all of them were perfect as well. Quickly, Delilah wrapped her body up again, as if she couldn't bear to look for one more moment. Then she held the bundle out to Tenika.

Sniffing back her tears, Tenika gingerly took her daughter in her arms and settled into the rocking chair beside the bed. She looked into Ashanti's face and saw as innocent and helpless a soul as she'd ever seen. Powerfully, Tenika felt her heart crack open right then and there, and once again, she just shook her head.

Slowly, she began to rock her daughter.

As Tenika held the feather-light bundle of their dying baby, the two sat together rocking for a long, long time. She wanted to know this little slip of a person, and she tried hard as she sat with her daughter to tune into some kind of essence or understanding of who she was. But as she sat rocking and gazing at her daughter, it eluded her.

What she found, instead, as the rocker moved them both gently back and forth was something she'd never realized she had. It was a peace, a rightness, an overwhelming urge to protect. To love.

It all came clear as Tenika sat and rocked her dying daughter. She was, indeed, a mother. And she cared intensely about this baby, no matter whether she lived or died.

Finally, she rose and handed the baby back to Delilah. Then

she put her hands on her hips. "Okay," she said with a sigh. "I want everyone to meet her before she dies," she said. "That okay?"

"Yeah. I do, too."

"We have to, for our sake. We need witnesses. You know what I'm saying, Delilah? We need them to know her, too."

Delilah was nodding, her eyes fastened on Ashanti. "Call them in," she murmured.

"Cause this is it," Tenika continued. "This is about all we get with her. Then after that… " Her voice trailed off. "Let's at least get Lizzy in here to start."

Giving herself a moment, Tenika wiped the last of her tears from her face. Squaring herself, she pulled out her phone and typed out a text to her friend.

It was time to make this whole damn thing real.

*

By now, both Lizzy and Monroe were caffeinated and pacing in the hallway outside the waiting room. They were the first to see Tenika's text to Lizzy, asking her to come to their room.

"Hey!" Lizzy called over to Sally and Rosalind. "I can go see the babies…or baby?" She peered at her phone a little more closely. "I'm not sure what this means."

The text just said, *Got a baby for you to meet.*

Quickly Lizzy replied. *Just me alone?*

Tenika's reply came immediately. *Yeah.*

Lizzy read the texts aloud, and the cluster of friends all looked at each other. This did not bode well.

"It specifically said the word 'baby'? Not babies?" Sally asked.

"Yeah," Lizzy affirmed

"Wow. You don't think one of them…" Monroe didn't finish their sentence.

Meanwhile, Sally closed her eyes, as if to staunch the imminent flow of more tears. No one said anything for a moment, as if their silence might keep them safe from the obvious tragedy that lay just ahead.

Rosalind stood up, restless and ready to leap into action. "Okay. Is there something the rest of us should do?"

"Just stand by. I'll text you, or I'll come back. Or something," Lizzy said as she headed out of the waiting room. Turning, she looked back at them briefly. "Honestly, I don't know what's happening. But I won't keep you guys waiting. I promise."

Then she was gone.

*

Cautiously, Lizzy peered around the edge of the door to Delilah's room. Inside, Tenika was sitting on Delilah's bed, and the two mothers were bent over a bundle of baby in Delilah's arms. The tenderness in the room was palpable. Instantly, Lizzy could feel the adrenaline that had been building in her body ease and begin to drain away.

"Is there a baby in the house?" she asked, trying to keep it light. But all attempts at levity disappeared when they both looked up at her. On their stricken faces, Lizzy could clearly see a crisis was taking place.

"What?" she asked simply.

Reaching over, Tenika picked up her daughter and cradled her in her arms.

Then walking over to Lizzy, Tenika nodded to the bundle she held. She looked up at Lizzy intently. Lizzy couldn't read her expression exactly. It was halfway between devastated and struck by God.

"This is Ashanti," Tenika finally said simply, her voice breaking.

Lizzy's eyes fastened on this gorgeous baby. She was so perfect in every way. Tenika looked down at the baby in her arms, and as tears began to trickle down her face. Finally, Tenika spoke, her eyes on the floor.

"She's dying, Lizzy. Not going to live until tomorrow."

Instantly, Lizzy was thunderstruck. "Wha—wait, come on, Tenika. This little baby? She's beautiful! She's perfect."

Tenika just shook her head in response, and Lizzy realized then that it was true.

Now Tenika cleared her throat. "Ashanti has a rare birth defect," she explained. "She's missing most of her brain." Then she sighed. "She'll be gone by tomorrow."

"And…the other baby?"

Delilah spoke up now. "Aiden's okay. He's in the nursery right now. He's perfectly normal, and we're going to take him home tomorrow or the next day."

"Thank God!" Lizzy exclaimed. But then she, too, could feel the threat of tears. Her eyes filled as she looked at the dead-quiet, tightly swaddled little bundle before her. "I just…Jesus, T. I can't believe this."

Tenika and Delilah were silent, just gazing at their baby.

"What are the chances of this happening?" Lizzy pressed, but still neither woman answered.

Delilah held Ashanti out to Lizzy now. "Do you want to hold her?"

Lizzy swallowed. "You sure that's okay?"

Tenika looked at her. "She's just a baby, Lizzy. She's not made of glass. Go on," she said. "Hold her."

Suddenly intimidated, Lizzy carefully took the bundled baby from Delilah's arms.

She'd never held an infant in her life, yet somehow her body knew instantly what to do. Ashanti was warm in Lizzy's embrace, and her stillness was strangely comforting. Lizzy watched her face for a moment. The baby seemed to exude a sweet, peaceful calm.

Lizzy could feel the stir of emotions that had been racing through her body begin to settle as she held the infant. Even though she could feel the heartbreak of the situation in every fiber of her being, something else was happening now, too. Something that was bigger than life or even death.

This baby had a quality that Lizzy could feel, but she couldn't quite name.

"Ashanti," Lizzy finally said, looking into the baby's face. "You are so beautiful." Then, the tears that had been threatening began to roll down Lizzy's face. Embarrassed, she sniffed hard and wiped at her wet cheeks with the back of her hand. "Oh God," she said. "I'm sorry."

"It's okay."

Lizzy looked up at them. "There's…something about her," she said, groping for the right words, and Tenika nodded.

"I know."

Lizzy was quiet for another moment, as she studied the baby in her arms. "Damn, I wish Kate was here right now."

She looked over at Tenika. "She'll never meet her," she said grimly. "But we're here, at least. The rest of us." Carefully, Lizzy handed Ashanti back to Delilah. "Can I take her picture?"

"Okay," Delilah said gently, setting the baby back into her arms. Lizzy pulled out her phone and took a few shots of the baby in Delilah's arms and of the two mothers with Ashanti.

A moment later, Lizzy sent the images off to Kate via text. There was just no way she was going to meet this baby, and not share the slender thread of her life with Kate. It was too big, too precious. And this was too important a moment to waste.

Then straightening herself again, Lizzy blew her nose and took a deep breath.

"Okay," Lizzy said, grounding herself.

It was time to go tell the others.

Chapter Twelve

Ronnie pulled open the refrigerator door and stared at the contents. She contemplated what she saw—a selection of yogurts, the remains of a rotisserie chicken, an open pint of half and half, a kombucha and some wilted salad greens, for starters.

Skeptically, Ronnie also eyed Frankie's workman's lunch ingredients: salami, string cheese, English muffins, brown mustard. Ronnie had watched her make the same damn lunch most of the days she'd been there. And here, Sally kept describing Frankie as a 'foodie'.

Foodie my ass, Ronnie grumped to herself.

It had been a very, very long time since she'd had the run of someone's fridge, not to mention their liquor. Pulling a designer IPA from the door, Ronnie shut the refrigerator, twisted open the bottle cap, and took a long, thirsty sip. The beer seemed to loosen her mind the minute it made contact with her throat. Immediately, she relaxed.

Moving on, Ronnie now opened the freezer. There had to be something decent in here to eat. The aging chicken and wilted greens on the refrigerator shelves seriously weren't doing it for her. Relentlessly, Ronnie began to dig, trying to ignore her frozen fingertips as they worked their way past a bag of frozen peas, some ice trays and injury gel packs, and several nearly empty ice cream cartons.

Knowing Sally as she did, Ronnie assumed that somewhere in this freezer were delicious things. There were the kind of meals Ronnie, herself, once enjoyed. She'd been savoring them on all of those nights of canned beans on the hotplate in her crummy SRO room. Or on the days of white bread, peanut butter and pasta served up in the city's soup kitchens, when she showed up hungry with no money for food, and there was a distinct odor of stale urine in the air.

The fact was that Sally actually was a foodie. And she was a frugal one. So it was Sally's habit to carefully save her leftovers from special meals at restaurants. Then she'd bring them home, label them and freeze them. She'd pull them out months later to enjoy them a second time, often with a glass of wine and some candlelight. "High End Leftovers," Sally used to call them when they'd lived together.

Ronnie remembered it was a remarkably big deal to Sally, Usually, she wasn't even up for sharing. Presumably, especially in the company of the fabulous Frankie, Sally was still saving a few entrees here and there.

Finally, Ronnie's hands found gold. Her now numb fingertips closed on a small flat plastic take out box in the back of the freezer, and she extracted it. She wiped at the frost that had clouded the lid of the box. The words "Anniversary Lamb" were marked on it with Sharpie with the date. Ronnie gave a satisfied smirk.

Now this was precisely what she was looking for. Something substantial that might feed her hungry maw, which had been so deprived for so very long. She was pretty sure Sally would never miss the treasured box of leftovers. Even if she did, by the time Sally discovered it, Ronnie would be long gone.

After prying the lid off the box, Ronnie opened the microwave. Shoving the box inside, she whistled as she punched a few buttons. The machine turned on with a hum. Then Ronnie set a place for herself at the table, complete with knife, fork and carefully folded linen napkin. She had no idea when her hosts would return. And honestly, she didn't much care.

Presumably both of them were over at the hospital by now, cooing over the much-talked-about babies. That ought to keep them busy for a while, she thought to herself. She'd probably have the place to herself all night long.

Whatever the issue was hadn't been particularly clear as Sally rushed out the door. All Ronnie knew was that she now had room to stretch out and enjoy the place. As far as she was concerned, it was time to indulge in a little self-care.

A moment later Ronnie drained the last of the beer, chucked the bottle in the blue Recycle bin, and let out a beer belch. Then she selected a nice Russian River Pinot Noir from a stash of bottles she discovered in one of the cupboards. Easing the cork out a moment later, she poured a good amount into a balloon goblet for herself, and placing it on the table, she decided to let it breathe a bit.

This is the life, she thought contentedly to herself. Ronnie wondered how long she could make it last.

A moment later, she transferred the steaming slices of lamb roast and savory new potatoes in a red wine sauce to one of Frankie's white china plates. Ronnie thought she detected a hint of rosemary in the sauce as she carried her perfectly heated dinner to the table. It all smelled delicious.

Now it was time for the final touch. Pulling a small box of matches from a nearby drawer, Ronnie lit the two candlesticks and sat down to her own version of Sally's so-called Anniversary Dinner. Taking a long sip of the Pinot Noir, she began to eat.

It really wasn't so bad, living on someone's couch.

You could take it a remarkably long way if you did it right.

*

Frankie shut her locker with a slam and looked over as Simone, one of the other officers, came walking in. Simone stopped at the sink and washed her hands. "Hey," she said. There was no reply for a moment. Curiously, Simone studied Frankie in the mirror as she dried her hands.

"Hey," Frankie finally responded dully.

Simone turned around. "What's up, Sarge? You got a bug up your butt today, if I may casually observe."

Frankie gave a wave of her hand, dismissively. But of course, it was something. A very big something.

Simone stepped up to her locker, just a few doors over from Frankie's. Pausing, she looked over at her commanding officer once more. "Oh, come on, Sarge, you're always doling out the advice to me when we're in here. Maybe it's my turn this time, huh? Tell me what's going on."

Frankie gave a small embarrassed chuckle. "No, no. Really, Simone...everything's fine. Honestly." She looked up with what she hoped was a convincing smile. But Simone wasn't buying it.

Instead, Simone stood there, hands on her hips and a skeptical expression on her face. Slowly she tapped her long, ornate fingernails against the gun belt on her hips. "Let me guess," she said. "You and Sally havin' a great big cat fight?"

"No, no...well..." Frankie sighed. Then she hesitated. Once again, she'd been busted. By now, the few women in her station could all read each other like books. And she had, indeed, talked Simone down at least twice in her own personal life.

It was what Frankie did—her superpower as sergeant of Parkside Station. She was mother confessor to all the guys, and Oprah to all the women. The question was whether she could finally let her guard down and get real with Simone.

God knew she needed to talk to someone, and hey...it was Simone. A cop and a fellow lesbian at that, not to mention one of her closest friends in the station. It wasn't like they didn't know each other. They drove around together in a squad car for the better part of two years.

Frankie weighed the options for a moment longer. Then she took the leap.

"So there's this…uh…other person," she began.

Simone looked up sharply. "Wait—you slept with someone else? Sarge, seriously?"

Frankie looked offended. "Simone! Please. No! It's that we've got a freaking grifter living in our house. And she used to be Sally's girlfriend."

Simone was aghast. "What? You got the ex staying with you? As in sleeping on your couch?"

"That's right," Frankie said, equally outraged. "I guess she and Sally are tight, or whatever. But I'd never even heard of this person before. Didn't even get a vote in whether she stayed over or not."

A text message suddenly pinged on the phone in Frankie's back pocket, but she ignored it and continued. "And the thing is, she's obviously a con artist, and Sally's totally under her thumb. Simone, I can practically feel the sleaze oozing out of her."

Simone stood there, arms folded, rapt. "Go on."

"So she tells Sally she's got some terminal blood disease—she doesn't even freaking know the name of it."

"And she's sleeping on your couch? Oh, Sarge…" Simone shook her head in disappointment.

Frankie put up a hand in protest. "Believe me. I know it's ridiculous. But here's the problem. When she showed up we were just getting over this huge fight about the wedding." Frankie's voice dropped. "Sally met my mother, and you can imagine how that went."

"Uh oh."

"Right?" Frankie continued. "There's no way out, Simone. The ex has to stay for a little while if I want Sally to marry me. She's totally bent on helping this woman! And as we all know, Sally can be a very soft touch."

Simone shook her head sympathetically. "Sally may think she has to put her up, but it's your house, Sarge. Get this chick out of there. Like, today." Simone crossed her arms skeptically. "Pretty soon your silver and jewelry are going to start walking out the door. You know what I'm saying?"

"I know…" Frankie shook her head. "I haven't even had time to do a check on her—" At this, Simone's eyes grew big. Doing background checks on potential lovers was standard fare for the women of Parkside Station.

Frankie felt her phone ping again and, sensing something was wrong this time, she pulled it from her pocket and looked at it. Then she started. "Oh, Jesus…"

She looked up at Simone. "I have to get out of here. Some friends are having twins, and there's trouble over at the hospital."

"And what about your perp—I mean, your houseguest?"

Frankie rolled her eyes. "Well, I can't just throw her out, Simone. She's going to have stay there for now. At least until I can talk to Sally about it."

"Girl, I would totally throw her ass out," Simone said, shaking her head. "And get the damn background check done."

Frankie sighed.

As usual, Simone was totally right.

*

Lizzy walked down the hospital corridor, toward the waiting knot of friends. Looking up from phones, they all stood somberly as she approached.

"What?" Monroe said, as soon as Lizzy was in earshot. "Just tell us."

Lizzy shook her head and hesitated. This was harder than she thought it would be. Telling them about Ashanti's fate would now make it frighteningly real. But she had to do it.

Lizzy cleared her throat and put her hands on her hips. "Okay, so here's the deal," she began.

The group looked at her, expectantly, but for a moment no words would issue from Lizzy's mouth. Lizzy searched the floor for courage, or something she couldn't even name. Then finally, she looked up into the expectant faces of her friends, now clustered around her.

There were tears in her eyes as she began. "Uh, okay...so there's a problem with one of the babies."

Sally turned away from the group with a shuddering sob, unable to even hear what Lizzy was about to say. But somehow this inspired Lizzy to continue. She had to get her message out. Better to be direct she thought. *Just get it over with.*

"It's bad," she began again. Hesitating for the briefest moment, Lizzy finally forced herself to continue. "Ashanti is missing most of her brain. She won't live much past tonight."

Monroe and Rosalind both gasped; Sally sank down in a nearby chair and put her face in her hands. "Oh, God," she moaned, and she began to sob in earnest.

"It's a rare thing. Anenceph—something. You know...it's so weird. I mean, I saw her, guys. I held her, even, and everything. She looks perfect. Perfect!" Lizzy paused, as she, too, was trying to process what had happened.

Lizzy shook her head, barely able to believe it herself. "But she's not okay. Not at all. She's not really moving, or making any sounds." She paused, almost breathless. "But the other baby, Aiden...he's fine. And so is Delilah, so that's good."

The group looked at her silently, as if she was going to tell them more. But there was no more to share. Meanwhile, something gave way in the pit of Lizzy's gut as she stood there. Exhausted by her effort, she dropped into a nearby chair and folded her arms across her chest. She closed her eyes, wondering what would come next.

There was the sound of footsteps coming around the corner, and now a voice called out. "Lizzy?" The group turned and looked at the stout, middle-aged Black woman coming toward them. She was wearing the uniform of a security guard, and she had a look of deep concern on her face. It was Keisha, Tenika's cousin.

Keisha was the sort of relative who showed reliably for holidays and birthdays, but little else. She was pretty much the only family Tenika had. And although she'd been an occasional part of their gatherings for years, Keisha was still a bit of an enigma to Lizzy.

For every bit of T's beautiful renegade streak, Keisha was the exact opposite—a church lady in the true sense of the word. Her deep Baptist faith had carried her through a number of crises in her own life, including the end of her marriage. And it had taken some years for her to embrace this tight group of lesbians. But to Keisha's credit she had.

"Lizzy!" she called again. "Where are they? How are they doing?" she asked anxiously.

"Hey Keisha," Lizzy said. The two shared a brief hug. "So... uh..."

Keisha put her hand on Lizzy's arm, and suddenly Lizzy's eyes filled with tears as she began to cry. "I'm sorry," she croaked, shaking her head as if to fling the tears from her eyes. Clearly, she was unable to stay strong for Tenika's own flesh and blood.

Keisha's eyes widened as she saw Lizzy's tears. "Lizzy, you've got to tell me what's going on." Her words were clipped with dread.

Whirling around, Keisha turned away in impatience as Lizzy struggled to speak. She turned to Sally. Then she glanced over at Monroe and Rosalind, whom she hadn't even met yet. "Will one of you please tell me what's happened?"

"Ashanti has a serious birth defect," Lizzy said tearfully behind her. "She's...uh..." Lizzy hesitated. "She's dying," she finished quietly.

Keisha's hand flew up to her mouth. "Oh, Lord sweet Jesus," she murmured, and she shut her eyes in pain. Immediately, Lizzy put her arm around Keisha, who began to wobble slightly. "We're going up to their room now," Lizzy explained. "Tenika wants us all in there. She'll be happy to see you."

Rosalind and Monroe looked at each other and nodded, and

Sally stood up slowly, a sodden mess. Keisha glanced around at the group uncertainly. "All of you?"

"Yeah," Lizzy nodded. "T wants us all to come right now, to meet Ashanti. But…uh…" Lizzy hesitated.

But Keisha didn't hear her. She was already gone, fast-walking up the hall. "This way?" she called over her shoulder.

"Room 314," Lizzy called after her. "Up ahead and make the first left."

This was so much bigger than anything she'd ever dealt with in her life. Maybe even bigger than the time they almost lost the garage.

Monroe looked at her. "What is it, Lizzy?"

Lizzy drew closer to the three others. "Let's just…you know. Try to be cool. Or at least, cry quietly." She said, her voice lowered. "You'll see. T and Delilah are freaking devastated." Then she sighed. "That baby just looks so perfect."

Lizzy's voice broke, and her own tears started up again. "We have to go in there and be strong, people," she said, as if to convince herself. Still, her voice wavered. "So, you know, prepare yourselves."

Frankie can't get here soon enough, thought Lizzy, as she moved toward the still-keening Sally. Putting her arm around her friend, she slowly began to steer her toward the restroom to wash her face.

They really needed someone with some serious emergency skills.

*

"Tenika? Where you at?" Keisha called, trying to keep her voice calm. Tenika looked up as Keisha burst into the room.

Keisha stopped dead in her tracks at the unfamiliar sight. Her cousin, a sometimes testy butch lesbian who was one of the strongest women she'd ever known, now looked completely and utterly undone.

Tenika's expression was both devastated and vulnerable. She had the rawness about her that Keisha hadn't seen since they were kids growing up together. Back when her single mother was working all the time and Keisha, two years older, was the adult in her life.

Now, here was Tenika, as broken down as she'd ever been. "Oh, T," she said, instantly reading the level of despair in the room.

Wordlessly, Tenika held the baby out toward Keisha, and Keisha came and took her. Delilah wanly said her name from the hospital bed. "That's Ashanti."

As Keisha took the swaddled baby in her arms, all she had learned raising her own son came instantly rushing back. The tiny, quiet, warm body in her arms was nearly weightless.

Ashanti's silence and stillness undid Keisha as well, and she looked up, crestfallen. "Lizzy told me," she said simply.

"Yeah." Tenika put her hands in her pockets. Then she turned away, retreating to the window once more. Delilah looked over at her woozily. "We can't believe it."

Keisha could only nod her head. It was just as Lizzy had said. This baby in her arms seemed so very perfect, it really was unbelievable that she would be dead in a matter of hours. Sitting down in the rocking chair, Keisha gazed into the baby's face. Keisha's lips, meanwhile, moved silently as she prayed to Jesus for the baby's safe passage to Heaven.

She had just finished her prayers, as Lizzy appeared in the doorway. "Can we come in now? I've got the others with me."

Tenika did not turn around, her gaze still fastened out the window. "Sure, come in."

Sally, Monroe and Roslyn all gathered in the doorway, as if entering the room would somehow make matters worse. Tenika finally turned around and looked at them. "Come on, y'all," she insisted. "Don't be afraid. It's just a baby."

Monroe and Rosalind slipped into the room somberly, followed by Sally, who'd managed to get hold of herself. Still, her tear-stained face revealed exactly what she'd been going through.

As usual, it was impossible for Sally to hide a thing.

She walked over to Delilah's bed, and bending down she gently gave her old friend a hug. They'd been through so much, going all the way back to college. She took Delilah's hand and squeezed it. "I'm so sorry," she said in a whisper.

Tenika walked over to the group of friends. "Listen up everyone," she said, clearing her throat. "This is Ashanti. And she's not going to be with us for long. So I want everyone to hold her, and try to just have something to remember her by."

Her voice broke as her strong woman demeanor began to fade. "I need y'all do this for me," Tenika said. "so I don't forget."

Lizzy wrapped an arm around her best friend. "We've got you, T."

"That is, you all can hold her if Keisha'll let go of her," Tenika remarked with a nod in her cousin's direction. Her strained attempt at levity was met with silence.

Wordlessly, Keisha just held the baby out to Rosalind, who was standing nearby. The heaviness in the room was unmistakable, as everyone tried to come to terms with what was happening in real time, right in front of them.

Now they all watched Rosalind as she scooped Ashanti up. She gazed into her precious face, just as everyone else had done. She ran a finger gently across the baby's cheek, then she bent to kiss her downy soft forehead. "Hi Ashanti," she said. Then, she turned to her partner.

"Here," she said quietly, putting her into Monroe's arms.

They'd never held a baby before, and Monroe awkwardly accepted the bundle, as Rosalind hovered nearby to correct any mistakes. She still remembered her role as big sister to her baby brother many years ago, and all of her instincts were still there, guiding her. But Monroe was far less experienced, and far more uncertain.

"Like this," Rosalind said, adjusting the bundle of baby in Monroe's arms. Monroe looked mildly shocked as they gazed into the baby's face. Then Monroe glanced over at Rosalind.

"This is…whoa…"

Lizzy watched them from the doorway, where she'd retreated to try to restore her equilibrium. She'd never felt so powerless in her life, watching as each of her devastated friends passed the dying baby around the room. Finally, her eyes came to rest on Tenika and Delilah, who sat together numbly, watching the proceedings. *How would they cope?* she wondered.

There truly was nothing more to say.

Chapter Thirteen

Taking the parking garage stairs two at a time, Frankie bolted up toward the Emergency entrance of the hospital. Lizzy had texted her the floor and the number of Delilah's room only moments before. She swung into a crowded elevator in the lobby, just as the doors were closing, and jabbed the button for the third floor.

'Maternity' it said on a small metal sign beside it.

It was Lizzy's text that had finally gotten Frankie's attention. Not that she generally ignored her own partner's messages. It's just that Sally tended to be a bit more emotional when things really got challenging. And who knew what the facts of the situation actually were.

Sally's texts had been painted with pure alarm.

Must come now—babies soon to arrive! I'll be at hospital. and *Please come NOW. We need you, Frankie. Babies are on their way!!*

Much as she loved her partner, Frankie knew in her gut how long labor and delivery took. She'd escorted more than one laboring mother in dire panic to the hospital, only to hear later that the baby wasn't born until the next day. So when Sally's texts came rolling in, Frankie figured she definitely had time to change out of her uniform, and maybe even grab dinner if this was going to take a while.

Lizzy's message, on the other hand, made Frankie stop short. *Serious problems at the hospital. You are needed ASAP.*

Poor Tenika and Delilah, she thought as the elevator made its painfully slow rise to the third floor. And poor Sally. By now, she was probably a puddle on the floor that Frankie would have to somehow clean up. She had no idea what the term 'serious problems' meant, but she also knew that Lizzy was no alarmist.

Furthermore, a few days earlier, Sally had predicted all of this. Though she'd been coy with Frankie about exactly what she'd seen. She'd just let Frankie know they'd have to be prepared because it really wasn't going to be easy. And now, here they were.

Once again, against all odds, Sally was right.

Slipping through the open elevator doors, Frankie paused at the nurse's station for quick directions. Then heading up the hallway on her right, she found Delilah's room. She paused in the hallway for just a moment, taking a breath and composing herself.

It was the babies and little kids in trouble that always got her the most at work. She knew without being told that she had to prepare herself for what was to come. Years earlier, finding the body of a child on Ocean Beach had set her up with a case of PTSD that had been hard to shake.

Frankie cautiously peered into the room. A Black woman she'd seen at one of Tenika's parties was now kneeling beside Delilah—her hands clasped before her, her head held low in prayer. Everyone around her had their eyes closed. Frankie bowed her head and listened from the doorway.

"Help this baby, Jesus, as she makes her transition into your loving arms," the woman said. "Please help her, God. Take her straight up to her place in the Kingdom of Heaven," she continued. "Thank you, Lord Jesus." A few sniffs could be heard in the room, as those around her were stifling their tears.

The Kingdom of Heaven. The infant—Tenika's own baby daughter —was evidently dying.

A wave of shock ran through Frankie's body, as she realized what was going on. Taking a deep breath, she reached for her professional composure. Squaring her chin, she tried to keep her head bowed to join those who were praying. But somehow she couldn't.

Raising her head, Frankie looked directly into Sally's eyes. They were now fixed on her from the other side of the room.

Sally. Thank God, she thought.

They exchanged a gaze that Frankie tried, unsuccessfully to read. Tentatively, Frankie tried a smile as she worked to understand the full extent of what was going on. Sally just shook her head. Then quietly, Sally slipped across the room to her side. Taking Sally by the hand, Frankie led her out into the hallway.

"Ashanti died," Frankie said, more a statement than a question.

"Dying," Sally corrected. "Some time tonight." Pulling a tissue from her pocket, she blew her nose and took a deep shuddering breath. Sally explained what had happened to Ashanti and that Aiden was healthy and still stabilizing in the nursery.

The two were silent for a moment in the darkened hallway. Frankie reached for Sally's hand as she felt all the tension between them suddenly melt away. She pulled Sally to her, and wrapping her arms around her, she buried her face in Sally's hair. Immediately, Sally began to sob into her shoulder.

Wordlessly, they hung on to each other for a long time. Finally Frankie pulled back and looked at her. "Honey—" she began, but Sally shook her head.

"Not here. Not now, Frankie. It's okay. It's okay. We've just got to get through this first. We've got to be there for them."

"Right. Of course, we will," Frankie nodded. "Even if it takes all night."

"It probably will," Sally said. Briefly, they kissed, the kiss of partnership. Already, the balance between them was righting itself.

"I'm sorry," Frankie said simply.

"I am, too," Sally agreed.

A nurse passed them and they both looked over at her. She was pushing a small bassinet on wheels toward Tenika and Delilah's room. In it lay a beautiful bi-racial newborn. He looked straight up at them as he passed with dark, glittering eyes.

Frankie couldn't take her eyes off of him. She and Sally watched as the nurse pushed the baby into their room.

"That's Aiden?" Frankie asked.

"I'm sure it is," Sally replied. And they both smiled, their fingers still entwined.

Suddenly Frankie turned to her. "Is Ronnie still at the house?"

A dark look passed over Sally's face, and her smile disappeared. "Don't start, Frankie."

Frankie held her hands up, eager not to get into another fight. "I'm just asking."

"Yes, and everything will be fine," Sally said curtly. "I'll text her that we're going to stay here all night."

"Okay, fine," said Frankie, hoping to strike a conciliatory tone. Her hands headed for her pockets. She hoped everything would be fine. She seriously did.

Meanwhile, every fiber of her being seriously doubted that would be the case.

Things back at their house would be anything but 'fine'.

*

Inside the hospital room, a whole new scene was unfolding. Tenika had a look of complete tenderness on her face as she gazed down at her brand new son, now in Delilah's arms. Beside her on the bed, Delilah was nursing the infant for the very first time, as the nurse stood by to assist.

Apparently he'd had no trouble latching on, and the group cooed and smiled as they watched him. A few pictures were shot, and the mood had become considerably lighter for the moment.

Meanwhile, across the room, Sally was now holding Ashanti. Instinctively, her body rocked the baby back and forth.

It was the same age-old rocking that women had been doing for generations through time, in a universal, maternal need to comfort. It was the same rocking Tenika had discovered herself, only a little while earlier.

Sally was doing this almost in spite of herself, and quite honestly, it was probably most comforting to her at that moment. For in her arms, the inert little baby remained motionless. *But it didn't matter*, she thought. It simply felt right.

"Ashanti," Sally whispered to the silent child in her arms. Ashanti still had not opened her eyes or even whimpered in response to being held. Nor would she at all.

Aiden, by contrast, was now crying, a lusty, wide-open yell as he finished nursing across the room. It was ear piercing, as only a newborn's cry can be. Delilah looked up at the nurse a little alarmed, hoping for some kind of fast instructions. Leaning over, the nurse deftly picked him up, patted his back gently and jiggled him delicately as she supported his head.

"It's gas. Always gas," the nurse said with a sigh, and there was a collective chuckle in the room.

The baby has gas! The room seized on this detail with gusto. Evidently, Aiden was going to be just fine. Their collective relief in that moment was palpable.

Tenika collected herself, and standing up, she walked over to the others. "Can you guys stay tonight?" she asked. Her voice was exhausted, and she looked truly shell shocked "I think... well...we don't really know what's going to happen," Tenika finished vaguely.

Though, of course, everyone did know exactly what was going to happen. Aiden would finally get enough nursing and would eventually nod off to sleep. And Ashanti would drift off to her final rest, without whimpering a single cry.

Lizzy put a hand on her arm. "Of course, T. No worries." Then she turned to the others. "Right guys? We'll all stick around..."

There were general sounds of agreement from all of them. Then Keisha piped up. "And I'm not going in to work tomorrow, T. I'm calling in sick."

"Yeah, me neither," said Monroe. Rosalind echoed a similar thought, and Sally looked over at Frankie beside her, who gave her a silent nod of agreement. And as she looked away, Sally felt reaffirmed.

Frankie was beside her, strong and true, and Frankie would help her get through this. And together, they would support Delilah and Tenika, and everyone else. It was simply what they did at such times.

Really, there was no other place she'd rather be right now, Sally thought to herself as she looked down once more into Ashanti's face. She would do her best to memorize it. To memorize all of this, for this was life unbounded.

It was a sacred place, indeed.

*

Self-consciously, Lizzy glanced around the vending lounge, as her call to Kate once more attempted to connect. She felt like the others in the room could hear the tinny ring of the international line. And she worried her voice was going to be too loud as she tried to speak to her wife.

Yet, the only other people in the room didn't seem to notice her at all. It was just an elderly couple. They sat at one of the tables, drinking tea.

Once more the international line gave its static-filled ring— a persistent, mechanical 'beeeeep'. Lizzy closed her eyes, hoping against hope. *Please pick up. Please pick up.*

It was now 6AM in Ireland, and she still had heard nothing from Kate. They were going on five days now since their last contact.

But this time, Kate picked up after the third ring. And as she did, Lizzy's heart gave a leap and soft relief spread throughout her body. *Thank freaking God*, she thought.

"Honey?" she said, her voice a little ragged with emotion. It was only then that Lizzy realized how much she'd been through in the last six hours, since she'd first walked into the hospital.

Kate's voice responded. "Lizzy?" she said.

Lizzy's whole nervous system seemed to give a sigh as it cycled down a notch. There was such comfort to be found in hearing Kate's voice. It was grounding, a homecoming of sorts for her. *Thank God*, she repeated to herself.

"Oh my God—Kate, did you get my texts?"

"No, but I know you called me several times…" Kate said, and now Lizzy noticed how groggy she sounded.

"Uh oh, did I wake you up?"

"Not at all. I'm getting ready to go see Da. Must take the bus and it takes a while, you see," Kate explained. Her Irish accent had already come roaring back, and it took Lizzy aback for a moment. "You know it's just six in the morning here, love," Kate added gently.

"Yeah. Yeah, I'm sorry I called earlier. I…I had to." Lizzy lowered her voice. "Something's happened, Kate."

Kate's voice ratcheted up to a note of alarm. "What? Are you okay?"

"Me? I'm fine. Well, I guess that's relative. It's the babies, T's babies, honey." She paused. "Delilah had to give birth yesterday because she broke her water…" Lizzy's voice trailed off.

"Oh, no…"

"It's their daughter. Ashanti." Lizzy paused. How she hated sharing the news, but once more, she plunged in as she told her wife what was happening. "There's nothing to be done," she concluded. "Ashanti's still alive. As far as I know."

Kate gave an audible gasp. "Jesus," she said.

In fact, none of them had been in Delilah's room for the last hour. A nurse had asked them all to step down the hall to a waiting room, hoping Delilah might get some sleep. Tenika had chosen to stay by her wife's side as they waited for the baby to die together. Aiden, meanwhile, had gone back to the nursery for the rest of the night until his dawn feeding.

"I guess they're going to come get us if she passes in the next few hours," Lizzy continued. "So we're all pretty much here until then—sitting in a waiting room at the hospital until she goes."

"God, how awful." Kate said. "Sweetheart, I wish I was there."

"Believe me, I wish you were, too."

Together they sighed in the sanctity of their shared air waves. "Oh, honey…God," Lizzy said, feeling herself wanting to break down. "This is so hard. And poor T and Delilah…they're going through hell."

On the other end of the line, Kate's voice was filled with pain. "Are you crying? I hate that I am not there."

"It's okay—it's okay. You're exactly where you need to be," Lizzy reassured her, trying to sniff back her tear. She wiped at her wet cheeks with the back of her hand, and gave an embarrassed chuckle. Pulling a bandana from her pocket, she blew her nose, and gave a shuddering sigh. Then there was a pause.

"How's the other baby?" Kate asked.

"He's great." Almost involuntarily, Lizzy began to smile. "I held her. I held Ashanti. I've never held a baby before. She was—she is so beautiful."

She thought of the exact moment that Tenika put Ashanti into her arms. It was strangely anticlimactic because the baby was so very still. Yet, she was alive in Lizzy's arms for that brief moment, and Lizzy could feel how important it was that she get to have this tiny moment of connection.

She had held Ashanti's tiny hand with its perfect fingers, and wondered at the pure fragility of life.

"I love you," she said suddenly to Kate. "I hope you know that."

"I do. And I love you, too," Kate replied. Her words were like warm honey pouring through the phone line, and Lizzy breathed them in. She closed her eyes, a silent prayer of thanks.

"How's your dad?" Lizzy asked.

"Maybe he's dying. But honestly, I don't really know. He just seems so old, Lizzy, and so frail. Nothing like he was when I left." Kate gave a twisted laugh, and Lizzy could tell then that she, too, had begun to cry.

"Oh baby—" Lizzy began.

"But I'm glad I came. I'm just…I'm sorry I'm not there."

"No, no, you're doing exactly the right thing, Kate," Lizzy insisted. "Don't even think about this. He's your dad!"

"True," Kate demurred.

Lizzy paused, fighting the urge to ask Kate when she was coming back.

If she was coming back.

How much Lizzy wanted to blurt out a plea. *Just never go away again, okay? Or at least give me a chance to get a little more emotionally prepared the next time.* But Lizzy said nothing, knowing she couldn't be needy. Not now. This moment was demanding something much more from her.

Instead, something opened up as Lizzy listened to her wife breathe on the other end of the phone line, so very far away. "Take care of your dad," she said. "He needs you, Kate."

"I know he does," Kate replied. "He's got my sister, and our mother, but still I need to be here. For me." She paused. "Does that make sense?"

Lizzy nodded. "Of course it does," she answered. Whatever Kate was going through—and clearly it was a lot—there was a time and a place for everything. That much Lizzy knew.

Lizzy half-smiled at the realization that she was finally giving Kate her much needed space she'd been asking for since they'd gotten together. For it was always Lizzy's habit to love her partners so much that she dedicated herself to their every last need. And in Kate's case, that was all just a bit too much at times.

Yet here they were, technically in a Green Card marriage, yet with something so much more profound at play. And now separated by thousands and thousands of miles of physical space, not to mention an ocean, Lizzy could feel it more deeply than ever. It was taking everything she had to play it cool, and not to cave to the insistent hungry wolves in her belly who longed to urge Kate to come back soon.

"So..." Lizzy began.

"I have to run," Kate said now, and Lizzy nodded. She'd been expecting this. The hasty departure. It was Kate's specialty. Still, her partner loved her, and Lizzy knew that.

"I'm sorry, Lizzy," Kate suddenly said.

"For what?"

"That you have to do this alone," Kate said, and Lizzy closed her eyes against yet another incursion of tears.

"S'okay," she murmured. *Stay strong*, she chided herself.

"Going to go now, love," Kate said in her lovely, lilting Irish accent, only one of the many things that drew Lizzy to her.

"Okay," Lizzy said. "Love you." The line went dead then, and Lizzy felt the pit in her gut sink like a stone.

Once again, Kate had slipped away like a sylph.

Dispiritedly, she slid her phone back into her pocket and she stood up. And as she did, a short, dark woman walked in, her face creased with worry. She appeared to be an immigrant, perhaps Latina. Lizzy eyed her curiously.

Suddenly, she looked up, and she and Lizzy made eye contact. Immediately, Lizzy was struck by the misery in her face. She wore an expression of complete and utter defeat—as if there was simply nothing more to be done. Whatever was going on for this poor woman, it was big.

Lizzy's heart opened up to the woman for just a moment, and she felt like she was looking straight into this woman's soul.

That's me, she thought. *That's how I feel.*

Whatever she was going through, well…she was in damn good company.

*

Half an hour later, Lizzy found herself walking the hospital corridor with Aiden in her arms. His tiny warm figure was different from Ashanti's—bigger, warmer, and full of life.

The infant squirmed a little, his eyes still scrunched shut. He made a few small nonspecific sounds as he wiggled his head to the right and left. They weren't coos, and they weren't cries. They were something in between, and Lizzy stopped for a moment, trying to read what the baby needed.

Not that she could provide it. She'd never held an infant in her life before Ashanti was placed in her arms a few hours earlier. In fact, this entire experience was about as foreign to Lizzy as flying to the moon. Yet, as she walked slowly back and forth along the corridor, the squirming baby in her arms, she wanted to get better at it.

Anxiously, she searched his tiny face, and the furrow that now appeared on his brow. Perhaps he could tell just how inexperienced Lizzy was at holding newborns. Or perhaps his ever-present tummy gas was back. Lizzy could tell he was gearing up to start wailing again.

Then, as if on cue, Aiden's back stiffened and his face grew red, as he let out another ear piercing howl. Instantly, she was seized with something like panic. Yet at the same time, she tried to calm herself, wanting to get this right. Wanting not to go running back to Delilah and thrusting the screaming baby at her.

Lizzy took a breath, trying to remember exactly how the nurse had positioned the baby's body when she was patting his back. Gently, she placed her hand behind his head, where her arm had been cradling him. Slowly, she lifted Aiden up to place his cheek against her shoulder. His warm body nuzzled in against her own breast.

He was so close now, she could smell his utter baby-ness and it gave her a warm, trenchant feeling of hope. *I like this*, she thought to herself as she began to rock her body, swaying gently. Humming next to his ear now, Lizzy eeked out a few bars of "Oh Susannah."

Well, I come from Alabama with a banjo on my knee, she sang.

What a random choice, she thought with a smile. Yet, boldly she continued.

And I'm gone to Louisiana, my own true love to see…

Something shifted now and the baby in her arms quieted slightly. His ear-splitting cry had now cycled down to a long, tired whine. Perhaps it was the lull of her singing, or perhaps it was the rocking, or even her soft, steady patting of his back. Somehow, something was working.

Quietly, Lizzy felt a thrill she'd never before experienced. She didn't just like this…she loved it. Immediately, she thought of Kate. And her. And a baby of their own. Lizzy smiled, a grin of insight and awareness.

She could do this—they could do this.

All of this was possible. Perhaps Kate would come back, and their life really could continue. Maybe her anxiety was nothing more than a whole lot of misplaced worry. Maybe they'd get through this, and life as they knew it would return. Then perhaps they, too, would get to have a baby of their own.

Lizzy nuzzled her cheek closer to the baby's soft, cotton covered head, and as she did, a wave of pure love overtook her. In spite of her middle of the night exhaustion, she was buzzing with energy now.

Somehow, in the periphery of this entire scene lay hope.

*

Ronnie stretched and yawned as she leaned back in Sally's desk chair. Pressing the print button on the document she'd created on Sally's computer, she waited for the whir and click of the printer beside her to begin spitting out copies of her resume.

Might as well make hay while the sun shines, she thought to herself. Who knew when she'd get unlimited use of a computer and a printer again.

Reaching over, Ronnie pulled the top sheet from the printer and studied it critically. She'd been here more often than she'd wished in recent years, always trying to stay one step ahead of the next axe to fall. Which, admittedly, sometimes didn't actually work.

Her resume felt light and cheap in her hands, a thoroughly unimpressive document. Wearily, her eyes scanned her so-called credentials, some of which were real, and some of which weren't. This always made her smile, because somehow no one ever stopped to question any of it. It still hadn't gotten her a job, but you never know.

Tomorrow was another day.

Paper, thought Ronnie. Specifically, she needed some decent stationery for her resume. Something in a nice, muted color, with a little linen in the weave. If anyone would have something as gracious as that, it was bound to be her former lover. Ronnie just hoped Sally's stationery didn't have unicorns on it.

She pulled open the top desk drawer and began her hunt. She pawed through a few piles of papers, a box of paperclips and two staplers. Immediately, her eyes came to rest on a letter folded in a pale pink envelope that was tucked in the back of the drawer.

The words 'Misty Kennedy' were written on it in Sally's handwriting. Ronnie picked it up, fascinated, her resume task now completely forgotten.

Holding the envelop up to the light, she peered at it for signs of cash or even a check. Instead, it appeared to contain a hand-written letter. Ronnie considered the envelope in her hands for the briefest of moments. *Why had Sally tucked this into the back of the desk drawer? What was she trying to hide?*

Throwing caution to the wind, Ronnie tore into the envelope with her index finger. Within seconds, she was reading Sally's very contentious letter to her soon-to-be-mother in law.

Hello Misty, it began. It continued in a tone that Ronnie could scarcely believe. *Sally—my Sally—actually wrote this?* Quickly, her eye darted down the page, wondering who Misty Kennedy might be. A relative of Frankie's she assumed.

...your rudeness to me was so egregious that I left feeling nothing less than traumatized. Frankly, I was shocked. And I still am.

Ronnie read on, mesmerized. Where had Sally, of all people, learned to kick ass?

...you couldn't even be bothered to have lunch with us on a rare visit from your daughter...

Ah. That explained it, then. Misty was Frankie's mother, and Sally had just written a letter calling her out.

Ronnie smiled. This was just getting better and better. She read on.

Clearly, you only care about yourself and no one else, and that's just plain sad.

Ronnie looked up for a moment. Perhaps she'd underestimated Sally. She shook her head, amused. Then her eyes skipped down, scanning the rest of the page.

Ronnie reached the part about marrying Frankie. Here Sally's handwriting became even more emphatic, as she pressed her pen more fervently into the paper.

Sniffing in disdain a second later, Ronnie now returned the letter to its envelope. She really didn't need to read that part. Folding the letter in half, she shoved it into her back pocket and closed the desk drawer.

She wasn't sure yet how, but this little discovery was going to come in mighty handy indeed.

The possibilities seemed endless.

Chapter Fourteen

Frankie slouched against the wall just outside of Delilah's room and waited. Maybe it was all those years of standing patiently around in hospitals that had trained her. This was right where she always seemed to be, hovering just outside of the x-ray labs and emergency rooms, waiting for her injured assailants and perps, or perhaps the victims themselves to get treated. There was often a concerned parent or family member along for the ride as well.

Frankie liked to be right on the edge of the action, keeping an eye on things. It felt better this way. She really couldn't sit around the waiting room, obscured by all those walls and doorways. No, she had a gut-level need to protect her vulnerable friends, her people. And protect them she would.

Frankie studied a passing young man in green scrubs. Judging from his exhausted look and the lanyard ID around his neck, she assumed he was a med student. Once again the hallway returned to silence, and Frankie gave a long stretch and a yawn. Bending over, she touched her toes a few times. Then she returned to her post at the wall and considered grabbing a little medicinal caffeine from the vending machine up the hall.

Glancing inside their doorway once more, Frankie refocused her attention on Delilah. For the last hour, neither she nor Tenika had shifted much. Frankie could just make out their movements in the lowered nighttime light, as only one small lamp now lit the hospital room.

Tenika reclined beside Delilah on her hospital bed, her back propped up with pillows. The two of them were awake, eyes wide open, as they watched the dying baby in their arms. Together, they'd taken turns holding Ashanti in the near darkness, but most of the time, they were painfully still. As if too much movement might upset the fragile balance of life in the room.

Sometimes Tenika would hum a soft tune to the baby, one that was unrecognizable to Frankie. Other times Delilah would raise the baby to rest Ashanti's cheek against hers. It was a scene so tender, so full of portent and the lurking presence of death, that Frankie could barely bear to watch.

Earlier, she'd heard Tenika ask the night nurse how long she thought the baby had left. The nurse had murmured something Frankie couldn't hear. Then the nurse turned away with an inestimably sad look on her face. It shook Frankie, seeing that, and she related. Her own trauma watching a teenager jump from the Golden Gate Bridge a year earlier had nearly ended her career.

At least once, she heard both of them crying together, no words exchanged between them. Yet, the space in their room was comforting to her now. Indeed, Frankie couldn't leave if she wanted to. She needed to witness what was going on here, mostly because the room's tender air was raw and beautiful as it stretched on, minute by painful minute.

This was why she wanted to be here. It was the raw emotion of this place that she needed, and the pure kinship. Somehow it refreshed her soul. It was the adrenaline of life and death, and Frankie feasted on it. In fact, it woke her up.

Gradually, now, Frankie came to recognize a key truth as she stood by, watching. What was happening in this room was love personified. And it was profound. Tenika and Delilah were helping each other get through the worst crisis they would ever know.

It made Frankie stop and think.

In an instant, a clarifying flash of insight filled her mind; the insight landing on her like a first drop of cold rain. Frankie thought of Ronnie, parked on their couch in her men's pajamas. And she thought of Sally, fighting off sleep in the waiting room down the hall. And in that moment, Frankie was filled with regret.

Suddenly, she could see how jealous she'd been of Ronnie, as well as her obstinacy about welcoming her. She could also see her many unfair judgements of her own fiancée, all of them so harsh and unnecessary. And she could even see her refusal to defend Sally in front of her mother, who had, admittedly, been a monster.

Why had she done this?

Frankie had no answer. Instead, a wave of hard shame hit her, full force.

How could I have screwed up so much?

And how is it that Sally is still speaking to me...and even forgiven me?

Frankie marveled at yet another vast apology that now stretched before her. Standing up, she put her hands on her hips, wondering where to turn first. Distastefully, she wet her lips. And she sighed as she considered what had to be done.

When am I ever going to get this right?

She shook her head.

Probably never.

*

Kate walked up the darkened stairwell toward the bleak little garden on the roof of Good Sisters of Mercy Hospital. It was the well-intentioned place of cheer in an otherwise depressing facility, known for its starchy nun-nurses and dreary old paintings of Jesus on the green waiting room walls.

Clutching her sad cafeteria coffee, Kate made her way to a bench along the brick exterior wall of the hospital. Around her was a rock garden of sorts, really just a smattering of half-dead succulents that had been drowned in the endless rain. The tattered garden did nothing to lift Kate's mood.

She'd left her sister back at Da's bedside, waiting for the moment when the angels would finally show up and usher him off to the great beyond. If that was actually going to happen anytime soon. It occurred to Kate that it might not, despite the doctor's insistence that this was the end.

Kate had no idea why she thought this—she just did. Perhaps it was because her father had always been a fighter. Or maybe it was her own resistance to the idea of Da finally dead and gone. A person who simply no longer existed.

Leaning back against the brick wall behind her, Kate closed her eyes and felt the weak sun on her face. It came as a sweet relief as she became aware of her own jet-lagged exhaustion. Reluctantly opening her eyes a moment later, she sighed as she took a sip of the tasteless coffee.

Kate felt empty. So far, her return to Ireland hadn't been nearly as welcoming as she'd hoped it would be. For even with her father on his deathbed, this was a return home for her, a chance to finally come back to the place where her life began. So many times over the last eight years, she'd imagined her triumphant return— the daughter who went to America and came back successful and solvent.

All this time, she'd been thinking so hopefully about home. And now, here she was. Successful and solvent, yes. But still firmly an outsider.

All of it was just like this garden. Everything in her childhood home looked small and provincial, and the people depressingly the same, if a little heavier. The same old grease-tinged pub and dusty church were still the focus of all their affairs.

Nothing was heart-warming and familiar, or even nostalgic. Instead, each place she moved through was like a sepia tone print that was now curling and faded, well past its prime. It was as if not one person, place or thing in the home she'd left behind had progressed.

Kate kept waiting to see something that perked her up, or even caught her eye. Yet, nothing had. Instead, the city and its streets simply looked industrial. It was all slightly dingy and definitely worn. This applied to her mother and her poor dying father, as well.

Really, she'd barely spoken to her mother at all since she'd arrived home. Sheila now had a permanently worried look on her lined face, and her workaholic avoidance of her husband's imminent death was absolute. It was as if Da wasn't sick and Kate wasn't even there.

Her father, meanwhile, was already halfway gone. She kept chatting on and on to fill the empty space in his hospital room; yet, she wasn't entirely sure what he could and could not understand. So Kate relied on her sister to fill her in on the family's daily maneuvering. Yet, Eileen was understandably busy with her baby. Most of the time, she was also too busy to talk.

Consequently, no one had anything much to say to Kate. It was as though her absence all these years had erased her from their consciousness. No one had even asked her a single question about her life in the States since she'd arrived. But then, her father's passing was a huge, preoccupying event on everyone's minds. Or so she told herself.

The truth Kate didn't want to admit was that somehow they'd all moved on without her. And she had moved on without them. The starkness of this realization was a truth she could barely touch. Yet, here it was.

She no longer belonged here.

Taking another sip of her coffee, Kate considered her options. There was, of course, her life with Lizzy in California. *Lizzy.* The moment she thought of her, a pang of longing rattled through her body. How she missed her wife.

Kate shook her head at the mere thought. What was she doing here? And why hadn't she even told them she was now legally married? Lizzy was the best thing to have happened to her in the last ten years—or maybe ever.

Yet, when Kate was objective about telling her family this important fact, she knew there was no hope here. The parish priest had already been to their house twice to see her mother since she'd arrived. And her mother had disappeared to the church for half the day on Sunday, where she was now a member of the Ladies Guild. This was the same church that had taken an openly homophobic stance, even in recent years. Even in a country where same-sex marriage had been legal for some time.

One of the few real conversations she'd had with her mother was about coming to Sunday services. Which Kate did grudgingly, mainly because she was too tired and too sad to fight with Sheila about it. The idea that she might come out to her mum seemed obscure, almost laughable, as she sat in Mass with its swirling, smoky thuribles and its endless litany. Kate couldn't even imagine how that conversation would go.

Her sister knew about Kate's marriage to Lizzy, but as requested, she'd kept her mouth shut about it. She hadn't told a soul. Yet, even when they were alone together, Eileen asked her no questions. It was as if learning anything about Kate's life in America would shine an unfavorable light on her own.

Instead, there was now this strange invisible wall between Kate and her sister. She discovered it as soon as she arrived. Their lack of interest was simply a fact now. If she wanted any sort of relationship with these people, she'd simply have to get used to it.

Automatically, Kate pulled a small bag of crisps from her tote bag and opened it. *Screw it*, she thought. Who cared if it was only 9 AM? Placing one crisp after another in her mouth in a rapid succession, she savored the salty crunch and closed her eyes for a little hit of pleasure.

A thought descended on her then. Really, what did she expect? Of course, the family wasn't suddenly going to warmly accept her lesbianism. Why would they? Nothing else had changed in their lives. That much was obvious.

Still, Kate kept hoping against hope. She'd played out numerous scenarios on the airplane here. Perhaps there would be one shining moment around that final, inevitable stroke of death they were all waiting for. Then she and her mother would finally hug. They'd look at each other, say that they loved each other, and she would finally feel close to her mother again.

*Ma...*she'd begin, *there's something I need to tell you about my life in America.*

Having such a talk still seemed unfathomable to Kate. Yet, she also knew she could not go back to Oakland without telling at least her mother about Lizzy. She really couldn't. Kate could practically see the crushing disappointment painted on Lizzy's face. It would certainly be something she'd ask her as soon as they'd left SFO.

Kate had to take a stand. She simply did. It was that or lose the life she'd worked so hard to build.

Crumpling the crisp bag into a ball, Kate shoved it inside the pocket of her jacket. Then she stood up and prepared to return to her father's bedside for the remainder of the morning shift.

Some way or another, she'd figure this out.

It was what she always did.

*

Sally followed Frankie up to the rooftop deck of the Fabiola Building. The hospital hallways were eerily quiet, and their footsteps made a soft, echoing patter. She still wasn't sure why they'd all been allowed to stay past the end of visitor hours, but she was grateful they had.

Sally felt exhausted to the point of silence, as she made her way to the elevators. Frankie pressed the button, the doors opened and they got in.

"Why the rooftop?" Sally asked.

Frankie looked at her and managed a small smile. "I don't know. Breathe a little fresh air? See the stars? I figured we both needed it."

"Okay," Sally said in a small voice. She wasn't sure what was happening here, but somehow everything had shifted in the last hour or so. Suddenly, Frankie had lost her edge. Now she seemed gentler and more worn down. As if, in the face of the unthinkable, even she was acknowledging defeat.

They stepped out of the elevator, as it came to a dinging stop a moment later. Turning, Frankie reached for her hand, and Sally took it, no questions asked. It felt good to be holding Frankie's hand. Necessary, even.

She realized, then, how much she'd been craving Frankie's touch. Ronnie's presence really had caused a definite strain. Sally sighed as she thought about it, and the complicated situation she'd put them both in. She had no idea what to do next.

Mostly, she just hoped Frankie wouldn't bring it up. Not now. Not tonight. Sally knew she couldn't handle it.

They stepped out into the soft night air of the rooftop deck. The fog that had been in play earlier was gone now, and some stars were even visible overhead. "Come on," Frankie said, leading her to the railing at the edge of the deck.

The two paused at the railing and looked out over the scene of a thousand lights burning in homes and buildings across the city. It was a nighttime panoply of lamp-lit windows and tiny lives, all interwoven into the web of the city spread out before them. And it was beautiful. Beyond all of it was a layer of still darkness, Lake Merritt, and well beyond that lay the vastness of San Francisco Bay. Here was the restoring water that all of life in Oakland seemed pointed toward. Its presence was reassuring.

Pulling Sally close to her, Frankie now cleared her throat. Slowly she turned, and she looked down into Sally's eyes. The two paused there, as if they were looking at each other for the first time in a very long time. Sally could feel the pull between them—something she hadn't much felt at all in the last two weeks. Yet again, it thrilled her.

Unexpectedly, here was a moment of portent.

"Sally...I'm sorry," Frankie said simply. "I have been unfair to you. And unfair to Ronnie." She sighed. "Basically, I've been running around like a smug, entitled jerk, and I really want to apologize. This time for real."

Sally leaned her head against Frankie's shoulder. "It's okay," she said softly into her fleece. "It's over."

"No." Frankie was shaking her head. "No, it's not okay. And it's not really over—not until I fully apologize." She turned to Sally. "Look, I didn't defend you in front of my mother, who was completely outrageous, first of all. She was way out of line, and I was acting ridiculous."

"Frankie, shhh—" Sally began, but Frankie carried on.

"No, Sally. Listen to me. Please." Reaching over, she held her arms intently, as if holding Sally still would help her get across her point. "I was a jerk to Ronnie, too. I mean, who knows? Maybe she really is sick. You could be absolutely right."

A look of surprise came over Sally's face. "Why are you saying all of this now, Frankie?"

Frankie set her jaw, looking more determined than ever. "Because I'm watching what's going on downstairs, and it's breaking my heart, Sally. All of it...it just makes me appreciate you more than ever."

They looked at each other for a long moment as Sally absorbed Frankie's words.

Leaning down, Frankie kissed Sally's mouth. Then she kissed her again, a spiraling kiss that deepened and then gently released. "Look, honey," Frankie continued urgently, her arms softly enfolding Sally and pulling her close. Sally looked up into her face, her goodness, as usual, on full display.

"We are meant to be together. You know it. I know it," Frankie said. "So let's just elope. Let's go get married next week. Screw my mother and the big wedding and all of it. Let's just do this thing."

Suddenly Sally laughed and pulled back from Frankie's embrace. "Wow! Really? You're ready to do that?"

"Oh, yes. I am," Frankie said earnestly, and Sally could see that she was. She smiled at the fierce look of feeling on Frankie's face. And she could feel it straight down to her groin.

But then a less reassuring thought stopped Sally. "But what do we do about Ronnie?"

Frankie hesitated for a moment, choosing her words. "Well... something needs to happen for sure. But I don't have to be an asshole about it. Obviously, I owe Ronnie an apology."

Sally looked down at the floor, her clasp of Frankie's hand tightening. "I do, too," she said slowly. "Owe you an apology, I mean. I didn't have to dig in so much about Ronnie. And..." Sally's voice disappeared for a moment as she hesitated.

Am I really going to get into this here and now, when there is a baby dying downstairs?

Yes, in fact, she was. She had to.

"Look, Frankie," she said, looking up into Frankie's eyes. "I want to tell you something, too. While you were at work, before she moved in, I went on some walks with Ronnie, and..." Sally hesitated.

Frankie's look suddenly grew grave, and her entire manner changed as she stiffened. "And what?"

"Nothing happened!" Sally said, waving away any concern. "Honestly. But...I did find myself flirting with her."

Frankie grew quiet, her face a study in forbearance. "And?" she asked again, this time more steadily.

"And nothing. That's all," Sally said. Then she paused. "But isn't that enough?"

"Enough for what?"

"Well, I feel bad."

Frankie turned to her, her expression darkening with concern. "But you said nothing happened."

"Nothing did... I just..." Sally threw up her hands, hopelessly. "I mean, she has this weird power over me. I can't resist her, Frankie," she said, turning away. Now she had her back to Frankie. "I guess that's why she's sleeping on our couch," Sally continued in a small voice. "She still has some kind of control over me."

Frankie cleared her throat and put her hands in her pockets. She continued to gaze at Sally, preparing for the worst. "You still in love with her?"

"God no!" Sally burst, turning to face her partner. "I'm truly not, Frankie. I just...feel sorry for her. That's all it is."

Frankie shook her head and grinned in spite of herself. "You and your big heart."

Slightly embarrassed, Sally smiled, as well. It seemed Frankie was actually okay with her confession. "I know," she said. "So you're not mad?"

"That you flirted with your ex?" Frankie shrugged. "It's not my favorite news, but what am I going to do? Anyway, I haven't been perfect either."

She held out her arms to her love. "Come here," Frankie said to Sally, and Sally willingly swam into her arms. They kissed deeply, fully, surrendering to the starlight and the softness of a June night in the East Bay. And to each other.

There was hope on the horizon. They could both feel it as they kissed, and kissed some more.

The repair had already begun.

*

Ronnie padded out to the couch in her burgundy silk pajamas, one of the last vestiges of her former life.

She'd considered going to sleep in their bed. Her first night in a real bed with an actual box spring in God knew how long was incredibly tempting. But then Ronnie stopped herself. If they suddenly showed up, she couldn't blatantly piss them off. For the truth was, she needed Sally and Frankie.

At this moment, they were her only source of shelter. Then there was the money. About ten grand would do it, she figured.

Judging from Frankie's salary, which she'd found listed in some online public records, Ronnie had managed to construct a picture of Sally and Frankie's finances. Then she searched the house for cash. She went through their closets and drawers, their cupboards, storage areas, and even their filing cabinets, carefully looking for the random stash that was undoubtedly here somewhere.

She'd even checked out the garage, where people sometimes cemented safes in place, which they filled with undeclared cash. She also checked the basement for an emergency go bag full of small bills.

But, so far...nothing.

Ronnie was still pondering how to handle the next step as she snapped off the table light beside her, plunging the living room into darkness. Settling back under her covers on the couch, she watched a pair of headlights move across the living room ceiling from a passing car.

She could do this—she really could. In fact, Ronnie was so close to the needed money, she could taste it. It was the closest she'd been in months, ever since it became clear how much she needed to leave the country.

The plan was to go to Costa Rica. She'd check into the nearest airport hotel, bleach her hair, and just slip away to some obscure village where no one would ask questions. There were plenty of American retirees down there, so Ronnie figured she could fit right in. As soon as possible she'd get a fake identity—which was part of what the ten grand would go toward. The whole thing seemed pretty easy. For if there was one thing Ronnie was good at, it was reinvention.

Then the tax evasion charges she'd been avoiding could just hang out in limbo for a good long while—decades even. It was a known fact that the Feds really didn't go looking for tax evaders like her south of the border. They were too busy trying to shut down the big guys: the mobsters, drug dealers and money launderers.

And it stood to reason, why on earth would the IRS care about her and her sixteen years of unfiled returns? They definitely had much bigger things on their mind.

Really, if it wasn't for that letter from the IRS, she wouldn't even be trying to leave. The letter had sat on her windowsill for a good week before she opened it. And when she finally did, she just shook her head as she looked at the projected amount that she owed them: $186,547.

The number sat there on the page accusingly. It was an absurdly huge amount, one she couldn't even wrap her head around, let alone pay. And how in the hell did they even find her here, hiding in an SRO?

How could this possibly be right?

That's when the last shred of normalcy and stability dissolved from Ronnie's life, and she'd begun to make her plan to flee. Really, there didn't seem to be any other choice.

Ronnie made a point of missing the designated appointment with her tax auditor. After which she burned the offending letter. Sitting on the fire escape at the hotel, she watched it go up in flames in front of her, as if burning the letter could make the whole problem just disappear. Then she'd left the hotel for the last time, determined to disappear in plain sight.

So now Ronnie was officially an outlaw. That she should be sleeping on the couch of a police officer gave her a kind of perverse satisfaction. These were federal crimes she'd committed, something an officer with the SFPD would never hear a thing about.

No, neither Frankie nor Sally would ever know what was really going on. And they couldn't. Ronnie needed them too much.

And if she had to play hardball with them, well, then she'd do what she had to do. Ronnie had complete faith in Sally's weakness—and ultimately, in Frankie's as well. For if there was one thing she knew, few could resist the eternal appeal of love.

Clearly Frankie was already on the hook, without a chance of getting off.

Thank freaking God their Sally was such a catch.

Chapter Fifteen

Carefully Tenika placed her ailing daughter back in the bassinet the nursery had brought her in.

As far as she could tell, Ashanti was still alive. Tenika knew this because of the faint wisp of breath that still issued from her tiny nostrils. It was the only sign of life she felt from her daughter. She clung to this tiny bit of information, checking it again and again.

It was growing fainter and fainter.

On the hospital bed beside her, Delilah had fallen asleep. And now, Tenika was dangerously close to falling asleep herself. Putting the baby down for a few moments, she gave a much-needed stretch and walked out into the hallway.

Tenika looked around the deserted corridor, her hands on her hips. She had to get up and move to somehow keep on going in spite of her grief, her despair, her exhaustion. Coffee would definitely help.

Her footsteps sounded unnaturally loud as she walked down the hall. Suddenly, it seemed like there wasn't another single person awake in the entire place. Passing a clock above the now quiet nurse's station, she observed the time. 4:23AM.

She stopped at the door of the waiting room. Tenika was all too aware what her appearance in the doorway could mean to her gathered friends—that Ashanti had already passed. And really, right now, the last thing she wanted to confront was all the worry and grief on their faces.

Yet, in this moment, the others had mostly fallen asleep. Keisha sat snoring softly, folded into herself in a chair in the corner, her arms tucked across her ample breast. Meanwhile Rosalind and Monroe were curled up together in a seated sprawl on the loveseat, hands entwined and eyes closed. There was no sign of Frankie and Sally.

Only Lizzy was still awake, and she sat studying her phone. Looking up, she caught Tenika's eye and she rose suddenly.

Silently, Lizzy gave a gesture to ask if the time had come. Tenika shook her head and motioned for her to come.

"I had to get out of there for a minute," she explained as Lizzy joined her. "Think there's some coffee around here?"

"There's a vending machine area up on floor seven."

Silently, Tenika followed Lizzy up the half-lit stairwell. Lizzy didn't ask any questions, and Tenika didn't offer any replies; what was there to say? Both of them inherently understood they were all just hanging on, minute by minute at this point.

"Here," Lizzy said, guiding Tenika into the fluorescent-lit vending lounge she'd discovered a few hours earlier. Some tables and chairs were arranged in the center of the small room, and three vending machines flanked one of the walls.

Tenika looked around as she entered. And at first, she didn't notice the woman sitting in a chair near the corner. She sat bent over, her head in her hands. She was sniffling, and it struck Tenika that she might actually be crying.

She cast a weary look in the woman's direction and sighed. Then she looked at Lizzy as if to say, *Life sucks, no matter where you look.* Heading off to the nearest machine, Tenika shook her head as she went through the motions of buying herself an instant espresso.

Meanwhile, Lizzy hung back, motionless, her eyes still on the woman in the corner. It was the woman she had noticed earlier in the same room. She'd changed her chair, but that was about it.

A moment later, Tenika returned, a fresh cup of espresso in her hands. "You want something?" she asked. Then she took a long sip which she hoped would be bracing, but it wasn't. "It was warm brown water, basically, but right now it's good enough."

Lizzy looked up at her, distracted. Then she shook her head. "No thanks, T. You go on back. I'll be down in a moment."

Tenika left, making the sad walk back to the room where her family waited in suspended motion. She walked along one corridor and down the next, all the while wondering how they were going to survive the next month. Or three months, or six months. Or even the next year.

Tenika had no earthly idea; already this baby had imprinted herself on her heart and soul, and Delilah's as well, simply by lying in their arms. *How are we ever going to get through this?*

Yes, they had Aiden. But they'd never have Ashanti, not more than they did now. She was going back where she came from before they ever got to know her.

A moment later, as she approached the waiting room, she saw Delilah's night nurse walking toward her. The woman had a somber look on her face. Instinctively, Tenika's gut tightened.

This was it, and she knew it.

Tenika approached the nurse. "Is she gone?" she asked.

"Almost. You should come now," the nurse confirmed. Then she turned back toward Delilah's room, message delivered.

The news was a gut punch, one for which Tenika realized she would never be prepared. She stopped in the doorway of the waiting room where her friends all slept. Tenika hung on to the door jamb for a moment, mustering up what little strength she had left.

"Y'all, come now," she said, raising her voice slightly to rouse the sleepers. "Rosalind…Keisha? Come on now—wake up. It's time."

Various sleepy heads raised up, and bleary eyes turned toward her, but Tenika didn't stop to make eye contact. She was already walking down the hall, draining the last of her coffee.

Crumpling the empty cup in her hand, she tried to draw up her strength from the last of her reserves. And she realized then, she was now on autopilot—a mysterious reserve of energy she'd never experienced before poured through her body. It wasn't just caffeine; it was resolve. And she needed it now more than ever. She had to be there for her wife and her baby son.

And for Ashanti.

*

Lizzy stood with her hands in her pockets for a long minute, studying the weeping woman in the corner of the vending lounge. She was small, rounded and dark haired, a Latina woman.

She was simply dressed in a dark sweatshirt, jeans and cheap blue sneakers. At her feet was a tattered, flowered diaper bag. An open bag of Doritos sat on the chair next to her, along with an empty coffee cup. She appeared to be in her late twenties or early thirties.

She was the very same woman Lizzy had seen in this lounge earlier in the night—when she was trying to talk to Kate. Trying to get Kate to reassure her that everything was alright.

The woman had walked in and sat down like a harbinger of death or defeat, of everything hard in life. And here she was again, falling apart right in front of Lizzy. She knew what this meant, of course, and it made her stomach tighten. It was as if the breakdown of her own life had officially begun, as well.

Lizzy focused anew on this broken-hearted woman. She seemed so devastated, sitting alone in this dreary, forgotten corner of the hospital, crying her eyes out. Lizzy wondered what circumstances could have possibly forced her to sit there like this, hour after hour in the middle of the night.

Walking over to the woman, Lizzy now sat down in the chair next to her. She cleared her throat, but the woman's head remained buried in her hands. She appeared to give no notice.

Lizzy cleared her throat once more, but again, the woman ignored her.

Finally Lizzy leaned forward in her chair. "Ma'am?" she said in a low voice.

Now, at last, the weeping woman grew quiet. Her crying stopped, but still her head didn't move. She appeared to be listening.

Lizzy paused. What was she supposed to say now? She really didn't know. Something conciliatory? And if so…what exactly?

Whatever happened to you, I'm sure it must be bad and I'm really sorry?

I really feel your pain, and I completely relate?

Awkwardly, Lizzy remained silent. It occurred to her that her chair was just a little too close to this grieving woman. As if to keep her space, the woman's eyes remained fixed on the floor. Apparently, looking at Lizzy was more than she could muster at the moment.

Lizzy began to doubt herself. Maybe the poor woman just wanted to be alone, and she should leave her be. Maybe getting up and walking away really would be the compassionate thing to do. Still, something had compelled her to take the chance, to sit down and try to talk to her. Lizzy found she couldn't shake that impulse. She wanted to help.

Lizzy sat there, thinking.

Do I seriously have time for this…right now? For all she knew, Ashanti could have just died downstairs. Yet here she was, trying to help a total stranger. She vowed to make one last attempt, and if nothing happened she'd leave. She'd offer a little comfort and then let it go.

After all, it was a rare chance to help a grieving stranger. Anyway, this was what Kate would do.

"I'm sorry for…uh…whatever it is you're going through," Lizzy heard herself say.

"Just wanted to say I'm sorry."

The woman looked up at her suddenly, her tear-stained face red and puffy from crying. Clearly she was reeling from some very bad news. "Thank you," she said, in a heavily accented voice. Then she repeated the words carefully, as if she wasn't sure what else to say. "Thank you, miss."

Lizzy nodded, and she remained quiet. The two women took each other in.

"It's my baby," the woman finally explained. "She's…" She couldn't finish her sentence, but instead, broke down into sobs once more.

Reaching over, Lizzy patted her arm awkwardly. But now the woman sat up straighter and blowing her nose, she looked back at Lizzy. Suddenly, she needed to talk. "My baby. She's just three months."

Lizzy nodded, listening. Gathering strength, the woman continued in her uneven English. "She's sick in her heart. Doctor says she will die."

Lizzy felt something give way. "The same thing is happening to my best friend. Right now—upstairs. Her newborn is missing part of her brain." Lizzy paused, unsure what else to say.

But then, tears began to stream uncontrollably down Lizzy's face. It was as if the truth was finally sinking in. "It seems so wrong—her baby is going to die tonight. Right upstairs."

"Oh my God," the woman said, and Lizzy nodded.

"She's so little… And she looks so perfect, but she's…. she's…. so messed up," Lizzy said. "And they wanted her so much," she explained to the stranger, who was nodding now with tears in her own eyes.

"I know," the woman said.

Suddenly, Lizzy's tears felt like a relief, like a great, heavy door finally opened up and let her through. She actually let a sob escape her as the woman also continued to cry in the chair across from her.

The two just sat there, weeping at their common dilemmas for a moment. Pulling out her bandana from her pocket, Lizzy blew her nose. "Are you alone?" she asked, and the woman nodded.

"I got no husband," she said. "I wanted to have my baby here. In America. But now… She shook her head, as if the entire venture had been an impossibly bad idea.

The woman didn't articulate the obvious—that soon she would be alone again, without her baby. And here she was, living in a strange land, most likely without any support at all.

"There's nothing the doctors can do?" Lizzy asked.

Now, suddenly, the woman fixed her eyes on Lizzy. "He said we needed a miracle, so I pray."

Lizzy nodded, uncertain what to do next. *Should I pray, too?*

She wasn't inclined usually to do religious things. But somehow, here and now, it seemed like the right thing to do. The only thing to do. "What's your baby's name?" she asked.

"Angelica," the woman said, pronouncing the 'g' with a soft 'h' sound.

"Angelica," Lizzy said, practicing her name for a moment with its correct pronunciation. "I will pray for Angelica," she announced, knowing that in fact, she would. "I'm Lizzy," she said, as she rose. She extended her hand, and the woman took it.

"I'm Yolanda," the woman replied. Her handshake was cool and limp, as if shaking hands was something she was not accustomed to doing. Or perhaps because she simply didn't have the strength.

"I'm sorry—I have to get back now," Lizzy said then. "To the other baby."

The woman looked up at her, and her expression was like that of a scared child. "I pray for her. What's her name?"

"Ashanti."

"Okay," the woman said softly, as if she was filing this info away. Then she managed a weak smile. "Thank you, Lizzy." She pronounced her name 'Leecy'.

Yolanda looked at Lizzy for one more moment, and there was warmth in her eyes now. Her face looked ever so slightly more relaxed. It struck Lizzy that Yolanda was pretty when she smiled.

"It's all gonna be okay. I know it is," Lizzy said, as she stood there. She had no idea why she was saying this, yet somehow it seemed true. "Keep the faith, Yolanda," she added.

The woman nodded somberly. "Okay."

"Bye," Lizzy said. Then reaching the doorway, she turned and hurried down the hallway.

She really had to get back.

*

Ashanti was in Delilah's arms, and everyone in the room had their head bowed. It was clear what was happening, and Lizzy silently slipped in to join the group. Next to her, Frankie gave a hard sniff, presumably to fight off tears. Beside her Sally was silently crying, and their hands were pressed tightly together. Monroe had an arm around Rosalind.

A nurse stood to the side, quietly surveying the scene.

Lizzy bowed her head like everyone else, and tried to move the image of Yolanda, broken down in her chair in the vending lounge, from her consciousness. But the image would not budge. It stayed insistently at the top of her thoughts. *I need to get a grip.*

"Did she die yet?" Lizzy whispered to Frankie who shook her head.

"Soon," she said.

The nurse bent toward Delilah and Tenika and asked them something. And just at that moment, a woman appeared just behind Lizzy. She was tall and red-haired, and she had a gentle air.

"Excuse me," she said, peering past Lizzy, and the nurse beckoned her in.

She walked toward Delilah and Tenika. "I was wondering if I could speak to you for a moment," Lizzy heard her say, and now she and Frankie exchanged a look.

The redhead walked over by the bed and, in a low voice, said something to Delilah and Tenika that Lizzy couldn't hear. The group stood there for a moment, listening, unsure exactly what was happening. This woman didn't appear to be a nurse, though clearly she was important. And she was from the hospital.

Tenika looked up uncertainly. "Organ donation!" she said in a startled voice. "Hasn't this poor baby already been through enough?"

Delilah took her wife's hand and nodded to the woman to continue. "Please go on," she said.

The entire room grew intensely quiet.

"It could be your baby's chance to save another baby's life," they could hear the woman say. The requester's gentle voice had a lulling effect on Lizzy, and she found herself listening intently as the woman described how organ and tissue donation could sometimes save four or five people. Sometimes even more.

Delilah and Tenika looked at each other. Tenika's face remained a mask of pain. "Hold on a minute—" she protested, clearly taken aback. But Delilah just took her hand.

"We need to think very seriously about this, T," she said.

Tenika cleared her throat. "Can y'all step outside, give us a minute?" she asked. A moment later, they all shuffled awkwardly into the hallway as Tenika shut the door behind them.

"I don't know about you, but I'm prayin'," Keisha announced, and she continued on with eyes closed, right there in the hallway. "We got to get Jesus on this… Please, Lord, help T and Delilah make the right choice," she said, her voice rising up from the group. "Help them do the best thing for all concerned."

And this time, even Lizzy bowed her head.

*

"T, please," Delilah said, her clear blue eyes looking up into the grief-hardened face of her wife. "We need to do this."

"I'm just saying, that's a lot of…well…invasive whatever.

How can we justify doing this to this poor baby?"

"Because it would be her contribution," Delilah answered evenly. "Her legacy. It's how she would carry on after her death."

By now, Delilah could see the path ahead. Ashanti would go, Aiden would stay, and they would all be altered.

But if one little baby could have her kidney or her liver, or even her heart, then maybe that would become the small light at the end of what seemed to be a very long tunnel. It was a tunnel whose length, and whose darkness, whose depth, they couldn't even fathom yet. This much, Delilah knew instinctively.

Donating her organs would be something for the two of them to hang on to. But only if Tenika could see it, too.

Tenika looked at her wife critically, her arms folded tightly across her chest. "You mean, it doesn't bother you what would happen to our daughter? I don't even want to think about it…"

Delilah regarded her wife. "Not if she could actually help someone," she said. "Look, honey—this is it. This is all she gets. What kind of life is it if she can't even donate her organs?"

The question stopped Tenika, and slowly she dropped her arms that had been clamped across her chest. "Well…" she said uncertainly. She shook her head, but now Delilah could see something was shifting. It was a transition she'd seen so many times, in so many circumstances with her wife. At this point, she knew it well.

Tenika was actually coming around.

She looked over at Delilah a moment later. "You sure about this?" she asked.

"Oh, I'm sure, alright." Delilah said, and she lay back against her pillow. She was so exhausted. Yet, in this moment, she felt calm, grounded and strangely alive. "I don't know why, T, but this feels like the beginning of everything."

"Well, then," Tenika said, "I think you must be on some pretty potent drugs."

"I am," Delilah agreed with a half-smile. "But I can also see where this is going." She took her wife's hand again. "And it's good, T. It's so good."

Unexpectedly, a tear ran down Delilah's face. And then another. She couldn't say for sure, but strangely, they seemed like tears of joy. For in that moment, she felt lit within—like her whole being was full of possibility. "Please," she said. "Let's do this. I swear to you, T…it's the right thing. I know it is."

Tenika closed her eyes, taking a breath. Half-broken, she sank down onto the edge of Delilah's bed. "I just don't want to lose her," she finally admitted as she began to cry.

"Then really let her go," Delilah urged. "Because, honey, she's already gone. And this way, we will send her off with love."

Tenika looked over and nodded her agreement. All of her fierce fury had finally, totally melted down to nothing. She, too, could see the inevitability of all of this.

There really was nothing more to be done.

The nurse had already explained what would happen next. Before Ashanti took her last natural breaths, she would immediately go on life support. And though she'd technically be completely brain dead, her body would continue breathing and pumping blood mechanically as they rushed to find the recipient and arrange the transplants.

It was a fraught, tricky and dramatic process. One Tenika could barely bring herself to think about. Yet, it was also one that Delilah had already, even instantly, made peace with. And that much Tenika could trust.

"Shall I call the nurse in?" Delilah asked, and Tenika nodded, her eyes still closed.

It truly was the next right step, and both of them knew it.

Chapter Sixteen

Kate lowered her tray to the café table across from her sister and steeled herself. She wasn't even sure exactly what she wanted to say. She just knew she needed to say something.

Carefully removing her chicken roll and her cup of tea, she placed the tray to the side and seated herself. Eileen, meanwhile, was jiggling a now well-fed Kaeli on her lap, trying to get her to stop fretting. A soggy, barely touched coffee sat before her. Soon it would be Eileen's turn to go upstairs and sit with their father.

Later that afternoon, Kate was scheduled to work behind the bar at the pub, taking Eileen's usual shift. Truthfully, it had been so many years that Kate could barely remember how to pull pints. And she hoped to God no one came in ordering anything more complicated than Black & Black. She figured she'd just have to keep her head down and fake her way through it.

Her mother was running the pub tonight, as usual. It would be one of the first times Kate had really spent much time at all in her mother's presence since she'd arrived—and, of course, they would be working. Kate wasn't looking forward to it.

Her mother's perpetual cloud of annoyance seemed worse than ever. "You'd never know her husband was dying," Kate remarked to her sister. The only sign of grief and worry on Sheila's face was the grim line of determination where a forced smile had once been.

The elephant in the room, of course, was Kate and her years-long absence from home. Kate recoiled at the mere thought of coming out to her mother. Most definitely, it would not go well, but she knew what she had to do.

God, I miss Lizzy. Briefly Kate shut her eyes against the tears that suddenly threatened to encroach. Then grabbing her sandwich, she unwrapped it intently, eager to focus on anything else for a moment. Suddenly, her attentive sister spotted her discomfort.

"You alright?" Eileen asked.

"Fine. Perfect," Kate bit into her sandwich and chewed. "And you?"

Eileen looked pained. "Oh, Kate…really?"

"What?" Kate feigned innocence. She smiled tightly, wishing she could just disappear into the wall behind her. There was no getting past her sister at such moments.

Of all the people on this planet, none knew her as well as her sister. Even if they hadn't seen each other in years. Eileen studied her with a practiced eye.

"It isn't Da, is it?" she murmured, half to herself. "So what's this all about then, Katie?"

Her baby now began to settle and coo softly on her lap. Kaeli sucked her fist and looked up at Kate, her wide, black eyes sparkling. Kate said nothing.

Eileen gave a sigh. "Katie, now come on, love. It's me. Your sister. You've been walking around like a tightly coiled spring ever since you got home. What is it? I know it's not just Da. What's the matter?" she demanded.

Kate was taken aback now. The question actually brought tears to her eyes, and she stared at her sandwich in her hand for a moment, composing herself. She wasn't going to get into any of this today. Not here, in the hospital, when they both had to spend hour after hour sitting by their father's miserable deathbed.

And yet, Eileen was doing what Kate had begun to think

impossible in their family. She was asking after her well-being. "Is it Lizzy? Are you two alright?" she pressed.

"Oh, God!" Kate gave a flustered laugh. "Is that all you're on about? Of course, we're fine. We're…wonderful! And very happy."

She paused. For she hadn't even told her sister the biggest part of this story. And if she was going to do it, well, now was certainly the time. Instantly, a small quiver of panic ran up through Kate's spine. She fixed her eyes on the soggy chicken roll before her, a single bite gone.

"Actually, we got married," she said in a low voice.

Eileen's eyes widened. "When was this?"

"A while back. There were immigration issues," she said. "But we would have done it anyway, you know," she added quickly.

Eileen fixed her sister with a curious look. She seemed genuinely confused. "So congratulations are in order then?"

"I suppose. But, mind you—we're happy. This is real, Eileen."

"Lovely," Eileen said evenly. Kate couldn't tell if she was genuinely pleased for them or not.

But then Eileen's next question betrayed the real trajectory of her thoughts.

"You going to tell Mum?"

"Oh, Jesus—I don't know, *I* don't know!" Kate burst. "I suppose I have to. I really do. If not now, when and all that? Anyway, Lizzy is beside herself that I haven't told them. She wants to come here, you know. She wants to meet you, and Kaeli—and them. And knowing Lizzy, that means she'll probably turn up here any day now, and you can imagine how that will go. Especially if I don't tell them."

Kate looked at her sister bleakly. "That's why I mentioned it." She began to cry in earnest, unable to stop herself. An older couple sitting a few tables away glanced over at her, then looked quickly away.

Eileen sighed as the baby stirred in her lap and gave a whimper. "I'm glad you did," she said gently.

"But what do I do?" Kate asked, tears welling in her eyes.

"I don't want to be a burden—you know I don't. I have to do something, but this is going to kill Mum. That or infuriate her. She'll probably stop speaking to me—and on top of Da passing. I honestly don't know what to do."

Eileen gave a tight grimace. "You couldn't tell Lizzy to hold on?"

"Oh, Eileen! It's been more than a year and a half. She didn't even know I hadn't told the lot of you until right before I got on the plane. It's bad," she admitted. Then she turned her eyes imploringly to her sister. "I don't want to lose her," she said, her cheeks now wet with tears.

"You honestly think she'd leave?"

"No, yes...I don't know! Lizzy has gotten me through so much—she really has. Helping me get out of the utter hell with Mindy. She even gave me a job until I could get new clients, and a new home. Then she found me the Sanctuary church when ICE was trying to deport me. Eileen, she even married me when I needed it most. And now...well, here we are." Kate paused, shaking her head at the enormity of it all.

And as she spoke, a new realization came pouring down through the tumble of her thoughts. It was as if the words themselves were shining a light on the reality of her marriage. Suddenly, Kate had an unexpected insight. It stopped her cold.

She wanted to tell her parents about Lizzy.

She honestly did. She wanted to tell them because she was proud of her life in America. She was proud of her and Lizzy, of all they'd shared, and how far they'd come together. Perhaps, if she could bring this message to her dying father, then at least he would know she was happy.

And maybe that was what really mattered in the end.

"I honestly love this woman..." Kate said, her voice breaking. "She's changed my life. And I owe it to her."

"But Kate," her sister said quietly. "Our father is dying right now. He won't like this one bit, will he?"

Kate bowed her head. *What am I thinking—being so self-centered at such a time?*

"I know."

But then, just as suddenly, she raised her head to her sister. "I was just thinking…perhaps…maybe Da should know about us. Before he dies."

"Why on earth would you do this to him, Kate?"

"Because Da wants me to be happy."

Sitting back with a sigh, Eileen looked at Kate and shook her head. "You are amazing," she said, a note of disgust rising in her voice. "Always on about you, Kate. Really you haven't changed a whit, have you? I thought maybe you'd finally grown up, after all those years in America, but apparently not."

Shoving back her chair, Eileen suddenly stood up, her hackles rising. "I'd better get up there," she announced. Now her tone was decidedly businesslike.

"Wait! Eileen—" Kate began. Reaching out, she placed a restraining hand on her arm. She couldn't lose her sister's alliance.

But Eileen shook her off angrily. And turning to her baby, she buckled her into her stroller with a snap. "I'll see you at home at five. That's when you're off to the pub for your shift."

Kate sighed. "Right." Walking quickly away without so much as a backwards glance, Eileen left, and as she did, Kate felt part of her give way and collapse completely.

She knew all of this was going to be difficult. But now she'd lost the support of the one person she'd counted on to get her through it. Kate stood and deposited her uneaten sandwich in the trash. Clutching her tea, she moved through the doorway of the cafeteria and headed for the sunlight of the exit. And as she did, a harrowing thought struck her.

Eileen could very well call her mother and be the one to break the news about her marriage to Lizzy.

Unless, of course, Kate got to her first.

*

The door opened as the requester stepped out and hurried up the hall. Lizzy's eyes followed her as she stopped at the nurse's desk. Intently, she bent over and spoke to the head nurse. Both of them looked back in the direction of Delilah's room.

"Okay, look everybody. Here's what's going to happen," Tenika began, as they all reentered the room. She hesitated, feeling the encroach of fresh tears. "Damn," she muttered, her voice wavering.

Delilah took her hand and squeezed it. Ashanti was still in her arms, cuddled up tight against her breast.

"I can do it, honey," she said gently. The room became silent and the only sound now was the slight, occasional snuffling breath issuing from the dying baby.

Lizzy watched, her heart aching for her friend as Tenika sank down on the edge of Delilah's bed, defeated, her back to the group. Hanging her head, her shoulders shook as she began to weep silently.

Delilah carried on calmly. "We're going to donate Ashanti's organs," she explained. "They say we can donate her heart and maybe even her liver and kidneys. There are a lot of babies who need them."

Delilah paused. Glancing over at her wife, she put her hand on Tenika's back. "So…that's it, I guess." She hesitated. Then her own voice lowered, betraying her loss. "We have to let her go."

A collective sigh went through the group, and Keisha let out an involuntary sob. "We knew this moment would come," Delilah continued.

"But this will be good," Monroe said, looking around at the gathered friends. "It's a good thing, organ donation…right?" The others nodded their agreement.

"So I've asked the nurse to bring Aiden in now," Delilah said. "So she can die in peace with all of us here."

Tenika got up and turned around, and facing the group, she wiped her tears from her cheeks with the palm of her hands. "Just don't leave yet," she said to them. "Stay y'all." Then she paused, looking around.

"Where the hell is Lizzy?" she asked.

*

"Excuse me," Lizzy said, leaning toward the nurse seated at the nurse's station. "I'm looking for that red-headed woman from the organ donation place."

The nurse pointed to a small office just behind the desk, where the door was currently closed. "She'll be out in a minute," she said. Lizzy glanced at her watch impatiently, knowing she needed to get back immediately.

"Can I interrupt her?" she asked, and the nurse shook her head.

"She's on the phone."

"It's just that my friend's baby is dying right this minute, and I really need to talk to her."

"Can't help you," the nurse said tersely, as she flipped through the clipboard of paperwork in front of her. She had the well-practiced air of someone who was used to dealing with the general public and all their dramas.

Lizzy checked the wall clock again and paused, wondering if she should run back to Delilah's room and see what was happening. The baby's death was imminent—she knew that. But Lizzy's task was equally urgent. She knew Tenika and Delilah would thank her in the long run.

She folded her arms, trying to calm herself as the requester's office door stayed firmly shut. "If I could just go knock on the door, maybe?" she asked the nurse, who just shot her a silencing look.

This is insane, she told herself. She had to get back there for Tenika. She had to. Still the old urge to help someone in distress kept pushing her forward. It was how she was wired.

Just then, the nurse picked up her clipboard and disappeared down the hall. Immediately, Lizzy darted over to the closed office and knocked. A moment later, the door opened, and the red-headed requester poked her head out.

"Yes?"

"Hi," Lizzy said. "I'm a friend of Tenika and Delilah's, and …um…I wanted to say there's a baby in this hospital who might need Ashanti's heart. At least I think she does. I was just talking to her mother, and her doctor says the baby's going to die without a miracle. Her name is Angelica. So maybe this is the miracle?" Lizzy paused. "I just wondered if…uh…you do this kind of thing?"

A half smile moved across the requester's face. "Sometimes," she said. "Rarely. But it's happened. Do you know if the baby is currently on the transplant list?"

"I have no idea," Lizzy replied.

"And Angelica and her mother—are they both here in the hospital right now?"

"I guess," Lizzy replied. She honestly had no idea. "I met the mom, her name's Yolanda, in the vending lounge a few hours ago. I could try to find her."

"And who are you?"

"Lizzy. Lizzy Edgewood."

"Well, we don't have much time, Lizzy. And I'm sure you realize we do have a transplant list, of course. There are always babies waiting for a heart."

"Right," said Lizzy. "But can you just give me a half hour? Let me at least try to find her?"

Rebecca, the requester, paused, wheels turning in her mind as she assessed Lizzy, a person she'd never seen before in her life. Requests like this came along every once in a while, usually from well-intentioned people. But seldom did they ever amount to anything because the transplantation process was complex and full of vulnerabilities.

All it took was one mistake to derail the entire process—including waiting to notify the next recipient on the list. Yet, fielding such requests was also part of Rebecca's job, as she was the first point of contact.

"Their blood types would have to match, Lizzy. There are a lot of reasons this may not work. A transplant might not even save her." Rebecca said gently. "So we don't encourage this kind of thing. But I suppose you could try. You'll have to hurry—twenty minutes tops, okay?"

Then Rebecca smiled and shut the door, leaving Lizzy to work her plan.

People were really surprising sometimes.

*

An even more somber air had settled in Delilah's room. Ashanti had passed away only moments earlier, and she lay in on a pediatric gurney in the corner. A ventilator directed breath into her lungs, while an array of electrodes were taped across her chest, recording the movements of her heart. They played a rhythmic pattern of tiny, even spikes on the portable monitor overhead.

Delilah and Tenika had asked to keep her with them until Ashanti was wheeled off to the operating room for the beginning of the transplant process. It would come all too soon, and they all knew it.

Lizzy hung in the doorway, hesitating for a moment as she tiptoed into the intense quiet in the room. Only the beeps from Ashanti's monitors disturbed the silence. The group appeared to be gathered in prayer, or possibly they were just deep in thought. Sally looked up and sighed.

"Hi, Lizzy," she said.

"Where you been?" Tenika asked. "Ashanti passed. We're just waiting for them to wheel her out of here."

"I know. I'm sorry, but I got an idea," Lizzy began. And she told them about her encounter with Yolanda hours earlier, and her conversation with Rebecca. "Maybe Ashanti's heart could—you know…" she fumbled.

"Keep the other kid alive?" volunteered Tenika.

"If you guys wanted," Lizzy finished, looking back at her friend. "That way you'd know the mom. And you'd always have her in your life somehow. And this mother...well, Tenika, you saw her."

"Barely," Tenika said. But then she waved her hand. "Yeah, sure. Whatever. At this point, if it's gonna happen it's gonna happen. I mean, Ashanti's gone—"

"Do it," said Delilah firmly. "I like it."

"I'm on it," Lizzy said, and she took off for the back stairs.

*

A moment later, Lizzy raced toward the vending lounge doorway. Yolanda had to be in there. She was going to save this baby. Suddenly the day was looking up.

Lizzy paused in the doorway, surveying the group now assembled in the room. Two toddlers eating cheerios at one of the tables looked back at her, along with a grandmother.

Yolanda was gone.

Stepping back into the hallway, Lizzy stood there for a moment, considering her options. There was a nurse's station just ahead, but who knew what for?

A blast of overwhelm clouded her brain, as she began to walk toward the stairwell. Lizzy realized she had no idea where to find the Pediatric Unit. Or even where to begin to find this baby and her mother in this vast city hospital full of pavilions and wings.

Where would a critically ill baby even be? The Pediatric ICU?

Lizzy realized that it all depended on how Yolanda had brought the baby into the hospital. Perhaps she'd come in through Emergency and somehow the baby was still there.

On the other hand, the pair might have left altogether. Yolanda might have packed up Angelica and taken her home to die peacefully in her arms, surrounded by candles and prayers.

Lizzy sighed.

She needed help.

Chapter Seventeen

An unlikely procession had begun as Lizzy hurried back from the stairway. Up ahead, she could see Ashanti's gurney being slowly wheeled out of Delilah's room by two attendants. The baby was being wheeled into surgery to begin the transplant process.

Lizzy stopped and watched the mournful parade slowly move up the hall. Slowly, Keisha followed Ashanti, a look of inestimable sadness on her face. Monroe and Rosalind trailed in her wake, hands clasped. Sally followed, her face still streaked with tears, as Frankie walked somberly by her side.

Tenika took the spot at the rear, cradling Aiden, as Delilah walked beside them, pushing an IV on a pole.

Lizzy fell in behind all of them, feeling her heart rise up in her chest. *We are doing this. This is actually happening.*

As they made their way up the darkened hall, Keisha began singing in a low voice. Her song was soft at first, and a little tentative, but then her voice grew in strength as they walked alone. Soon her song filled the air.

Jesus loves the little children
All the little children of the world

One by one, others in the group joined in as the song grew and grew. Remembering the words, they carried on, picking up steam.

Red and Yellow, Black and White

They are precious in this sight
Jesus loves the little children of the world

Now the procession slowly turned the corner into the bigger, broader corridor leading up to the operating theater. It was a well-lit thoroughfare, and as they rounded the bend, Lizzy was amazed to see the entire hallway up ahead of them was now lined with staff.

The blue-garbed technicians and orderlies, the nurses with their colorfully printed scrubs, even some surgeons and doctors in their long white coats, all stood in silence, heads bowed. Respectfully, they'd paused to pay silent tribute to this slow-moving caravan—to this infant who would save another infant's life.

As Keisha's song rounded the corner, they, too, picked up the song and began to sing.

Jesus loves the little children
All the children of the world

Lizzy watched as even some patients came to their doorways to see this early morning procession. And they, too, sang the old hymn as they passed by.

Jesus loves the little children
All the children of the world

Catching up with Tenika, Lizzy touched her arm. And her business partner, her best friend in the world, turned to her now with a look Lizzy had never seen. For a moment, it took Lizzy's breath away. Rather than grief, Tenika's entire face was now incandescent with love.

"Thank you," she said.

The two women stopped and hugged each other. It was a hug full of loss, of hope, of grief, and of the most improbable emotion of all—joy. For this was how it was at such a moment, when the edge of one life converges into so many others that everyone is collectively moved.

A moment later, Ashanti arrived at the swinging doors that led to the operating theaters. The song died down, the staff drifted away, and the group watched, their hands pressed together, as the tiny baby passed through the doors, never to be seen again.

Tenika and Delilah were both sobbing by then, and Aiden had begun crying, as well, his tiny, shrill cry filling the room. Sally reached for Aiden and, stepping to the side, began to comfort him while the others gathered in a massive group hug.

It was all over now.

And yet, it was also just the beginning.

*

Kate pushed her way into the darkness of the pub, leaving behind the natural sunlight of the street. She watched the last of the lunchtime stragglers down his final gulp of Guinness. Then, putting a bill on the bar, he weaved his way past her out the door.

Her mother was behind the bar, giving the bar top a final wipe. "Hi, Mum," Kate said.

Her mother looked up. "You're early," she remarked, as she placed his glass in the commercial dishwasher below the counter. With a snap, she turned it on and the ancient washer chugged into motion.

Sheila picked up a pouch with the lunchtime receipts in one hand and her coat in another. "Going to drop this off at the bank. Then I'm heading home for an hour's break."

"Mum. Wait," Kate said, a note of urgency filling her voice, as her mother came around the bar.

"What?" Her mother pulled her jacket tight and zipped it up. She put her hands in her pockets. A look of annoyance flickered across her face. "You don't want to work tonight?"

"No, I'll work. But can we speak for a moment, Mum? You and I?"

Her mother sighed. "Oh, Kate. Come on, let me just go home. I have to be back here in an hour—and so do you."

"No, Mum. Please. I need to talk to you." Kate walked over to one of the two tops and pulled out a chair. "Here," she said. "Can I get you something?"

Her mother's eyes rolled to the ceiling, and she hesitated for a moment. Then she marched over to the chair and seated herself in it. She didn't remove her coat. "I have a lot to do," she said. Kate, who was now behind the bar, poured herself a tall glass of Chardonnay. She knew she'd need it.

"You sure you wouldn't like anything, Mum?" she asked again.

"To go home."

For years now, Kate had been dreading this final moment of truth with her mother. She'd thought about it so many times in high school, when she had her first crushes on the girls in her class. And when her mother kept pushing her at this boy or that on Sunday mornings at the church.

She'd mulled it over again and again, especially since marrying Lizzy. And always, she landed at the same place. Eventually, she'd have to tell her mother she was gay.

And, well...here she was.

Over the years, Kate found herself imagining a million possible reactions—from her mother's highly unlikely proud embrace and congratulations on her marriage, to the more likely stony silence and strategically flung insults. Sheila was almost certain to give her a hard time.

"Mum," Kate began, as she slid into her chair across the table, wine glass in hand. She looked at her mother, who sat there, her arms firmly crossed against her purple nylon jacket.

"Helping yourself to the good wine, are you?" Sheila said in an acid tone, nodding to Kate's glass of wine. Kate didn't answer.

Her tightly pulled back bun had grayed since Kate had left, and her mother was twenty pounds heavier. But she was still essentially the same, a downtrodden woman who'd given her everything to a man and a cause, in this case the family pub. Yet it was a cause that even she no longer believed in.

Kate could see it all in front of her. Her mother had been utterly defeated by life. And now she was just plain angry.

"What's all this then?" her mother asked. Impatiently, she glanced at the aging gold watch on her wrist.

"We've scarcely had the time to talk since I got home, and I thought"

Her mother stood up. "Well, if this is just about chitchat, now is not the time, Kate. I'm bone tired. Been here all day, you know, and I have to work tonight."

"I know it's your break, Mum. I'm sorry…" Kate hesitated. Then she took a large fortifying gulp of her wine. Once more her courage rose. "Look, I need to tell you something, Mum." Kate paused, adrenaline coursing through her veins. Her mother eyed her curiously. And slowly, she sat once more.

"I want to tell you something important about me and my life in the States," she continued.

"Go on." Once again, Sheila's arms folded across her chest. "I'm listening."

Kate's eyes fastened on the illuminated Harp Lager sign over the bar, just past Sheila's shoulder. The neon letters shone blue below the golden, glowing harp, witnessing what she was about to do.

"I'm…uh…"

Kate's mother just regarded her, her face betraying nothing.

Kate closed her eyes, her own childish way to protect herself. "I'm gay. I'm a lesbian, Mum," she blurted. "And I have a wife back in the States. Her name is Lizzy and she owns a garage."

There was silence.

Gingerly, Kate opened one eye, then the other, and she looked at her mother. Sheila's face was frozen, almost as if she was unsure how to react. For one long, fearful moment, Kate remained silent as the two women just stared at each other.

"Well," Sheila finally said, as the hostility came pouring back into her face. "Bully for you, Kate," she said. Then her voice dropped into a low hiss. "You think coming in here and telling me this as your father lays dying in the hospital is in any way helping?"

Sheila's tirade began to gather steam. "You think you can just go running off to California and think it's perfectly fine not to come home for nearly ten years? Huh? That your poor father and I didn't even wonder what the hell had happened to you?"

"I've explained! I couldn't leave," Kate insisted. "There were immigration problems—"

Sheila pushed on through, her voice rising. "And that you can just waltz in here now, all fine and mighty in your ridiculous California clothing and your silly haircut and tell your own mother such nonsense?" Sheila gave a derisive snort.

Then she stood up and leaned across the table, so she was only a foot or so from Kate's face. Her face was shaking with rage. Behind her, a dishwasher poked his head out of the kitchen door to see what was going on.

"Well, I'll tell you what you can do, Kate. You can go home and pack your bags and get the hell out of here and never come back." Sheila paused, breathless now, as one strand of her tightly pinned up hair worked its way loose and fell across her cheek.

Standing up, Sheila folded her arms for her final pronouncement. "We don't need your kind in our house. You're not welcome here anymore."

"But, Mum—" Kate cried.

"Not discussing it," Sheila shot back as she headed for the door, giving her jacket a final zip. Then pausing, she fixed Kate with one final look. "Go on… And don't even think about telling your father. This will truly kill him."

"Mother!"

"We're done here!" Sheila roared. The door closed behind her with a slam, and Kate was left to sit there in silence. And shock. Putting her head down on the table, Kate felt the cool, linoleum surface beneath her and she clung to it for strength. Her mother's reaction had been all too predictable, of course. But never did she think she'd be asked to leave.

But here it was. Everything she'd been afraid of for so long had finally come to pass. The final confrontation—the completion of all she had begun was now set in motion. She realized, as she sat there, that she felt oddly relieved.

Downing the rest of her wine in one long gulp, Kate looked around at the family business for what she knew would be the very last time. Jimmy was in the kitchen, so really all she had to do now was go home. If you could call it that.

Kate shook her head in amazement at all that had just occurred. She would, indeed, be gone within the hour.

*

"She's Latina, you say? How tall approximately?" Frankie was asking her questions with the practiced calm of a seasoned first responder. "What was she wearing?"

Lizzy continued to generate a verbal picture of Yolanda for the group of friends, now gathered by the elevator. Tenika and Delilah had sent them off to find her with their blessings, and now find her they would. Frankie, ever the pro, had stepped in to take charge.

"I've been all over the floor where the vending machines are, but she's not up there," Lizzy explained. "I went by the Pediatrics ICU, too, but they just had a shift change. Someone said a Latina woman passed through there about a half hour ago."

The knot of anxiety that had been churning in her gut for the last hour tightened. The fact that they had less than twenty minutes to find this woman wasn't helping. "We've really got to get moving," she added.

"Yup," Frankie agreed. "So you guys clear on what she looks like?" The group nodded. "Monroe and Ros, you two head out to the sidewalk outside the garage exit, and start looking at every car that comes out. Sally, you check the cafeteria, then join me in the garage. Text me when you get there." She paused. "Lizzy, you and I'll go to the garage right now. We'll divide up and scour the place."

"Why the garage?" Lizzy asked her, as the elevator door opened.

"She might be sleeping in her car." Frankie looked around. "Everyone got my cell?" They all nodded in agreement. "Okay then," she said. "Let's go find this woman."

*

Lizzy peered into car after car as she did a slow jog through the B2 Level. Then she headed up to the B1 level. There had to be hundreds of cars. She had no idea how they'd be able to check every one of them.

She was catching her breath beside an old Honda Accord with corroded paint when she looked up then to see Sally running down the ramp toward her. "Lizzy!" she called.

Lizzy stood up straighter. "You find her?"

"No. Net yet." Sally stood there panting for a moment. "But I just had a vision that she's up on L1. Where's Frankie?"

"Probably L3 by now," Lizzy said. "Go on up to L1 and check it out. I'll be along—I just have to cover these cars." Sally ran back up the ramp as Lizzy resumed her hunt.

It seemed so unlikely that Yolanda was anywhere in this garage. Lizzy was shocked that Frankie had even suggested it. But here they were, going car by car, and strangely it did feel right. Perhaps Frankie knew something she didn't. Or now, maybe Sally did.

At this point, Lizzy was dog-tired, but at the same times she was also wired. Early morning adrenaline pumped through her like potent caffeine. She was determined now. She was going to find this woman if it was the last act of her life.

Her phone rang now, and she grabbed it, thinking it was Frankie. It was a number she didn't recognize.

"This is Lizzy."

"Honey?" asked the staticky, far off voice. Against all odds, Kate was calling from Ireland.

Lizzy stood stock still, warmth spreading through her body. "Kate? Is that you?"

"Yes! It's me!" It sounded like Kate was laughing and crying at the same time.

"Oh my God, are you okay?" Lizzy began hurrying along once more, past car after car, peering inside each one as she made her way toward the ramp up to Level 1.

"I'm…well, I'll tell you about it later. But here's the thing, Lizzy. I love you and I miss you. I miss you something fierce, Lizzy." Kate continued. "And I'm coming home tomorrow."

Lizzy stopped short. "Tomorrow! What's happened? Did your dad die?"

"No. It's a long story." Now it sounded like Kate was just flat out crying.

"Hey—are you okay?"

"Yeah, but I need you. I just—"

Suddenly another call came in, interrupting Kate. Lizzy looked at her phone. Now it was Sally.

"Wait. Honey, I'm sorry. I have to go right now. I love you. Text me your flight info and I'll be there. I really have to go."

"Lizzy?" Kate's voice was asking as she was cut off.

Lizzy couldn't believe she was doing this, as she pressed the disconnect button. Here was her love. Her wife. Her life. And she was telling her everything she'd been longing to hear ever since she left.

Sally's voice came on the line now. "I'm here with Yolanda and her baby on 1," she said. "We're over by the elevator. Call Frankie."

Lizzy gave a shout of jubilation that echoed through the concrete car park. An old man in the corner looked up at her as he was getting into his car.

Maybe this was going to work out after all.

218

*

"Yolanda!" Lizzy threw her arms open to the woman as she ran toward her. "Oh my God, I'm so glad we found you."

Yolanda was shaking her head, a wary smile on her face. Clearly, she didn't understand what was happening. Sally's complete lack of Spanish wasn't making it any better. She looked over at Lizzy with something resembling relief. "Thank God you're here," she said.

"Angelica's heart…her heart." Lizzy pointed to her chest in a pantomime.

"Yes?"

"We have a new heart for Angelica," Lizzy tried to explain. "New heart…organ transplant?"

Yolanda shook her weary head, still confused. And now she looked just plain dismayed.

Just then, Frankie came hurrying down the ramp from L2. And as she came, she began spewing a loud, non-stop stream of fluent Spanish in the young mother's direction. Yolanda looked around now, trying to see who was talking to her.

As Frankie reached them a little breathlessly, she took over, continuing her fast rush of Spanish. The two women conversed back and forth rapidly. The words *de donación de órganos* and *trasplante* kept popping out as Lizzy tried to follow along.

Yolanda was nodding more and more now. Then a wide smile broke out on her face.

"Oh, *Leecy*," she said as she threw her arms around Lizzy. And Lizzy gave her a modest hug back as a shy smile broke across her own face.

"Well, don't get too excited yet. We have to get you up to the organ donation woman right now." Frankie translated as they all hurried toward the elevator bank.

Stepping into an elevator, Lizzy glanced at her phone, still marveling at the call from Kate only moments earlier.

Kate was coming home. And she still loved her.
Maybe everything really was going to be alright.
For all of them.

Chapter Eighteen

Kate hesitated outside the door of her father's hospital room, uncertain exactly what to do next. So far the last hour had flown by in a disconnected blur. She just kept putting one foot in front of the other. Filling her suitcase. Booking her flight. Charging her phone. She could do this. She really could.

Sequestered upstairs in her childhood room, Kate had had little time to think or even plan. She just kept taking care of one task after another, her hands shaking but her mind strangely clear. Downstairs, her mother slammed one door and then another as she crashed around the house, pounding out her frustration and her anger. She'd become a roaring beast who Kate now needed to avoid as best she could.

She called an Uber and half an hour later, slipped silently out of this house she'd grown up in. It was a home that had sometimes been a safe haven, but more often a prison. And as she quietly closed the front door behind her, Kate felt only one tiny nostalgic wave of longing for her past.

But then it disappeared as she loaded her suitcase into the trunk of the waiting car.

Kate rode to the hospital in silence, contemplating all that had just happened and all she had let go of. As she did, a new sense of liberation began to course through her veins. Reaching for her phone, she called Lizzy.

Briefly, Lizzy came on the line and her voice sounded tired and somewhat harried. Something intense was clearly happening in the background, though Lizzy didn't say what it was. And she ended the call quickly.

But she said she'd meet Kate at the airport, and that she loved her. And that's what mattered most.

Just hearing Lizzy's voice had its usual tonic effect. She began to laugh and cry at the same time. Then her mind relaxed, and her raw wounds began their healing And she knew, once again, she was doing exactly the right thing.

She reached her father's room well past four in the afternoon. By now, her father would most likely be alone.

Taking a deep breath, Kate pushed open the door to his room, for it was still a shock to see him in such frail condition. Her Da lay still in a shaft of late afternoon sunlight, his eyes closed. He looked as pale and fragile as ever, yet now there was a look of peace on his face. Kate hadn't seen this before.

As she approached, he opened his eyes.

"Da," Kate said, rolling her suitcase to a stop behind her. She pulled a chair up to the side of the bed and sat down. Then she took his hand. He gazed over at her. Then suddenly, seemingly out of the blue, he spoke.

"You're leaving?"

Kate turned around and glanced at the suitcase behind her, as if to make sure it was still there. Yes. She was doing this. She was actually leaving.

"I came to say good bye," she explained. "Mum and I…well, we both thought it best if I go back to the States sooner rather than later."

Her Da just looked at her.

"I mean, it's really my decision as well. Going back," Kate fumbled. "It's…here's the thing." She took a breath. "I wanted to come talk to you about something, Da. I told Mum, and I realized you should know, too."

Kate stopped. Suddenly, sitting there by her father's death-bed, it felt like ice was filling her veins. She was about to drop a huge bombshell on her dying father. *Maybe Mum is right.*

Maybe this information really would kill him. Maybe Da would be so upset, he'd breathe his last breath right then and there, and collapse and die right in front of her. And then she would be the one to blame for his death.

Kate looked down and studied the wedding ring on her left hand. She'd tucked it away in her purse on the airplane ride over to Ireland. But in the last hour, she'd dug it out of her toiletries bag and put it back on her ring finger, where it belonged. Now, of course, she no longer needed to hide her marriage. Just looking at it gave her the needed shot of courage.

Kate cleared her throat and looked at her father. His eyes met hers.

"You see, Da, I need to tell you something before I go."

Stop rambling. Just get it out, she chided herself. Leaning forward, she looked into her father's eyes. He was studying her intently, trying to figure out what was going on.

"The thing is, Da, I'm married."

His eyebrows rose, and a weak smile actually crept across his face. "It's a good marriage," Kate continued. "We're happy, Da. And...uh..."

She looked down at the ring on her hand and she twisted it. Then she looked directly back at her father. "I'm married to a woman, Da."

There was silence. "I'm a lesbian," she continued. "Turns out I always have been."

Briefly, her father closed his eyes. Then he opened them once more, and he focused on her. Then he opened his mouth. "Love?" he managed to whisper.

"Yes. Love."

He nodded, then, and he said nothing more. But his grip on her hand tightened, and he gave a weak squeeze. And in that moment, tears sprang into Kate's eyes.

Leaning over, she kissed the faint freckles on his bony hand. And suddenly, all the grief she'd been avoiding came pouring in. She placed her cheek against his hand, and she began to cry in earnest. "I'm sorry I have to leave," she wept, as she pressed her cheek into his hand. "I am really sorry, Da."

Her father withdrew his hand, and with a light, shaky touch, he began to stroke the hair on her lowered head. His touch was filled with so much love in that moment, it broke her heart.

Then closing his eyes, his hand dropped. Her Da drifted off to sleep once more.

After a moment, Kate slowly rose. "I love you, Da. And I will miss you," she said aloud, and she found she meant it. Then bending over, she left a parting kiss on his weathered cheek. His eyes did not open.

Taking her bag, Kate rolled it toward the doorway, aware that in some barely perceptible way, her life had just been seriously changed. She looked back for one last moment at the inert figure who'd once been her strong, strapping Da, and who would soon be gone.

Her redemption had happened through one small touch.

All it took was finally telling the truth.

*

Sally pulled her car into their parking pad, right behind Frankie's. They'd hit more than one light in tandem, and even pulled up next to each other at an intersection. Lowering the window, Sally had leaned over and blown her lover a slow-motion, Marilyn Monroe style kiss she'd hoped was fairly hot. And Frankie had smiled and winked back at her.

Her reaction had thrilled Sally straight down to her vulva.

The entire ride home from the hospital had been filled with

hope for Sally. She'd even sketched out a brief seduction scenario in her mind, in the scant hour Frankie had before she had to drive into work. Frankie would love it, she knew.

It would be her way of acknowledging her love for the triumph they'd just had together, getting Yolanda's baby a new heart. The transplant process had already begun, and indeed, the prognosis was good.

They were saying goodbye to Delilah and Tenika when the donation coordinator came in to tell them Anjelica's blood type matched Ashanti's. They would, indeed, be able to save Angelica's life.

Tenika just shook her head, amazed at the intensity, the miracles, the loss, the abundance and everything else this new day had already brought them.

Sally and Frankie had looked at each other then, and the hugeness of what they'd just done together filled all the space between them. And in that moment, Frankie had leaned over and kissed Sally. It was a kiss she was going to remember for a long, long time, so filled with appreciation. And tenderness.

She wanted Frankie more than ever, Sally realized. But as she pulled the keys from the ignition, a sudden thought stopped her cold.

Ronnie.

Ronnie would undoubtedly be asleep in her usual position on their living room couch, under Sally's comforter. Now the presence of her ex suddenly seemed wrong. Overnight, she'd become an uninvited guest, and they really did need to ask her to leave. Sally's mind began to turn in circles, as she contemplated just how to extricate Ronnie from their home.

"Honey?" Frankie called, walking toward her.

Sally got out of her car. "Yeah?"

Frankie pulled her close and kissed her, a longer kiss. Then an even longer one followed. She could feel Frankie's body pushing into her own, as her own vast floodgates of desire opened up. Clearly she'd been thinking the same thing.

"I was thinking about you on the drive home," explained Frankie, as she kissed her throat, and moved her hand firmly across Sally's hip.

"Sweetheart, we're in the front yard," Sally murmured, as the heat between her legs grew.

"Yep," Frankie chuckled. Then she pulled back and looked at Sally. "Might be more private than our house at the moment."

"I know," Sally sighed, shaking her head. "We have to ask her to leave."

"That's your job," said Frankie. "She's your ex." Then she smiled a little wickedly. "Unless, of course, you need me. Believe me, honey, I'd be happy to help."

As they let themselves in, an impeccably dressed Ronnie sat waiting for them in the corner of the living room. She was wearing her best three-piece tweed suit, her crossed legs showed off her freshly polished wingtips.

There was a strange look of satisfaction on her face. Ronnie resembled a cat who'd just eaten a canary.

"Ronnie."

"Frankie."

The two women regarded each other coolly. "Hey, Sally!" Ronnie enthused. She got up, walked to Sally, kissed her chastely on the cheek. "How did it go?"

Sally and Frankie looked at each other. "It's been a long night," Frankie said.

Sally now fell silent. She had zero capacity for Ronnie and her antics. In fact, Sally had literally nothing to say to her. Nonplussed, Ronnie sat down once more. She motioned to the couch.

"Would you two mind taking a seat for a moment? I need to talk to you both."

Frankie looked at Sally uncertainly. Then giving a sniff of

derision, she began walking away. "Sorry. I have to be at work in an hour."

"Wait, honey—" Sally began, but Ronnie cut her off with a wave of her hand.

"Hey, Frankie, you are definitely going to want to hear this," Ronnie called after her.

Frankie stopped and looked at her houseguest. Then remembering all that had passed in the last twenty-four hours, she turned back and walked humbly over to the couch. She sat down and regarded Ronnie. Meanwhile, Ronnie's expression had become downright smug.

"What is it?" Frankie asked. "I actually don't have much time."

"Sally," Ronnie said, gesturing to the couch. Sally looked at Frankie with a flicker of annoyance. Then she, too, seated herself on the couch across from Ronnie and gave a yawn.

Ronnie began by patting her tweed jacket pocket. "I've got an offer for you two," she began. "An offer I think you'll find difficult to refuse."

Sally and Frankie just listened.

She paused dramatically. "As you know, my life has been really difficult the past few years. Well, ever since Sally left me."

"You actually left me, Ronnie," Sally chimed in.

Ronnie gave a wave. "Whatever. All I'm saying is things have been hard for me, right? And now I anticipate I'm going to have some very big medical bills with the illness and all…"

"The illness you can't remember the name of," Frankie remarked, arms now folded.

"But because of your…largesse," Ronnie continued, "putting me up here on your couch and all, I've made a few discoveries."

Frankie shifted uncomfortably on the couch, and glanced at her watch. Ronnie proceeded, unfazed.

"What I'm hoping we can work out is a loan," she began. "You'd finance my medical expenses and I'd pay you back, with interest of course." Ronnie gave a little cough, for effect. "I'm sure I could repay you in a year, once I get back on my feet. All I'd need is about ten thousand."

"Dollars," Frankie concluded.

"Yeah."

Frankie stood up. "I've got to get ready for work," she said, disappearing rapidly toward the bedroom. Frankie slipped out of sight for a moment.

Meanwhile, Ronnie jumped to her feet. "Hey! Frankie—wait!" she called. "Don't you want to see what I have in my pocket?" She turned to Sally. "She's really going to want to see this…"

Sally stood up now. "Ronnie—" she began, but Ronnie cut her off.

"Ten thousand isn't that much when you think about it. It's probably just a month's pay for Frankie."

Suddenly, Frankie came out nowhere. She rushed at Ronnie and put her face right into hers. "Don't make me do something I might regret," she warned in a low growl. "I think it's time for you to get the fuck out of here."

Sally watched, mouth agape, but Ronnie carried on unfazed. Now she smoothly extracted a folded pink envelope from her pocket. "I wanted to read you a letter I'm about to send," she continued smoothly. "It's addressed to Misty Kennedy, and it looks like Sally wrote it."

Sally was on her feet now. "Hey! That's private!" she yelled.

Stock still, Frankie looked at Sally in alarm. "What the fuck?"

"I believe Misty Kennedy's your mother?" Ronnie asked calmly, as she began to read the letter. "*Your rudeness to me was so egregious that I left feeling nothing less than traumatized.*"

"Don't read it!" Sally pleaded as she grappled for the letter, but Ronnie jumped up on the chair and held it out of reach.

She continued to read "*…it seems to me you have ice in your veins…*"

"Give me that!" Sally lunged toward the offending letter, but Ronnie kept the letter up out of reach.

"So I found your mother's address, and I'm just about to mail it," she explained. "Unless, of course, you folks want to pony up that ten thousand we talked about?"

"What are you asking us to do?" Frankie asked slowly, as if she wasn't quite believing what she was hearing.

Ronnie tucked the letter back into her jacket pocket. "Sounds like your little bitch here's gonna make some real trouble with your mom, Frankie."

"And you want money for this, Ronnie?" Frankie asked, still disbelieving.

"Yeah. Just give me ten thousand in cash, and you can have the letter back." Ronnie finished with a polite smile. "All done."

Now Frankie was the one to smile. "Thanks, Ronnie. That's just what we needed," she said, reaching into her own pocket.

She pulled out the phone that was just visible, and turned off the audio recording she'd just made.

Moving in, Frankie gripped Ronnie's arm. "Did you know that extortion is illegal in the state of California?" she asked. "Did you know it can even get you jail time, especially with the evidence I now have on my phone?"

Ronnie looked at her, as if she'd forgotten to connect a few critical dots. Frankie gave a weary sigh.

"Give me the fucking letter, Ronnie."

Grimly, Ronnie sighed. Then she turned it over.

Frankie continued, her grip tightening on Ronnie's arm. "You know, I'd love more than anything to run you in, and I will. But only if you ever speak to me or my wife, or you turn up here again. Is that understood?"

Ronnie lowered her head and nodded, aware that she'd blown it, yet again. "So get your things and get out of here right now," Frankie commanded.

Then she and Sally stood there and watched silently as Ronnie packed her bag and rolled it to the door. "Bye guys," she said. "Sally."

Then opening the door, Ronnie slipped away. Frankie locked the door behind her.

"Did that just happen?" Sally asked, shaking her head.

Frankie put her hands on her hips. "Apparently."

Then Sally smiled. "Did you know you called me your 'wife' just then?"

"Yeah," Frankie smiled. "I know. Feels like it, right?"

"Glad you agree," Sally said, nodding to the letter now in Frankie's hip pocket. "Actually, it's all in that letter. If you've got a minute, you might want to read it."

Frankie smiled. "Oh, you know I do."

Leading Sally by the hand, Frankie walked over to the couch and pulled her down beside her. Then together they read Sally's letter.

Hello Misty,

Thank you for hosting me on our very brief visit to Santa Barbara. Unfortunately, your rudeness to me was so egregious that I left feeling nothing less than traumatized. Frankly, I was shocked. And I still am.

People like you think you can spout off about anything you want to say, simply because you have wealth and power. But you don't have power over me, Misty. Instead, you have my pity.

Though we don't know each other, it seems to me you have ice in your veins. The fact that you couldn't even be bothered to have lunch with us on a rare visit from your daughter says a lot. Clearly, you only care about yourself and no one else…and that's just plain sad. Especially for Frankie.

If you think you can stop me from marrying Frankie, you're wrong.

We will get married because we love each other deeply and this is what we want. Frankie is an exceptional woman who does not deserve your disapproval even slightly.

Instead, she deserves love and understanding, which you seem to be incapable of providing.

I am determined to give her this, myself. And if you don't like it, then too bad. Maybe you'll adjust to the idea over time. Or maybe not.

Regardless of your feelings for me, I wish you peace, Misty. Your future daughter-in-law, whether you like it or not, Sally Pruett

When Frankie looked up, she had tears in her eyes. And leaning over, Sally put her head on Frankie's shoulder in sweet surrender. Frankie kissed the top of her head and laid her cheek against it.

"So when do you want to get married?" Frankie asked.

"Tomorrow?"

"Sounds good," said Frankie. "I'll take the day off."

Then rising, she took her soon-to-be-wife's hand, and she led her back to the bedroom.

It was time for a brand new beginning.

*

Lizzy waited nervously, a bouquet of Kate's beloved yellow roses in her hands. The plane had circled overhead for more than an hour due to the Bay Area's ever-present fog. Lizzy watched the arrivals board intently, until finally the notice was posted that her flight had landed.

Kate would be coming through the arrivals gate any moment now.

To Lizzy, it was as if her wife had been gone for weeks or even months, not just five short days. So much had happened that at this point, she was simply exhausted. The garage was still closed, and probably would be for a good part of the coming week. Delilah and Tenika were taking Aiden home from the hospital tomorrow, and both of them were going on maternity leave for the rest of the month.

The transplant had happened, and Angelica's life had been saved. Yolanda had even managed to come by their room for a teary thank you in broken English. And both Tenika and Delilah told her how grateful they were she'd made it happen.

And now Kate was coming home.

At any moment, the swinging door in the International Arrivals at SFO would push open. After the well-dressed gaggles of Japanese ingénues, the Indian grandmothers in their saris, and the tired European businessmen all walked out, Kate would finally emerge. Lizzy couldn't wait.

She saw her moments later, and Kate beamed as soon as she caught her eye. She waved a weary hand, and Lizzy gave an enthusiastic wave. And then they were together, kissing long, hard and deep right there in SFO's Terminal 2 as everything around them faded away.

It felt so good to have Kate in her arms, and Lizzy smiled down into her face. "I seriously missed you," she said. She pushed a strand of hair from Kate's face.

Kate chuckled. "God, you have no idea how much I missed you."

They began to walk toward the truck, as Lizzy pulled her bag along. "So your dad didn't die yet?"

Kate looked over at her. "No, no, love. But I did say goodbye. And I'm glad I did." She stopped, then, and looked over at Lizzy.

"The fact is that I told my mum about us and she threw me out."
She shrugged. "So that was that."

Lizzy's mouth dropped open. "Wait. Seriously? She threw
you out? Told you to leave and never come back?"

Kate nodded lightly, as they walked along. "Mm-hmm. Never
wants to see me again." She entwined her hand in Lizzy's. "I told
all three of them about us getting married. Even my Da. And,
Lizzy, he actually understood." Kate shot her wife a look. "I think
he even approved. At least he was in our corner." Kate chuckled as
they walked along, hand in hand. "Anyway, I'm so glad I did. And,
honey, I hope your heart wasn't set on going to Ireland any time
soon."

Lizzy squeezed her hand and looked back at her lover gratefully. "I'm just here to follow you," she said. "Wherever you want
to go."

"Ah, Lizzy," Kate stopped, and they hugged happily. "I'm so
glad to be home."

"Me too," Lizzy muffled into her hair. "It'll probably take me
a week to tell you everything that's happened. But first—have you
had dinner?"

"Not yet."

"Then let's get right home," said Lizzy. "I've got some Irish
Stew for you."

And Kate smiled at Lizzy, knowing she was, indeed, in exactly
the right place.

And she was married to exactly the right person.

Also by Suzanne Falter

Fiction
Oaktown Girls series
Driven
Committed
Destined
Revealed

Transformed series
Transformed: San Francisco
Transformed: Paris
Transformed: POTUS

(All titles by Suzanne Falter & Jack Harvey)

Non-Fiction
The Extremely Busy Woman's Guide to Self-Care
The Joy of Letting Go
Surrendering to Joy
How Much Joy Can You Stand?
Living Your Joy

Acknowledgements

Thank you to all who made this book possible. Your help has been invaluable!

Dr. Rima Goldman gave me extensive information on all aspects of delivering babies. Pat Murray was a cultural consultant, and the esteemed Terrance Kelly gave me key advice about gospel music.

My super production team came through again. Danielle Hartman Acee provided copy editing and layout, and Caroline Manchoulas created our cover.

Jack Harvey provided critical support to this project, and the entire Oaktown Girls series.

Working with you all has been a privilege.

About Suzanne Falter

Suzanne Falter is an author, speaker, blogger and podcaster who has published both fiction and non-fiction, as well as essays. Her queer fiction titles include the funny romantic suspense series Transformed. She also writes and speaks about self-care and the transformational healing of crisis, especially in her own life after the death of her daughter Teal. Her non-fiction books include *The Extremely Busy Woman's Guide to Self-Care, How Much Joy Can You Stand?* and *Surrendering to Joy.* Suzanne's essays have appeared in *O Magazine, The New York Times, Elephant Journal,* and *Thrive Global* among others. Her free flash fiction can be found at www.suzannefalterfiction.com, as well as on Facebook, Twitter, YouTube, and Pinterest. She lives with her wife in the San Francisco Bay Area.